LAST DESCENDANTS

VITARIAN CHRONICLES

VOLUME 2

S. L. WATSON

S. L. Watson www.slwatsonauthor.com

ISBN 978-1-954440-02-9 print ISBN 978-1-954440-03-6 hardcover ISBN 978-1-954440-05-0 ebook

Cover Design by Rena Violet

For my Family. You are my rock, my compass, and my inspiration.
I love you infinity times infinity infinities forever!

CHAPTER 1

*A*s the students settled into their Nadi Shodhana, I held the burning sage high while I circled the room, contacting each unique energy field. The pungent smoke filled my nostrils and clung to my skin as sweat trickled down my body. Deep exhalations of expelled energy whirled, forming into dark shapes. The more toxic the energy, the more hostile it became once outside the body. The energy hovered above, struggling to reconnect with its hosts, but my protected space trapped it, rendering its attempts useless.

I continued to circle the room, weaving the earthy smoke into the air. There were always one or two students in every class who couldn't release the soul-draining energy that leeched off them, and they needed extra help. I sensed this resistance now as I stopped in front of a shaking young woman. Her aura was dim and webbed with black tendrils. A whimper escaped her lips as she sat in her pose, unable to free herself. Heat burned in my stomach. This darkness had fed off the poor girl for so long that it'd tangled her aura into a knotted mess.

"Very good," I called out to the class. "Continue to let the energy flow through you with each exhalation." I bent down near the shaking student and placed my hand on her back and corrected her spine upright from her hunched position. "It's okay," I told her. "Just let it out." I closed my eyes and drew the heavy darkness from her as I stood. It resisted, but its fight was futile against my power.

The young woman stopped shaking as her body relaxed into the pose, and her aura immediately brightened. Silent tears slid down her cheeks as I moved away to give her space. It was time to cleanse the rest of the room of the furious energy soaring above the group.

"Now, on your next exhalation, allow any remaining toxic or negative feelings to flow away from you. Feel the energy traveling down your arms and flowing out through your fingertips. Once you've done this, place your palms flat against your heart and imagine a bright protective light shielding you."

I set the burning sage onto a plate and headed to the back of the room. The air became dense and nearly tangible with dark, menacing tendrils that swarmed together to resist my power. One by one, I drew each tendril from the swarm and into my own biofield, where the energy dissipated upon contact.

Exhaustion settled over me as relieved sighs mingled with tears spread across the room. The group had no idea what I'd just done; they only sensed their sudden release from the burden of something toxic and heavy weighing on them. It was normal for pent-up emotions to follow the expulsion of dark energy.

"Now, gently lower your hands and elbows onto the mat, and push back into Child's Pose, stretching your arms and fingertips out in front of you, and resting your forehead on the floor. As your hips relax down toward the—"

Before I could finish, the door to the studio swung open,

and a blast of cold air hit the room. I glanced to see who'd ignored the Hot Yoga in Session sign hanging on the door.

"Oh, wow! Did I interrupt? Phew! The smell in here could rival a boys' sweaty gym locker room." The intruder waved her hand across her nose.

I swallowed my irritation and pasted a friendly smile on my face. "We're just finishing up our session. I'll be right with you."

She quirked her eyebrow like she wasn't used to being dismissed and smoothed her flat-ironed platinum hair. The humidity in the room was causing it to frizz.

That's what she gets for ignoring the sign.

My gaze landed on the basket dangling at her side. I recognized it as the one I'd packed with my homemade candles, tea, and honey, and left with the front-desk attendant of the new yoga studio across the street. Was this the new owner of the studio? And why was she carrying the gift I'd left her?

I shrugged away my curiosity for now and turned my attention back to the class. "On your next inhalation, slowly push yourself up and come to standing. Take a deep breath as you lift your arms over your head and release into prayer. Namaste."

"Thank you, Everly," said the students in unison.

The haughty girl stood giving me dagger eyes as I walked around the room answering individual questions. She definitely wasn't used to being made to wait.

I smiled inwardly at her obvious annoyance as I meandered my way toward her.

Molly marched to my side, flicking her sweaty ponytail just as we reached the girl.

"You didn't see the Do Not Disturb sign before you barged in, interrupting our class?" Molly demanded before I could get out a word.

3

"I must have missed it." The girl brushed at her arm as if wiping away something offensive.

"Mm—hmm," Molly hummed.

Before any claws were bared, I gave Molly an appreciative wink and interjected. "I'm sorry. Is there something I can help you with?"

Her green eyes raked me over. "You're Everly?" The girl lifted the basket and set it on the front desk, next to us.

I nodded. "You must be Bree. I see you got my welcome package." I smiled.

She didn't return the gesture. "I won't be using these things, so I'm returning them."

"Oh, okay," I responded, taken aback. *How odd.*

"See you tomorrow, Everly." Some students waved as they stacked their yoga mats and headed out of the front door.

I waved back, then turned my attention back to Bree, giving her a more thorough look-over. Her clothes were likely designer by the look of the finely tailored threads, and the glossy, pointed red stilettos she wore begged to catch an eye. I wondered what had brought someone like her to our rural town of St. Helens, Oregon. She looked to be in her early twenties, maybe a year or two older than Molly and me. But where we preferred hanging out at my mom's café, drinking tea and chatting about books and recipes, Bree had the air of someone who preferred big-city life and night-clubs. Yet she had opened a yoga studio here. Why?

"You're returning a gift?" Molly stepped in, her tone peeved.

"Who's returning a gift?" Darion asked, coming up behind Bree and positioning himself next to Molly.

Bree's eyes widened and then turned calculating as she took Darion in. "I'm Bree." She extended her hand. Her tone flipped a complete one-eighty when she addressed Darion.

"Pleasure." Darion gently took her hand and then released

it quickly. He'd been trying hard this last year to get past his distaste of common human gestures. Handshaking was one of them. Most Vitarians weren't fond of the hand-to-hand greeting.

Molly narrowed her eyes at Bree. "Bree here is returning the welcome gift that Everly gave her."

Darion glanced at the basket. He reached in and pulled out the candle I'd made, and popped the lid off. "Hmm ..." He breathed in deeply. "Patchouli and lavender. My sister makes the finest candles in town." He peered into the basket. "And is that your baby's breath honey?" He plucked the jar out.

Bree watched Darion hungrily. "There must have been a misunderstanding. I was actually bringing the basket over to thank Everly," Bree backstepped. "I love candles and honey." She smiled only at Darion.

Molly huffed. "You said you would not be using them and were returning them." She stomped her foot.

"Back off," Bree hissed at Molly, edging closer to Darion and slipping the candle and jar of honey out of his hands and into hers. "Maybe you'd like to come over to my studio and share the basket with me?" Her teeth grazed her bottom lip. "I'll put together a cheese plate to pair with the honey." Her unnaturally long lashes fluttered as her eyelids drooped with hidden meaning.

"Studio?" Darion's brow quirked with curiosity.

Molly's face fell when Darion didn't move away from Bree, but he seemed entertained by her invitation. Unable to resist an opening for a snarky retort, Molly added, "Bree's the owner of the new yoga studio across the street, Bree's Yoga. You know, like the smelly cheese."

I stifled a giggle while Bree rolled her eyes.

"Actually," Bree said. Her tone had pitched up an octave. "It's B-r-e-e, as in a hot summer breeze." She trailed her finger across Darion's arm.

He watched her hand skim his skin without a hint of emotion, while Molly's face flushed the color of a fire truck.

Heat flared inside me, and before I could rein it in, the jar of honey cracked open, and honey oozed out all over Bree's hand and dripped down onto the hardwood floor.

Bree screeched and dropped the jar and candle to the floor. Shards of glass and globs of honey scattered at our feet. "What did you put in that honey?" Bree demanded.

"We'll grab some towels," said a student who'd been locking up her equipment in one of the personal lockers I had for rent. Another student came running over with the broom and started sweeping the glass into a pile.

I folded my arms to hide the tremble that had taken hold. I couldn't think of what to say and just stared at the broken glass on the floor. Luckily, Molly was quick to reply to Bree's accusation. "You probably cracked the glass the way you swung the basket up on the counter."

"Whatever," Bree snapped. "Just fetch me something to get this sticky mess off."

"I'm so sorry," I muttered. "I'll grab you some wet towels." Turning abruptly, I dashed to grab fresh towels from the supplies shelf.

Darion followed me to the sink. "I saw the look in your eye," he whispered in my ear. "It's Siobhan's magic. You need to learn to use it instead of stuffing it away. You could've injured her."

"Oh, look who's talking," I whispered back. "I have it under control, Darion."

"I can see that," he taunted. "And all this dark energy you're siphoning from your students every day isn't doing you any favors."

I turned on the faucet and stuffed the towels under the tepid water. "Drop it, Darion. It won't happen again. And I'm helping people with what I do here."

His mouth quirked up into his usual sly grin. "Okay, sister, but don't say I didn't warn you."

Fire burned in my chest, and water sprayed upward from the faucet unnaturally. I huffed in exasperation.

Darion didn't say a word, but the look on his face gave away his thoughts. He raised an eyebrow and strolled away as though nothing out of the ordinary had just happened.

"Here." I handed Bree the warm towels.

She didn't say thanks.

"So, what's the name of your studio mean?" she asked as she wiped at her hands and eyed the students who'd helped clean up the broken glass and spilled honey.

The unfriendly glares she was giving people weren't going to help her business. If she planned to have anyone signing up for her classes in this town, she'd need a warmer approach, but I doubted any advice from me would be welcome, or from anyone else she considered gum under her heel.

I kept my other thoughts to myself and just answered her question. "Pranayama," I said. "It means 'extension of life force.'"

Molly clicked her tongue. "Pranayama is a type of yoga that focuses on breath work. How can you not know that if you're a yoga instructor?"

Molly made a good point. I let my guard down and scanned Bree's energy as she answered.

Bree glared at Molly. "My studio is a more modern version of today's yoga."

Her responses were snotty, and her vibes capricious, and without a doubt volatile. But I didn't pick up any indicator she wasn't telling the truth.

Molly placed her hand on her hip. "*Modern*? Have you ever even practiced yoga?"

"Okay." Darion stepped in. "Molls, let's go get that breakfast we talked about." He pulled Molly in by the waist, and she gave Bree a hot smile as she sauntered off with Darion.

"So, are those two, like, a thing or something?" Bree asked me, glancing one last time at Darion.

I watched Molly and Darion make their way out to the street, arm in arm, and wondered the same question.

"Or something," I mumbled, not sure myself what was going on between Darion and Molly these days. They'd been spending more and more time together over the last year and seemed to have grown close, but neither one would admit to being more than friends.

A familiar bark drew my attention back toward the door, which had been left propped open. Luna came catapulting in and slid across the floor. She barely came to a halt as she jumped up and licked my face. I laughed and held her paws as I guided her back down onto all fours. My entire body relaxed in Luna's presence.

"Oh my God!" Bree stumbled back. "Where did that beast come from?"

I struggled to keep a straight face, looking at the expression Bree had plastered on hers. You'd think a dragon had just burst into the room spitting fire, instead of a boisterous dog.

"Bree, this is my German shepherd, Luna."

Luna regarded Bree skeptically, but offered her a warm welcome by bouncing over and licking Bree's hand. She must have smelled the scent of sweet honey on Bree's fingers. She sat and looked up at Bree with her big brown eyes and goofy dog smile.

For a flicker of a second, it looked like Bree might reach out and pet Luna, but then she seemed to rein in her softening expression and returned to her cool countenance with a tone to match.

"You let animals in your studio?" She scrunched up her

face at Luna and took a step back, folding her arms across her chest.

Luna ignored Bree's unfriendly demeanor as she pranced back toward the door and cheerfully yelped.

"Luna isn't just any animal. Are you, girl?" Jasper walked into view and bent down, giving Luna a good full-body scratching while Luna's leash dangled over his shoulder.

Bree's eyes trailed over his long body as he stood and ran his hand through his dark-cocoa waves.

I didn't miss the way her eyes lingered on his biceps before she finally drew her attention upward.

Luna licked Jasper's hand and darted toward the few remaining students, who always stayed after class to help clean up the supplies for the next class.

"I haven't seen you before," Jasper said to Bree. "Are you a new student?"

Bree's cheeks brightened with a hint of crimson. "I'm Bree" was all she said, and she coughed to clear her throat. Her aura turned a shade of red to match her cheeks. She was nervous. A feeling she probably wasn't used to experiencing.

I jumped in before Bree's silence could get any more awkward. "Bree, this is my best friend, Jasper." I turned my attention to Jasper. "Jasp, this is Bree. She just opened the new yoga studio across the street."

The anxious energy surrounding Bree relaxed a bit, and for the first time since she'd walked into my studio, her expression softened with gratitude. *Maybe there's more behind that snobbish exterior, after all.*

"You don't look small-town. Are you a transplant?" Bree asked Jasper.

Okay, I guess I'm wrong. Maybe she's just as vain as she seems.

Jasper's expression twisted with confusion. "Transplant?" He glanced my way, and I shrugged.

"You know," Bree said. "Did you move here from California or something?"

Jasper's amber eyes met mine for an instant, and we shared a hidden smile. If Bree had known where we were both really from, she'd have run screaming from the building.

Jasper winked at me before answering Bree's question. "Not a transplant. Born and raised in our beautiful small town." His answer was a part truth.

"Not to be rude," he continued, appraising Bree's haughty posture, "but why would you open a yoga studio across from an existing one? Everyone who takes yoga in this town already comes to Ev's studio."

Bree recovered from her bout of nervousness, and without missing a beat, she flipped her hair and answered, "Well, I'm sure Ev won't mind if people want to try something a little less … traditional." She flicked her hand around the room and batted her eyelashes at Jasper. She huffed when she didn't get the reaction she was hoping for.

Bree was definitely not Jasper's type, although, based on my brief interactions with her, I guessed she'd find it hard to believe she wasn't anyone's type.

"Bree's right," I offered. "There's nothing wrong with some friendly competition."

Jasper edged closer to my side as he studied Bree. "I don't think *friendly* is in her vocabulary," he whispered in my ear, earning himself a green-eyed dagger glare from Bree.

I nudged him in the ribs with my elbow and added, "Besides, my wait list is always full." I smiled at Bree. "There's more than enough business to go around."

"Great!" Bree announced. "Then I think it's time I go open my doors. May the best studio win." She spun, her heels clicking against the wood floor as she whisked out the door, and left the gift basket and its remaining contents behind.

Luna moved between Jasper and me and watched Bree go. She glanced up at us like she was thinking the same thing we were: What was that all about?

"Is it just me, or did she seem overly enthusiastic about taking your clients?" Jasper wondered, concern etched upon his brow.

I leaned my head on his shoulder. "Don't worry about her. I won't."

"That girl is trouble," Jasper mused.

I laughed. "You would know. You dated enough like her in high school."

Jasper placed his hand on his heart. "Oh, ouch. Don't remind me. Those days are long past."

"Hi, Jasper," chirped the remaining students as they passed to leave the classroom. They couldn't resist glancing back at Jasper several times before finally turning out of the door.

The laugh I'd held in burst free once the room was clear. "Those days might be long past for you, but you're still the heartthrob you've always been. Why don't you ask one of those nice girls out on a date?" I suggested. "Who knows? Maybe it'll turn into something special."

The smile faded from Jasper's face. "You know why."

A knot formed in my stomach.

I glanced around the studio at everything I'd worked hard to build over the last year, and a crushing weight settled over me.

"Yeah, I know."

CHAPTER 2

*L*una barked happily as I curved into the driveway. She sat in the passenger seat with her head sticking out the window, looking toward the thick forest that bordered our property. She was probably imagining all the animals she'd be chasing momentarily. I laughed at the big cheerful dog grin on her face.

I drove past the main house and pulled around into the carport near the guesthouse that'd been my apartment for nearly the last three years. My mom had insisted on having the guesthouse remodeled when she'd agreed to let me move into it after high school graduation as part of our compromise over me spreading my wings. I hadn't planned to live in it as long as I had, but after everything that'd happened last year, I knew my time on this planet was limited. Felix was handling the affairs on Aenoas-Vita, but his updates continued to remind me they needed my presence.

I knew that by remaining on Earth; I was only delaying the inevitable and that eventually, I would have to return to the planet where I had been conceived. But I wasn't ready to leave my home, or my mom. She had no plans to return to the planet she'd spent most of her life on and had fled from during her pregnancy with me.

Felix believed fate had chosen me as Oria's heir.

Destiny or not, Aenoas-Vita held nothing for me but a duty I'd sworn myself to in order to save Darion's life. Earth would always be home in my heart.

I got out of my car and opened Luna's door. She immediately bolted out and into the field of wildflowers that fed the bees for my homemade honey. She bounced after the honeybees, spinning in the air as her jaw clamped down over her prize. If she ever got stung, it never seemed to bother her.

My heart ached at the thought of leaving my family and all of this behind for a planet I'd only seen in memories that weren't my own. But I'd made a deal and had accepted my role. There was no turning back from it.

I drew a deep breath and stuffed the dark thoughts away.

Soft jazz echoed from the open kitchen windows of the main house, a dead giveaway that my mom was in the kitchen preparing a meal.

I decided I'd pop in and say hi before heading into my place. Luna would be fine out in the field. She'd come into the house through her dog door when she was ready, or go to the apartment. She never strayed from the property.

"Hey, Mom. It smells amazing in here." The sweet scent of vanilla bean greeted me as I entered the kitchen through the back door.

She glanced up from whisking custard in a bowl. Wisps of raven hair fell from braided twists on either side of her head and framed her face at chin length. Her sapphire eyes beamed at me as she bounced to the jazz beats playing from her Bluetooth speaker.

"Thanks, sweetie." She licked the spoon before tossing it in the sink and then dipping another and handing it to me.

13

"I'm making *Monarda* tarts, Jasper's favorite, for dessert tonight."

"Hopefully, you made extra for the rest of us." I nudged my mom's hip with my own, and we both did a twirl to the saxophone solo.

She laughed. "Oh, I made plenty."

"What's for dinner?" I asked, glancing at the bounty of dishes in the sink. I tugged open the dishwasher and started rinsing and loading.

"Well, let's see. Since it's Calista's first night back from her trip, I've made her favorite butternut squash lasagna, and I know how much you love my polenta cakes with fried sage, so we'll have those as an appetizer. Oh," she added, gesturing with her fork, "speaking of sage, did you include a sage candle in the welcome basket for the owner of the new yoga studio?"

"Yeah, but you're not going to believe it," I said, scrubbing some dried food from a bowl before adding it to the dishwasher.

My mom peeled off her apron while she waited for me to finish.

"She returned the basket this morning with everything still in it." I shook my head.

The creamy skin around my mom's eyes creased with her frown. "She returned a welcome gift?" Incredulity filled her tone. "What was her reason?"

"She said she wouldn't use any of it."

"Tsk." My mom clicked her tongue just as Molly had done earlier. Then she smoothed her navy-blue silk shirt, which complemented her eyes. "I'll drop by her studio with some treats from the café. No one can resist your lavender scone recipe." She ruffled my hair.

"I doubt she'll appreciate the gesture." I wiped a splash of water from my cheek as I rinsed the last of the dirty silverware.

Heat bubbled in me when I thought of how Bree had treated Molly. "You know, she was a real snot and not worth our trouble, and you should have seen how she ogled both Darion and Jasper, like some kind of panther in heat. Argh!" I looked down in time to see the fork in my hand bending. I tossed it into the dishwasher before my mom could see what'd happened. Inhaling deeply, I suppressed the magic inside me before turning around.

Furrows wrinkled my mom's forehead, and for a moment, I thought she'd seen what I'd done.

I prepared to explain, but then she tucked the fallen wisps of hair behind her ears and said, "Everly. You asked me to teach you Vitarian traditions, and this is one of them. We welcome new friends and neighbors. Regardless of how this young lady acted, she is new to our town and one of us now. If we stoop to her level, what type of people would that make us?"

She pulled me into her arms and kissed the top of my head. "You're a queen now, and the first Ever to rule for centuries. When you return to Aenoas-Vita, you're going to lead a planet of people, and the old fears of Orien's terror remain. Show them the strength of their new queen, who rescued her family and defeated Siobhan with mercy over malice."

"I know, Mom. I'm sorry. I shouldn't have let her get under my skin. It's just …" I couldn't tell her I struggled with Siobhan's dark magic inside me, and that each day it grew stronger, and my resistance weaker. I didn't want to worry her further.

"What is it, honey?"

I shrugged. "Not everyone will see Siobhan's punishment

as just. I absorbed her magic from her and sent her to the dungeons."

My mom sighed. "Let's talk no more of Siobhan. That woman took too much from me. She has her life, which is far more than she gave others."

"You're right. Let's forget about Siobhan." I forced my lips into a reassuring smile and pulled out of her arms. Reaching across the counter, I clicked the music volume up.

Trumpets buzzed over the speaker. Bright metallic beats filled the kitchen with an energetic tempo, creating a welcome distraction as we dipped our spoons into the custard and filled the mini pie crusts.

I smiled, watching my mom shimmy her hips and twirl her spoon. "You know, these will last about two-seconds once Jasper gets his paws on them."

My mom laughed. "Yeah, but they're so fun to make." Her finger shot across the edge of the bowl, scooping up a glob, which she plopped on the tip of my nose.

We giggled as our chins and noses dripped with custard, and both my sides ached, reminding me of all the times we'd spent in this kitchen laughing and making messes when something troubled me.

"I miss this." My mom passed me a clean towel.

I wiped my face. "Me too." I returned her smile, wishing sugar and laughter could tame the shadow that haunted me now. "I better go get cleaned up."

∼

*T*he guesthouse that served as my apartment was quaint and homey. Light filtered in through the tall windows that made up the wall on either side of the front door. The weather was on the chilly side, but I slid open a window anyway, letting a gentle breeze filter through the room. It didn't take long for the mellow scent of the wild-flowers from the field to permeate the space.

I pulled the long vertical blinds closed, relaxing in the solitude of darkness. Controlling Siobhan's powers was draining. I'd buried her magic deep within me on the night that had sealed my fate, but each day, a little more seeped past my barrier and wormed its way through my blood, luring me with its intoxicating rush.

Darion was right. I needed to do something soon, or it wouldn't be a matter of *if* I hurt someone, but *when*.

Suddenly the sweet, decadent scent of Daphne "Eternal Fragrance" that filled the air turned rancid, and I turned toward the vase of flowers I'd just cut earlier this morning to find them bending and blackened with rot. I heaved a groan, resolved that I'd have to ask Darion for his help sooner rather than later.

With a gentle touch, I caressed the brittle, lifeless flowers before crushing them in my hand. *Is this what's happening to me? Am I blackening inside just like these flowers?*

More and more, I found myself drawn toward a darkness I didn't understand. Something unseeable had sunk its claws into my soul. It fed on the light inside me, and I feared what would happen when no light remained.

I snatched the vase from the table and tossed the flowers into the trash.

Was it Siobhan's dark magic inside me causing the change, or something else?

It'd been a little over a year since I'd discovered my true origins; maybe it wasn't Siobhan's magic alone affecting me, but something deeper, more genetic. What if Darion wasn't the evil twin, after all? Siobhan had manipulated him his entire life, and once he'd learned the truth, he'd helped us, and chosen to remain on Earth to be with me and my mom. He'd spent every day since atoning for his past deeds, while I continued to slip further into darkness.

I squeezed my eyes shut and swiped away the tear that pressed free.

Everything will be fine. Darion will teach me to control Siobhan's magic, and I'll go back to feeling like my old self.

Glancing back down at the rotted flowers, I hesitated before removing my foot from the garbage can pedal.

My feet lifted heavily as I made my way into my bedroom. The energy it took to absorb the darkness from my class was still taking its toll. I peeled off my yoga clothes and dressed quickly in a pair of navy-blue skinny jeans and a soft cobalt cotton off-shoulder top. The vertical slits opening on the sleeves gave the shirt an airy feel. After adding a spritz of detangler to my hair, I brushed it out and added a French braid along the top and over to one side, leaving thin wisps to frame my face. I slid on a pair of black flats and headed for the main house.

Luna bounded from the field and slowed at my side. "Did you have a good run, girl?" I smoothed the fur between her ears.

My answer came as a lick across the cheek. "Okay." I giggled and wiped Luna's slobber off with my shirtsleeve.

As we approached the back door, the tantalizing aroma of sage and fresh rosemary wafted through the air, making my stomach growl.

Just as I reached for the doorknob, the sound of familiar laughter on the other side brought a smile to my lips. A wave of joy washed over me as I stepped into the kitchen.

"Calista!" I flew into her arms and breathed in the sweet scents of coconut and vanilla. "You smell like the tropics. I've missed you so much. How was your trip?"

Calista's chestnut curls cascaded over my shoulders as she bent her head to kiss the top of mine. "I've missed you too, sweetie. And the trip was good." She lifted her head back and smiled down at me.

A pinch twisted in my gut. Calista held something back. She guarded her energy, but a murky blue-gray hovered over her aura.

She tugged away and diverted her attention to Luna, who'd just let out a happy bark as she spun around the two of us.

"And I've missed you too, Luna." Calista laughed as she bent down to let Luna lick her face, and she tickled Luna's tall pointed ears.

"I have something for you both," Calista said to me and Jasper. "Oh, and you too, Luna." She scratched Luna's furry belly, then stood and walked into the living room.

Jasper guarded an area of the counter while he shoved bites of *Monarda* tart into his mouth.

"Jasp, you know those are for dessert," I scolded him.

He nodded as he chewed a mouthful. "Yeah, but your mom made extra for me to graze on. She told me to help myself." He scraped the edges of the dish, scooping up any remaining bits of custard onto his spoon. Closing his eyes, he savored the last mouthful and sighed in delight. "I'm sorry, Ev, but your mom's tarts are the best on the planet. I love yours too, but hers are out of this world."

I laughed. "It's okay, Jasper. You don't have to like mine best, but I hope you saved some for the rest of us."

Luna's nails clicked on the hardwood floor. She pranced in circles around the gift bags Calista carried in and set on the marble countertop. She sniffed out her gift and watched eagerly as Calista unwrapped a flavored bone for her. "Good girl," Calista complimented her as Luna sat proudly, licking her chops in anticipation. She happily latched onto the bone with her teeth and took her gift, and ran out of the kitchen.

Forks and plates clinked as Jasper rinsed and loaded his

tart dish and spoon into the dishwasher. "All right, let's do this," he said, clapping his hands together as he leaned over the counter and wiggled his eyebrows at us.

I couldn't resist rolling my eyes at him and laughing at the same time.

Calista ruffled his dark waves and plucked out a bag from the bundle she'd brought in and handed one to Jasper.

The next bag was larger, and she carefully held the bottom while she lifted it. "This one's for you."

As I carefully took hold of the bag, her eyes sparkled with excitement.

"Oh, wow." My muscles tensed with the weight of it. I gently set the bag back down onto the counter, worried the bottom might tear out, and admired the tribal artwork that decorated the paper bag.

Calista noticed my curiosity. "A local woman in Bali handcrafted these bags. She painted her tribe's symbols on them. They're meant to be reused."

"Lovely." I admired the swirling lines.

"Seriously, Ev," Jasper groaned. "I can't take the anticipation. Can you open it already?" he insisted.

"Okay, simmer down." I lifted the tissue from the top of the bag. "You know, Jasper. Some of us like to enjoy the packaging before tearing it open."

"Yeah, yeah." He nodded eagerly at the bag as I slid my hand inside and lifted out a box.

Jasper wasted no time in whipping out his pocketknife and swiping it across the tape that secured the box together. I slipped my fingers under the folds of the box flaps to pull them open.

"Careful," Calista warned. "There're sharp bits."

I folded the box flaps back and placed my hands on the sides of the item inside and carefully lifted. The overhead light reflected on a stone statue. A golden crown glistened atop the head of the fierce warrior who sat upon her tiger companion, which bared its deadly fangs. Multiple arms wielded a sword, a trident, a knife, and other weapons.

My breath caught. The details carved into the white marble were done with beautiful craftsmanship, and the colorful glaze painted on the stone shimmered with life.

I glanced up to find Calista smiling from ear to ear. "You've always loved my Durga statue, and now you have one of your own. I thought it would fit nicely in your studio. I picked up some pure patchouli incense at one of the local markets for it, too. You place it in the back here." She turned the statue to show me. "And the smoke travels up through the statue and out of her hands and the tiger's mouth."

"I love it! Thank you! It's perfect, and I know just where it'll go in the studio." I wrapped my arms around Calista in a tight hug. "Your turn." I nodded to Jasper.

He quickly tossed out the decorative tissue paper and drove his hand into the bag. "Sweet!" he said, admiring his gift as he lifted out a handcrafted bamboo flute and beamed. He brought it to his lips, and the kitchen filled with haunting notes, causing goose bumps to spread across my skin.

"It's beautiful, Cal. Thank you so much."

Calista pulled Jasper and me into a group hug. "Of course, kiddo. I knew it was perfect for you the second I saw it."

A familiar energy floated into the room, and then I heard the soft voice to match. "Having a group hug without me?" said Selkie as she carried in a tray of stuffed mushrooms and popped them into the preheated double oven.

"Hey, Selk." Darion followed Selkie into the kitchen. "I'll grab a vase for these," he said, carrying an enormous bouquet of fresh-cut flowers.

The energy in the room tensed. Darion's gaze fell on Calista, and his silver eyes darkened with apprehension.

Calista had barely tolerated Darion before she'd left for

her trip three months ago, and her constant distrust of him had begun an unsettling rift between her and my mom.

"Hi, Cal," he greeted Calista dispiritedly. "It looks like you all are having a moment. I'll come back for the vase."

Calista slid from between me and Jasper. "Darion, wait. I have something for you." She offered him a bag.

Selkie took the flowers from Darion's hands. I caught the encouraging nudge she gave him before she left his side and went to look through the cabinet where we kept the vases.

Selkie had wholeheartedly forgiven Darion for what he'd done to her when he'd first come to this planet, under Siobhan's control, and she'd taken him under her wing to help teach him about plant magic. A strong bond had developed between them, and Darion admired Selkie just like I did, as if she were a beloved aunt.

Darion accepted the small bag from Calista with a blank expression. When he unfolded the tissue paper, revealing a large teardrop-shaped stone, he met Calista's watchful stare.

"It's an Indonesian stone," Calista explained. "It represents willpower and determination. Both your mom and Selk have told me how hard you've been working to change. You're supposed to carry the stone with you. It's up to you if you want to," Calista added.

I held my breath, hoping Darion wouldn't respond with one of the sarcastic comments he used to avoid showing his emotions.

My shoulders relaxed when his expression softened as he held the stone up to the light, examining the multiple shades of red, gold, yellow, and specks of blue and black.

Calista's gesture made his energy glow warm. "Thank you for thinking of me," Darion said, tucking the stone into the front pocket of his black jeans.

The low growl of Jasper's stomach broke the sudden silence, just as the oven timer buzzed.

"Finally!" Jasper hustled over to the oven. He shoved his hands into the oven mitts and pulled out the dish that'd been baking in the lower oven, as well as Selkie's stuffed mushrooms from the top oven.

"Was that the timer?" my mom called from the dining room.

I flicked Jasper's hand as he was about to dip in and sample the dishes he'd just pulled out.

He feigned injury as he called out to my mom. "I got it, Ms. C."

"Thank you," I whispered into Calista's ear as we all pitched in to help set the table.

Calista nodded and whispered back as she grabbed the fresh-made apple cider from the fridge. "I'm offering an olive branch. For your mom," she added, hinting at her remaining hesitation to fully trust Darion's transformation.

I didn't blame her. Darion had been atrocious when he'd first entered our lives, but that had been before we all knew the truth, that he and I were twins. So much had changed since then.

The dining room sparked to life as my mom lit the candles with a snap of her fingers.

The first few months after I'd learned the truth of our heritage had been strange, and Mom, Calista, and Selkie no longer kept their magic secret from me. Now I looked forward to these moments when it was just us Vitarians, and we didn't have to hide our abilities in the presence of humans.

❧

The dining room echoed with laughter as everyone sipped their cider and wine. The smell of buttered sage tickled my nose as I lifted a portion of the polenta and fried sage onto my plate. I grinned when I saw Jasper starting his meal off with another *Monarda* tart. He chewed a bite with a dreamy smile on his face. I didn't blame him; I looked forward to enjoying the creamy custard myself.

Darion fidgeted in his seat before lifting the wine bottle from the table and refilling our mother's glass and then Selkie's. The candlelight flickered with his movements, causing prisms of light reflected from the crystal chandelier above to dance across the table.

"So, Cal, did you meet any interesting practitioners on your trip?" Darion swirled his wine around the inside of his glass. "Isn't Bali a hot spot for witches and fortune-tellers? I've heard voodoo is a common practice there."

Here we go again, I groaned internally. Darion hadn't let up about his speculations since Calista's departure.

My mom's shoulders rolled forward. The constant tension between her son and best friend weighed heavily on her.

I was about to send Darion a jolt of energy to shut him up, but I froze at the expression Calista wore.

She sat quietly for a moment, as if lost in memory. When she glanced up, a shadow of anxiety haunted her eyes, and the murky blue-gray color returned to the outer edges of her aura.

My nerves buzzed. Calista's reaction to Darion's question made me think he'd been right all along. If she wasn't holding something back, she wouldn't have hesitated with such foreboding.

Darion studied her. "Did the Spider Witch give you a reading?"

Calista's eyes widened. "How did you know?" She glanced at my mom, who'd been observing the two with mounting uneasiness.

Darion's silver eyes narrowed to slits. "I'm a Tracker, or

did you forget?" He wasn't asking her a question, but stating the obvious.

Calista's voice lowered to a hiss. "You were *spying* on me? How?" She turned to my mom. "Cacsha? You can't be okay with this behavior."

My mom pushed her glass back as she turned toward her son. Her face had paled at Darion's revelation, and the disappointment was unmistakable when she spoke. "Darion. I don't understand. Why would you violate Calista's privacy?" Her dark lashes lowered.

Selkie's melodic voice floated across the table. "Why don't we all take a pause? I'm sure Darion has an explanation." Her hazel eyes pleaded with him to give some good reason for his actions. When Darion didn't speak, Selkie sighed and shook her head.

Jasper broke the tense silence and asked the question that burned at the front of my mind. "Who's the Spider Witch?"

Darion leaned forward, facing Calista. "Better question," he said. "Why were you seeing the Spider Witch, and what did you learn?"

All eyes shifted to Calista.

She placed her hands on top of the table.

Whatever she had learned, it wasn't good. Being evasive wasn't usually Calista's style. A tremble took hold of her fingers before she finally pushed her chair back from the table. "It would be better if I showed you."

I shot Darion daggers while we waited for Calista to come back into the room. The disappointment shrouding my mom's aura cut at me. Darion had no business spying on Calista, even if he'd been right. If it hadn't been for the pained expression he wore right now, while he tried apologizing to our mom, I'd have sent him flying across the room.

My mom tucked Darion's hand into hers. "We'll talk about this later."

He cast his gaze down, no longer feeling smug about his revelation.

Calista came back into the room carrying what looked like a deck of tarot cards. She sat down and stared across the table at Darion. "Never spy on me again."

She glanced around at the rest of us, settling her gaze on my mom. "I'm sorry I didn't tell you the real reason I went to Bali, Cacsha, but Darion's right. I saw a witch. She's known as the Spider Witch, and these were her cards. She insisted I keep them after her reading. Maybe she foresaw this moment. I don't know. She speaks in riddles and gives half answers. The experience was more than frustrating." Calista glanced down at the deck in her hands as she split the stack and shuffled the cards.

Everyone at the table leaned forward in their chairs, hanging on Calista's words. "I learned of the Spider Witch years ago, on one of my trips. She's a revered conduit of eclectic magic and highly respected among Vitarian warlocks, and the only human they consider worthy of consulting with."

She tightened her grasp on the cards she held. "You see, her readings are never wrong. And if she allows you into her den, she has a message from the spirits. She comes from a lineage of diverse practitioners who possess extensive knowledge of dark magic and maintain a deep connection to the forgotten ancient power of earth. I was hoping"—she turned toward me—"she might have some insight into how to break the curse linking you and Darion."

Being an Empath, I didn't need to hear what the Spider Witch had told her to know the news wasn't good. Calista's demeanor spoke volumes.

"Well?" Darion urged Calista to continue.

My mom watched her friend intently, hopeful for some good news to come from tonight's debacle.

Calista shook her head. "She invited me to come for a reading, but she had no information to offer about how to break the curse. Her message was a warning"—she placed the deck on the table and cupped her hands atop it as if to shield us from the cards—"of something else."

Calista hesitantly flipped the top card off the deck and set it face up in the center of the table.

My heart skipped a beat when I saw who looked up from the card. It was Erebus, the Greek god of darkness.

She flipped over the next card to reveal the Tower, another bad omen, signifying upheaval and destruction—chaos.

The last card she laid down was the ominous image of Death wielding a deadly scythe.

"I've reshuffled the cards a dozen times since my meeting with the Spider Witch. The reading is always the same: darkness, chaos, and death."

My eyes locked with Darion's, and then my mom's.

"What did she say, Cal?" My mom's tone darkened with her straightened posture. "The cards could have multiple meanings. Tell me exactly what this witch told you—word for word." She extended her hand out to Calista.

Calista nodded, knowing my mom's intention. She planned to channel her magic through Calista and use her ability to retrieve memories. Then we'd know exactly what the witch had said, as if we'd all been there in that moment.

When Calista slipped her hand into my mom's, the air in the room stirred with Vitarian magic. Calista closed her eyes, and when she opened them, they were as black as night.

A chair fell backward to the floor.

Without turning from Calista, my mom responded. "It's okay. She's fine, Jasper."

Jasper picked up his chair and sat back down.

The candles burned low, and maybe it was just me, but an

icy chill seemed to pass through the room. Goose bumps spread across my skin.

Calista sat frozen, her black eyes void as she eerily stared ahead.

I'd never seen my mom use her powers on another person like this before. I rubbed my arms, but the prickles refused to diminish. Then, suddenly, the candles flickered brighter, to an unnatural height, and a warm breeze flowed my way. I glanced around the table and met Darion's eye. He offered a supportive smile. He'd used magic to increase the light and heat of the candles.

Jasper came and took the chair to my left and scooted close, as if to shield me from some unseen threat. I used to think of him as an overprotective best friend, but now I understand that it's his nature as a Shield to guard and protect. I still thought he took it too far sometimes.

Calista sat on my right in her trancelike state. Her hand darted across the white tablecloth, scooping up the three upward-facing cards. She placed them back on the deck while her hands moved around them in circular motions.

Darion huffed impatiently, earning him a nudge from Selkie.

Calista's hand hovered over the stack. Then she flipped the top card back over, laying it once again on the table. When she spoke, it was her voice, but the words and the countenance belonged to someone else. Calista covered the upturned card with her hand. "A sinister presence from the depths of the past has resurfaced, determined to seize what he believes is rightfully his." She turned the second card, laying the Tower next to Erebus. "His destruction has no bounds. He has taken life and will take more." Calista's hand shook as she laid the third card down. "Darkness will consume light, and a soul will be lost."

Thick incense permeated the air, only no incense burned

in the room. The chandelier rattled above, and the lights flickered out, leaving only the candlelight.

Calista whipped around in her seat and snatched my hands, squeezing them tight. Energy sizzled between us.

"Hear me, child," she commanded.

A low growl vibrated from Luna, who sat below me. I tried pulling my hands free from Calista's, but her grip tightened. "Don't give him what he wants." She released my hands and grabbed either side of my face, forcing me to stare into the black pits of her eyes. "The stars hold the answer."

Tiny specks of white light took shape in the dark marbles staring back at me, but then her hands fell from my cheeks, and Calista's head drooped down over her chest.

The chandelier lights flickered back on. My heart hammered against my chest so hard I could hear the pounding in my ears.

"Someone's knocking at the front door." Jasper's voice cut through my shocked stupor.

My head snapped up. "What?"

My mom pushed up from her chair and knelt in front of Calista, ignoring Jasper's announcement. "Cal, honey, are you okay?"

Selkie quickly brought around a cup of water and handed it to my mom. The two women shared a distressed glance before my mom shifted her worried frown back to Calista.

"I'm sorry, Cal. I had no idea that would happen." She pressed the cup of water into Calista's hand. "Here, drink this."

Calista shakily lifted the cup to her lips and sipped, then set it down on the table. With a raspy whisper, her words hung in the air as she spoke. "It was the witch. She used magic to channel through me. I don't know how she did it, but I know it was her."

Darion's hand slammed down on the table, causing the

29

water to splash over the cup. "It was her cards. They're spelled." His features darkened into an expression I hadn't seen him wear since we'd first met, when he'd been a different kind of person. "She linked them to herself so she'd know when you were using them. She was waiting for this moment ..." His words trailed off as the knocks continued at the front door.

My mom tossed a linen cloth over the tarot cards. "Just in case," she said as she tightly wrapped the cards. "We don't know what kind of power this witch has or what her intentions are."

"A message," croaked Calista. "And she didn't finish. I felt her struggle to maintain the connection before her energy faded."

Whoever knocked at the front door persisted.

"I'll get it." I jumped up, and the room swayed. The nauseating knots in my stomach tightened, and the lingering smell of dense, smoky incense weighed heavily on my lungs. I craved a breath of the pure, untainted air outside.

I paused just before exiting the room. The persistent knocker could wait another minute. "Why does the Spider Witch go by that name?" I asked.

It was Selkie who answered. Strands of her strawberry hair frizzed out of her bun in every direction. You'd think she'd just gotten off a roller-coaster ride.

Glancing around, I saw everyone looked a bit frazzled and out of sorts.

Selkie's singsong voice brought my attention back to my question. "She's called the Spider Witch because of her ability to weave together ancient magic from many traditions and cultures. The Spider Witch practices every magic ever known on Earth."

Selkie's answer confirmed my suspicion. The witch had hijacked my energy when she'd grabbed hold of me. If she was powerful enough to tap into my energy field, what else could she do? Hairs on the back of my neck prickled. *She knows about us and isn't afraid to use her knowledge to her advantage.*

"Don't leave out the best part, Selk," Darion added, almost excitedly. "She collects venomous spiders from around the world and uses their venom in her spells. She doesn't exclude any magic from her repertoire." Darion locked eyes with me.

I turned for the living room, ignoring the chill that settled in my bones. As I neared the front door, I picked up the familiar energy that hovered on the other side. On any other night, I would have opened the door elated to see him, but tonight, of all nights, was not a night for outsiders. I pulled open the door with a forced smile.

"Lucas! What are you doing here?" I didn't mean for my words to sound accusatory, so I backstepped. "I mean, I'm glad to see you, but I wasn't expecting you until tomorrow."

His brows drew down, and the porch light reflected in his blue eyes. He passed his hand through his sandy-blond hair and shifted his backpack on his shoulders. "I'm sorry, Ev. I tried to call ahead but got no answer. There's something I found that will make you understand why I rushed over."

"Oh?" I muttered. The tone in his voice wasn't what I would have expected from someone with good news.

The witch's warning echoed in my ear as I moved away from the doorframe. Her words, "Destruction, chaos, death," filled me with a sense of dread.

"Come in."

The others had already started clearing the table when we entered the dining room. I no longer had an appetite after what'd happened, and by the look of it, everyone else felt the same.

Someone had blown out all the candles, and the scent of sulfur lingered as the smoke dissipated.

Lucas paused. "I didn't mean to interrupt." He glanced at me apologetically.

"You're not," I assured him, and slipped my hand into his. "We were just finishing up."

My relationship with Lucas was new. We'd only just started dating, and it was long distance, since he still lived in Eugene, where he attended college and ran one of Neil's bars. We'd met when I'd been investigating a lead on who my father was meeting with before his murder. Lucas had helped show me around the area, and we'd stayed connected ever since.

Luna yelped excitedly when she saw Lucas, and ran up, rubbing her body across his legs.

"Who was at the door?" Jasper asked as he came back in from the kitchen. "Oh, hey, man." He bumped knuckles with Lucas. "Good to see you. You ready for the gig tomorrow night?"

Jasper had been standoffish with Lucas in the beginning, but they'd slowly bonded over their shared love of music, and he'd invited Lucas to play in his showcase for the Halloween masquerade ball tomorrow night. It was our town's biggest event of the year, and Jasper's first year performing as the headlining entertainment.

"Absolutely." Lucas nodded. "I've got my gear loaded in the car."

"Sweet! Since you're here early"—Jasper threw me a glance—"maybe we can get some extra rehearsal time in tonight." He moved his hands in the air as if he were hitting drums.

"You bet," Lucas agreed. He shifted the pack on his back, eager to show me what he had come early for, but he seemed unsure now that there were others around.

I reached out a hand and smoothed his shoulder. "What was it you wanted to show me?"

32

He slid his backpack off his shoulders. "It's about the picture," he whispered.

"Oh," I breathed, knowing exactly what picture he meant. "What about it?" My heart thumped. The pictures had led to a dead end, and we'd found no other clues about what had happened to Creagan last year.

Lucas closed the distance between us. "I think he's back."

The room spun.

Lucas dropped his backpack to the floor, swooping his arms around me to steady my balance.

Darion darted to my side, coming in just as Lucas caught me. "What's going on in here?"

Jasper bolted to my other side.

I pushed away from all three of them. "Would everyone just chill? I'm fine. It was just a dizzy spell."

I grabbed a glass of water from the table and drank deeply, turning to hide the tremble in my hands. My skin flushed as the chilled water filled my belly. I forced my hand to steady as I set the glass down on the table. "Show me."

Lucas extracted a large manila envelope from his pack. "Are you sure?" His eyes darted toward the kitchen, where we could hear my mom, Selkie, and Calista talking while they cleaned.

I nodded. "They know everything."

Lucas slid a stack of eight-by-ten photos out of the envelope. He laid them exactly where the tarot cards had been only minutes ago, and the images on the cards flashed in my mind as Lucas spread the photos out.

"You recognize this top one." His finger pointed at the date printed on the photo. "It's the one we printed from last year."

How could I forget the hooded figure who sat next to my father shortly before his murder?

"Look at the ring he's wearing." Lucas had circled the ring

on the stranger's finger in red ink, a detail we hadn't noticed before. "It was blurry in the original prints, but I went back through the footage and caught a new angle."

The tips of my ears sizzled. *How could I have missed this?*

"Now, look at this one." He slid the second photo next to the first.

A hooded figure similar to the one sitting next to my father in the first photo sat at the bar, holding a glass. The camera focused closer on the man's hand in this photo, and the ring circled in red ink was the same as the first one.

"This photo was from last week." Lucas pointed at the recent date printed from the video camera.

A shiver raced down my spine as I bent closer and scanned the two photos. The masculine profile in each photo mirrored the other. The same broad shoulders and confident posture. And an unmistakable letter marked the top of each ring. I studied the E with such intensity, my eyes ached.

"You're the bartender behind the bar," Darion pointed out. "Do you remember what he looked like?" Darion's words came out as agitated as I felt.

"That's the thing." Lucas scrunched up his face and rubbed the back of his neck. "I have no memory of ever seeing or serving him." He grabbed the third photo. "Although I clearly did."

The third photo had a crystal-clear image of Lucas handing the man a drink. "I have a vague memory of seeing the ring and thinking there was something familiar about it, but that's it, nothing else. My mind goes blank every time I try to remember anything about the man."

Lucas squeezed the top of a chair, his knuckles turning white as he stared hard at the photos. "It's infuriating. I've been racking my brain, trying to figure out how I could forget." He turned his head toward me. "I'm sorry, Ev. This is huge, and I've let you down."

I shook my head. "It's not your fault, Lucas. We don't blame you for not remembering. You see a ton of people every day."

"Yeah." He tilted the chair back. "But it looks like I'm engaging in conversation. I just don't understand how I can't remember anything."

I knew how he could forget, but I couldn't tell him without revealing the truth about myself. Whoever sat disguised under the hooded sweater had made sure Lucas wouldn't remember his face by using magic.

A fiery heat burned up my esophagus as my gut screamed that I was looking at the person responsible for my father's death.

My fingers curled into balls as I imagined shredding the hooded figure into pieces.

Forks, plates, and candlesticks rattled atop the table as my nails cut deep into my palms. A pressure on my shoulder jarred me back to my senses. Darion knew I was losing control. Our link intensified when we touched and amplified our abilities. Darion wasn't a dominant Empath or Siphon, like me, but he had some similar abilities, and he used those now.

The tension eased from my chest, and my tightened fingers uncurled as the rattling on the table subsided.

Jasper shot me a concerned glare as he distracted Lucas with more questions. I'd have to tell him about my growing problem with Siobhan's magic.

"We need to show Mom," Darion said, letting his hand slide from my shoulder.

"Show me what?" asked our mom from behind. She came into the room, flanked by Selkie and Calista. Selkie had smoothed her strawberry hair neatly back into its floppy bun, while Calista's curly chestnut locks flowed past her shoulders, wild as ever.

The A-line of my mom's recently sheared raven hair framed her face with sleek edges. Her worried frown lifted into a welcoming smile when she saw Lucas.

"Lucas." She masked the concern that hovered in her energy. "It's nice to see you." Her dark sapphire eyes traveled to the table where the photos lay. The three women moved in closer. "What are these?"

I wasn't sure I had my power under enough control yet to explain the photos without causing another earthquake across the table.

Darion sensed my unease and jumped right in. "Lucas brought these photos," he began, and explained everything to her while Calista and Selkie both listened and examined each photo.

When Darion told them the part about Lucas's memory, the three women shared a meaningful glance.

There wasn't much we could speculate about in front of Lucas, since he didn't know about our magic or origin. But my mom seemed fixated on the ring the stranger wore. She turned the photo this way and that like she expected a new angle to reveal more detail.

"Do you mind if I hold on to this one?" she asked Lucas.

"Yeah, yeah. Of course," Lucas answered while I gave my mom a questioning look, but her attention stayed glued to the photo.

"Boys, would you three mind helping Cal and me carry some things out to my van?" Selkie took off toward the kitchen with the men in tow.

"What is it, Mom?" I asked as soon as Lucas was out of earshot.

She squinted at the photo. "This ring. I've seen it before, or one like it, in the Royal Museum back home."

When she said "home," she was referring to the planet she had come to Earth from, Aenoas-Vita.

"The E sits within a rune. It's the signet of the Ever family. Each member of the royal family had a ring made for them."

I shuddered. "Are you sure?"

She shook her head. "It's been many years, but I'm sure this ring belonged to a royal member of our family. But what's it doing in this photo, and who is the man wearing it? You, Darion, and I are all that remains of the Ever line."

"Well," Jasper's loud yawn warned that they had finished helping Selkie and Calista. He stretched his long arms over his head as Darion and Lucas trailed in behind him. "You still crashing at my pad?" he asked Lucas.

"We'll talk later." My mom kissed my cheek, then tucked the photo under her arm and dashed out of the room.

"Yeah, man. If it's cool that I'm a day early." Lucas scooped up the remaining photos and slid them into their envelope, then handed them to me. "I'm sorry I can't remember anything more useful." His lips curved down apologetically.

I shook my head. "No more apologies. It's not your fault." I handed the envelope to Darion. "I'm going to walk Lucas and Jasper out."

Lucas picked up his backpack and swung it over his shoulder. He and Jasper talked excitedly about their jam session as we made our way through the living room.

I paused on the front porch, breathing in the sultry floral scents of the wisteria that still bloomed.

"I'll meet you at my place," Jasper told Lucas as he grabbed his helmet from the porch bench.

I followed him to his motorcycle, and he pulled me into a hug. "See you at the party tomorrow." We both knew he referred to the not-so-secret birthday party my mom had been planning for me and Darion.

Jasper's amber eyes darkened when he whispered, "Don't worry. We'll take on whatever is coming."

I squeezed him tight before letting him go.

Lucas waited patiently. He understood the deep bond between Jasper and me and didn't feel any jealousy towards our friendship. I waved as Jasper straddled his motorcycle and turned out of the driveway. Our friendship had endured a lot over the last year, and I'd worried how Jasper would feel when I'd talked to him about my developing relationship with Lucas. When he confessed his love for me last year, I had hurt him deeply by admitting that I couldn't commit to anything more than our friendship. But we'd moved past that, and he'd been supportive of my feelings toward Lucas. He knew how hurt I'd been after receiving Arden's letter, and spending time with Lucas had helped me move past my pain. At least that's what I told him and myself, but the truth was I couldn't escape the constant presence of Arden in my thoughts. My hand instinctively reached my chest, gently massaging my heart to ease the familiar pain that came with thoughts of Arden.

I lifted my head toward the sky. Despite being conceived on a planet somewhere galaxies away, its looming presence felt closer by the day. I brushed aside the familiar apprehension that came with thinking about Aenoas-Vita, and instead focused on the captivating constellations that embellished the night as a new sense of unease took hold of my mind.

What threat was the Spider Witch warning me of? And what answer could the stars possibly hold?

I searched the flickering lights for some kind of meaning in the witch's riddle, but found none.

A warmth pressed close behind me as I closed my eyes and filled my belly and lungs with crisp autumn air. I relaxed against Lucas and listened to the harmonizing melody of crickets and tree frogs that sang in the night, oblivious to the woes of larger creatures.

My skin tingled as firm hands grazed my sides, traveling up my back and massaging my neck and shoulders. The tension melted from my muscles as Lucas supported my body weight with his own. His fingers swooped my hair over one shoulder, and soft lips brushed the side of my cheek before trailing down my exposed neck.

Flashes of another filled my memory: Arden's body pressed tight to mine as his touch electrified my senses.

No! I pushed Arden's image away, trying to banish the memory from my mind. *I have to stop thinking about Arden every time Lucas touches me.*

"I'm glad you're here," I whispered, and kept my eyes closed as Lucas shifted his body and turned me to face him.

"Me too." His lips gently touched mine.

I stood on my tiptoes and ran my fingers through his silky hair as images of blue-green eyes shrouded in a golden halo stole me away. My stomach stirred as his kiss deepened.

I want you. Arden's voice echoed in my mind.

I froze, frustrated that I couldn't seal away my feelings for Arden. No matter how hard I tried, I couldn't replace Arden's image with Lucas. I forcefully closed the door on his memory and then opened my eyes.

Lucas stared down at me with the same confusion I'd seen over and over. "I should probably head to Jasper's." The unanswered question lingered between us.

I'd been vague when I'd told him I'd just come out of a relationship when we'd first met. I hadn't expected our relationship to be anything more than friendship when we'd kept in touch after my research trip to Eugene last year. But now that it was, there was no way for me to explain why I pushed him away every time things got heated. How could I tell him that another had stolen my heart and taken it with him to another planet?

I knew Lucas hoped I'd invite him to my place. But I just couldn't, not as long as Arden filled the space between us. It wouldn't be fair to Lucas.

Guilt twisted my insides when Lucas smiled down at me with his usual understanding and lifted my chin with his finger.

"I'll see you tomorrow." He kissed me, then opened his passenger-side door and tossed his backpack inside. He walked with heavy steps to the other side of his car and paused before getting into the driver's seat. "Night, Ev."

The wind rustled his sandy-blond hair, and my stomach tightened. A halo of golden hair bled into my vision as my mind betrayed me again.

Stop! I silently begged my traitorous thoughts.

My lips curved up into a forced smile. "Night, Lucas."

As Lucas drove away, I glanced up at the stars one last time, not thinking about the Spider Witch's warning but about something else—someone else—then turned for the door.

CHAPTER 3

$\mathcal{T}$he next morning passed in a flurry of activity. Darion had stayed overnight at the house, in the spare room my mom had fixed up for him. He had his own apartment above the café, but I think he stayed over so frequently to watch over us.

So much had changed between us over the past year. Darion had been my enemy, and I'd hated him with every fiber of my being when we'd first met. He'd kidnapped our mother and tortured her. But that was before either of us had known the truth of his conception and birth. Darion still had his moments and still drove me crazy at times, but at some point, without even realizing it, the three of us had become a family.

I sipped my coffee at the counter, watching Darion flip omelets on the grill. I remembered the letter our father had left him before I'd known Siobhan wasn't Darion's biological mother. Creagan had apologized in the letter for not being the father Darion deserved and had asked him to look after my mom and me. He hadn't used our names in the letter, but now we both knew it was us he'd referred to. Each day since

41

that night on the beach when Darion had sacrificed his life to save our mother, his actions had proved his intent to fulfill our father's last request.

"Hey, you two," my mom chimed as she came into the kitchen through the back-porch door. The pile of herbs she carried, and the dirt smudged on her cheek, hinted she'd been in the greenhouse. "Darion, it smells wonderful."

He flipped one omelet onto a plate and added a scoopful of roasted garlic and rosemary potatoes. "Perfect timing, Mom." He set the steaming plate of food on the counter and nodded for my mom to help herself. He handed me the next and took the third for himself. My mom set her armful of herbs on the counter and dug into her breakfast. We didn't bother carrying our plates into the dining room. Instead, we leaned casually against the kitchen island and ate together.

In between bites, my mom asked, "Would you two mind helping me unload some boxes at the café this afternoon?"

I glanced over my plate at Darion, and he winked at me. We both knew the real reason she wanted to get us down to the café. "Sure, Mom," we said in unison, and laughed. After a minute, the room fell quiet, except for my mom's fork circling her plate while she seemed lost in thought.

"Everything okay, Mom?" Darion asked, his amused demeanor switching to concern.

She perked up, realizing we'd noticed her distracted attention. "Sure, honey." She rinsed her plate and filled a glass of water. "I hope you two don't mind, but I'll need to go to the masquerade separately tonight. There's someone I need to meet with first."

Darion's brow creased. "But the three of us planned to go together." He set his plate down. "Who are you meeting?" Darion never cared about crossing boundaries, which was why he hadn't thought twice about spying on Calista while she was on her trip. But this time I agreed with him. Our mom was hiding something, and I also wanted to know what it was.

She finished her glass of water and washed her hands, quietly biding her time. She leaned against the counter and glanced between us as she held the hand towel, drying her wet hands, then sighed. "I'm meeting with Freya Moon." She set the towel down and busied herself with separating her herbs.

"The lady who owns the crystal woo-woo shop and offers palm readings? What are you meeting her for?" Darion picked his plate back up and shoved a bite into his mouth.

I remembered the time I'd gone into the crystal shop with Molly. A girl our age had been working behind the counter and had helped us. While she gave Molly a palm reading, I pretended to browse the shop while homing in on a powerful energy that I'd since come to correlate with Vitarian energy. I scanned the crystals, charms, and tarot cards, all the while searching out the source of the energy. Then my eyes landed on a woman watching me from behind a beaded doorway. She slipped away deeper down a hall when I noticed her.

My eyes snapped to meet my mom's. "Freya Moon is Vitarian, isn't she?"

My mom set her herbs down and turned. The scent of fresh rosemary filled the air, masking the fading aroma of garlic from breakfast. She slid her hands inside the pockets of the overalls she always wore while gardening. Since Vitarians didn't age at the same rate as humans, she'd always looked younger than what you'd expect of someone at her supposed human age, and with her new stylish short bob, she didn't look a day over thirty.

"Freya is Vitarian." My mom's dark lashes drooped closed as she paused for a moment. "But she's very cautious of other Vitarians, and she's anything but woo-woo." She quirked a pointed brow. "Freya was a stone reader and a crystal worker on our planet, and well-known for her ability to cross into the spiritual realm. We've helped each other in the past, and I was hoping she'd be willing to help me again with the Spider Witch's reading, and she's agreed to meet with me."

Something worried me about how standoffish this Freya had been when I'd been in her shop. "Darion and I are coming with you." My tone brooked no argument.

"Agreed," Darion added.

A ray of sunlight shot through the kitchen window, appearing to slice through the air, and bathed the kitchen in a warm glow. After a moment, our mom took one each of our hands. "After we're dressed for the ball, we'll go see Freya on our way together."

~

In no time at all, we had arrived at the waterfront parking area for the café, situated right in front of my mother's building. The café occupied the ground floor, with rented apartments on the upper levels.

The parking spaces were all taken save the one that mom kept reserved for one of our vehicles at all times, for unloading products. She stopped and waited for the group dressed as ghouls and ogres to cross the parking lot before she whipped into her reserved space in front of the café.

Now that it was October, the thirty-one days of Halloween Town festivities that our town hosted to attract tourism were in full swing. Tourists flocked to the area during the entire month, visiting decorated shops, and riding on bus tours while listening to presentations on ghosts and aliens.

Our town gained a reputation as a local hot spot for haunted historic buildings, and it didn't hurt that we also had a UFO sighting on record, or that teams of ghost-hunting "experts" officially deemed some of our historic buildings haunted. October definitely added a change of pace to our normally sleepy town, and the local business owners enjoyed a nice economic boom.

I pushed the SUV door open and stood in the parking space, gazing out at the surrounding mountains and the Columbia River. A pang tightened in my chest every time I thought of leaving the town I called home for a planet I'd never known. There had to be an alternative to the deal I'd made with Oria. She wanted her bloodline back on the throne. If I hadn't agreed, Darion would be dead, and Siobhan would have successfully destroyed our mother. I had no other choice but to fulfill Oria's prophecy and accept her offer.

A gust of wind rippled past, and I felt a streak of envy at watching the sailboats tack back and forth along the estuary, taking advantage of this gorgeous fall morning and the calm breeze. The sun added a warm glow all around, while its rays sparkled over the river water, giving it a majestic appearance.

The loud horn of a school bus splashed with fake blood and guts, and doubling as a temporary tour bus for the dead, wicked, and immortal, brought my attention back to the present. The bus cruised through the parking lot, blasting spooky tunes from the open windows. People dressed as aliens, witches, vampires, scary red-haired clowns with razor-sharp teeth, and princesses waved from the windows as they hooted and hollered along with the music.

"Humans are so weird," Darion complained as he lifted open the trunk of the 4Runner.

I quirked an eyebrow at him as we piled our arms with boxes. "Vitarians don't celebrate Halloween on our planet?"

Darion barked out a laugh. "Halloween is a human holiday." Darion looked out at the passersby. "Humans have lost touch with the true meaning of their traditions." He pointed toward the crowds, taking selfies with Halloween props. "Do you think any of these people even know or care about the history of Samhain or Dia de los Muertos or any other cultural tradition that celebrates their dead?" His forehead creased with lines as he shook his head. "They only care about"—Darion's mouth turned down like he'd eaten something sour—"the number of likes and follows they get on their social media accounts."

I shifted the boxes, trying not to get irritated at the way Darion regarded humans. "Please don't go into another one of your 'Vitarians are far superior to humans' rants again. I've had enough. And"—my brow arched—"I see you've been reading up on human history. Maybe there's more to humans than you give them credit for."

He grinned. "Yeah, well, Vitarians like to know the history of their home."

Darion's response surprised me. I steadied the wobbling stack on my hip. "So Earth's home now, huh?" I couldn't hide the hint of sarcasm lacing my words.

He snatched a teetering box from the top of my stack. "Don't read too much into it." He closed the trunk door. "Now, remember, act surprised," Darion prompted as he pulled open the café door and held it wide.

As expected, a chorus of voices sang "Surprise!" when we entered. Someone came up and removed the toppling weight from my arms, and I looked around to find the space filled with smiling faces. A banner hung above the register and bakery case that read: HAPPY BIRTHDAY EV AND DARION.

I turned to find my mom. She gave us a beaming smile and waved excitedly as she came over. "I can't believe this is really happening." She squeezed us both into a group hug. "I finally get to celebrate a birthday for both of my children together." She wiped an escaped tear from the corner of her eye. "I hope you two don't mind the big party."

"Of course not, Mom." I snapped my mental guard into place to block the vibrations drawing nearer to me. A group this large took more conscious work to keep the tendrils of energy from latching onto me.

Since I'd absorbed Siobhan's powers last year, my own abilities had heightened, and lately, proved unpredictable. As my ability to siphon grew stronger, I unintentionally attracted energy everywhere I went, and if I wasn't careful, I could leave a person feeling drained for days.

Darion squeezed my shoulder. He knew the challenge I faced while being in large groups.

"Thanks, Mom." He wrapped his free arm around our mom. "I've never had a surprise party before. This is awesome!"

Molly came bolting in our direction. Her hair was nearly all one shade of blond now, save for the bright pink strip she kept dyed on one side. "Happy birthday, you two," she sang while hugging me and kissing my cheek.

Darion synced up with Molly as she linked her arm through his, and the two huddled in whispered giggles as they separated themselves from me and my mom.

Molly had been the first human Darion seemed to like. She'd won him over with her quirky and honest character, never hesitating to call him out when his serious sarcasm crossed the line.

I'd held my breath the first time she'd scolded him. He'd been more unpredictable than my magic when he'd first come into our lives. But his silver eyes had lit up at her bluntness, and he had truly smiled for the first time since being freed from Siobhan.

"What do you think is going on between those two?" I

quietly asked my mom while noticing brushed shoulders and meaningful glances between Molly and Darion.

My mom also observed their interactions. "I don't know exactly, but Molly has had a wonderful influence on Darion. It's been months since he's slipped into another melancholy episode. Who would have thought"—she waved at Molly and Darion as the two laughed while Molly shoved some kind of brie-stuffed hors d'oeuvre into Darion's mouth—"that our little Molly would someday be the ray of hope to lift my son out of the dark pit Siobhan buried him in? I love that sweet girl."

I glanced back at Molly and Darion with the eyes of an Empath. Their auras bloomed bright pinks, purples, and greens, blending as one. Energy sizzled in their surrounding space. They were in love. How had I missed this until now? I blinked and pulled my magic back, not wanting to invade my friend's privacy. A lump of saliva caught in my dry throat as I realized that I'd been so caught up in searching for answers to Creagan's death, and burying my feelings toward Arden, that I'd been an absent friend.

Well, that's changing right now.

I bristled as I remembered how upset Molly had been at the studio when Darion hadn't rejected Bree's flirting right away. I'd thought Darion was just being Darion, but now that I sensed his true feelings toward Molly, it ticked me off even more that he hadn't immediately put Bree in her place.

Energy built at my fingertips as I considered sending Darion a jolt that would teach him a lesson for acting like a tool with Bree. But it faded when Darion interlaced his fingers with Molly's, and the two shared a stare that I recognized.

Indecision gnawed at me as I rubbed my hands together, and the magic eased. Molly was great for Darion—no argument there—but was he good for her? I'd learned many things about Darion over this past year. He feared rejection and masked his feelings by acting in ways to turn people off. I knew it was a protective mechanism he'd developed as a child, desperate for Siobhan's affection. His moods could be volatile. Sure, he'd improved dramatically, but Molly had always been like a sister to me, and I couldn't ignore Darion's past and what he'd been capable of before, even though he'd been under Siobhan's manipulations. Molly hadn't known the Darion I'd first met, and I had to wonder how much of that Darion still existed. If he hurt Molly, even unintentionally, he'd have to answer to me, brother or not.

Fabric tickled my shoulder as my mom bent toward my ear. "You made this possible for him. If you hadn't saved his life and absorbed Siobhan's curse, he'd still be linked to her, or worse." She squeezed my hand. "I'm sorry we haven't found a way to free you both from that wretched curse, but we'll keep searching. There has to be a safe way to undo it. Maybe if you contacted Oria again ..."

"Mom. Please. I can't ask Oria for help again. She made it abundantly clear that unless I hold up my end of the bargain, she won't help me. She's cut me off from the ancestors until I sit on her damn throne." I glanced around to make sure no one heard me and kept my voice to a whisper. "I'm not ready to leave Earth. Darion's still adjusting, and I haven't found Creagan's killer, and I'm not leaving until I do. We don't know why he was meeting with the person in the photo. They could still be a threat. Besides, Siobhan happily informed us that she designed the curse with only one way to end it, and that's not an option, so Darion and I will have to accept that our lives are linked indefinitely."

Voices boomed around us as guests mingled, reminding me we were at a party that my mom had worked hard to plan. "How about we forget about the curse for a day and enjoy the celebration?"

My mom's lips formed a sad smile as she pulled me into a hug. "You're right. This is a special day, so let's forget about curses and witch's warnings and enjoy the company of all these lovely people."

Inhaling deeply, I strengthened my mental defenses and observed the room. The café was bursting with people. My mom must have invited half the town. Bodies flowed in and out, filling plates with food from the buffet or accepting treats from the trays circling the room. I leaned my head gently against my mom's, determined to make this day everything she'd imagined. "Thank you for all this. I know how much celebrating Darion's birthday with him means to you. Love you infinity times infinity infinities forever." I kissed her cheek.

"Love you infinity, honey." She sighed happily and accepted a glass of champagne from one of the catering staff and a glass of non-alcoholic cider for me.

I'd learned that alcohol made it harder for me to control my powers, so I refrained from it entirely. Occasionally I enjoyed a sip of the ever flower elixir at Neil's club, but even that had to be consumed in limited doses.

"Oh, here comes Lucas and Jasper." I sensed their energy and waved them over. My eyes went wide when I saw what the two wore. A glittering, skintight and neon-green alien suit that would most definitely glow in the dark covered Jasper. Shiny green makeup disguised his face, and he'd sprayed his hair to match.

Jasper had obviously convinced Lucas to join him in dressing up for the Halloween masquerade ball tonight. And by the look of it, they'd used Lucas's Australian heritage as inspiration. He was the spitting image of Mick "Crocodile" Dundee, from head to toe. Wavy wisps of his sandy-blond hair stuck out of the cowboy hat atop his head. A sleeveless, dark green leather vest accentuated his toned torso, revealing the full scope of his corded muscles covered in tattoos from shoulders to hands.

My eyes traveled the length of his tight leather pants that left nothing to the imagination. *Oh, boy.* A sting prickled in my cheeks as I dragged my eyes back up his body and gulped down my chilled cider.

A soft voice to my left broke my lingering appraisal of Lucas as he moved through the room, making his way in my direction. "Happy birthday, Everly."

I turned to see Piper and her dad, Sheriff Baze, walking up. "I made you some homemade soap." Piper held out a small wrapped package topped with a pink bow, matching the one she had tied around her dark, glossy hair.

"Pip, you're not supposed to tell what the gift is before the recipient opens it." The sheriff smiled lovingly down at his daughter.

"Thank you, Piper. I can smell the lovely scent through the paper, and it smells incredible. I can't wait to use it."

Her eyes twinkled at my delight with her gift. Her blue eye followed her brown eye as she looked nervously to the side, down at her feet, and then back at me. "Um, now that I've learned to make my own soap, I was wondering if you'd teach me to make your oatmeal butterscotch cookies."

"Piper," said the sheriff patiently. "I'm sure Everly is very busy."

"It's okay, Sheriff. I would love to teach Piper how to make her favorite cookies." I winked at her, and she jumped up and down, sending the ruffles of her dress into a frenzy.

"Well, if you're sure it won't interfere with your plans, and please, it's just Sam today," the sheriff—Sam—said, smiling, his gaze drifting to my mom as she neared. "Cacsha, this is a well-structured party." His cheeks burned. "I just mean, you've done a good job managing the flow of traffic coming in and out."

Was the sheriff trying to flirt with my mom? Albeit in an awkward sort of way, but his energy had that nervous, "I like you, but I don't know how to tell you" sort of vibe.

"Thank you, Sam," my mom returned, casually tucking her hair behind one ear. "I suppose, being sheriff, it'd be hard not to notice that type of thing." Now her cheeks had brightened.

Okay. What's going on here?

Before I had a chance to put any more thought into my mom and the sheriff, Molly came catapulting toward me. "Ev!" she squealed as she threw her arms around me. We both stumbled back with her enthusiasm.

"Hey, Molls. What's up?" I laughed as I hugged her back and breathed in the familiar smells of warm spicy cinnamon, sweet sugar, and earthy honey that drifted from her hair, a dead giveaway that she'd been in the kitchen helping prepare for today's party. The smell reminded me of not so long ago, when Molly, Ty, and I would bake together here at the café. I smiled at the memory of the three of us covering the kitchen in flour during one of our many flour wars, which had inevitably brought my mom scowling into the kitchen before she'd shoved her hand in the flour and anni-hilated the three of us. My stomach ached at the memory. I missed how things used to be between the three of us, before I'd lied to Ty the night I'd borrowed his dad's boat to rescue my mom and Jasper. When we came back, he didn't buy the story I told him, and I couldn't convince myself to let my mom wipe his memory of the night. Even though I knew our friendship would never be the same if Ty believed I had kept the truth from him, I couldn't bring myself to violate his mind, but I also couldn't tell him what really happened. The truth wasn't just mine to share, and exposure could put us all in danger.

"I can't wait for tonight! We're going to have so much

fun," Molly blurted, drawing me back to the present moment. "Did Darion tell you?" she asked, wide-eyed.

"Tell me what?"

"He's going to be my Gomez. He didn't say anything?" Her tone lost some of its enthusiasm.

Now I understood why Darion had been so concerned about being late to the ball tonight. He'd made plans with Molly. "Oh, he hasn't mentioned his costume, but I know that he's been looking forward to tonight." I searched the crowd for Darion. "We'll be a little late, since we have to help my mom with something first." I didn't want to give specifics. If I told Molly where we were going, she'd want to come and ask questions I couldn't answer. The weight of every lie settled on me like an anchor, causing me to drift further apart from my friends.

Molly's expression briefly flashed with something before she said, "Yeah, Darion told me about that. He was going to pick me up, but now we're just going to meet there." She shrugged. "It's okay."

A pang pinched at my chest as Molly twisted a strand of her hair, trying hard not to show how bummed she felt. I'd tell Darion to pick Molly up like they'd planned and let me go to see Freya with Mom alone, but I knew he'd never agree. Just like Jasper, he had a tendency to take his protectiveness to the extreme.

Molly's face lit up. "Ty's here."

"He is?" I turned, scanning the area Molly faced, and spotted my friend. My lips pressed together. I hadn't seen Ty since he'd taken a second job and scaled back his hours at the café several weeks ago. I chewed my bottom lip as I took in his new appearance. He'd cut his hair in a new, shorter style and wasn't wearing his usual bandanna and tie-dyed shirt. I wanted to ask Molly what'd inspired his drastic change in style, but there was no time.

"Hey, Ev." Ty's lips curved up, showing off his dimpled cheeks.

I returned Ty's smile, still in awe of his new attire. I glanced at Molly, and she shrugged like she didn't have a clue either.

"Hi, Ty. How are you?"

The guilt still stung as I met Ty's milk-chocolate eyes. This was the most we'd spoken to each other since I could remember after the night I'd returned his dad's boat.

Ty shifted and pulled at the top button of his collared shirt like he was a little uncomfortable in his new clothes. He glanced around the room as though he was searching for someone, before responding to my question. "I've been good." He stopped fiddling with the stiff fold of his collar and lifted his other hand. "Happy birthday." He held out his trademark gift bag, made of old comics.

As I looked at the cartoon characters, memories of the fun times Ty and I had reading comics together made me smile. He'd used our favorite comic to construct the bag. "Thank you, Ty." Accepting the gift, I held onto the hope that it signaled a possibility for our friendship to heal.

"Well, let's find out what's inside." Molly edged closer.

Ty and Molly both watched eagerly as I pulled the tissue paper off the top, then carefully lifted out a beautiful dream catcher. My eyes went wide as I traced the intricately woven web to the E that decorated the center. My chest tightened at Ty's generosity and thoughtfulness.

"Ty, it's absolutely lovely. Thank you so much."

The tension Ty carried eased, and his eyes beamed. "Yeah, you're welcome. This weaving technique"—his finger traced a delicate area of web—"has been a skill passed down through my family, originating among the first tribes in this area."

I admired the craftsmanship and how the string criss-crossed in a seamless and complicated design. "It's amazing."

"He made me a similar one with an M in the middle. I have it hanging above my pillow," Molly declared. "I've had the best dreams." Molly's eyes darted sideways toward Darion, who was standing near the buffet table, and her mouth turned down as her eyes narrowed into slits. "Oh, hell no," she blurted.

I followed Molly's gaze and understood what had riled her. *Who invited her?*

Bree stood with a hand on one hip, wearing a tiny strapless dress that clung tightly to her skin, and, unsurprisingly, a pair of matching stilettos. She reached out and took a bite of something off Darion's plate.

Molly's energy buzzed as a growl escaped her lips.

My jaw clenched, and it took all of my willpower not to send a blast of energy that would knock Bree on her perky ass.

To Darion's credit, he immediately backed up, putting distance between himself and Bree.

"That's it," Molly hissed as she took a step forward. "The claws are coming out."

I snatched Molly's hand. "Hold on, I'm coming with you." But before we even took one step, Bree's attention snapped in our direction. She flung her perfectly straight hair over one shoulder and offered us a satisfied smirk as she strutted our way.

She slid up next to Ty and wrapped a possessive arm around his waist. "There you are." Her finger traced his earlobe. "I've been looking for you." Her syrupy tone made me want to vomit. By the look on Molly's face, I could tell she felt the same way.

What the double hell? I stared wide-eyed at Ty and Bree,

then glanced at Molly, whose eyes nearly bugged out of her head as she whispered, "WTF?"

"Who are you?" Piper chirped from below.

I'd almost forgotten she was standing with us while her dad wandered off with my mom to chat with friends.

Bree's eyes flicked down at Piper, and before I knew it, my magic was burning to be released. I instinctively moved closer to Piper.

"Oh, aren't you a sweet little thing!" Bree cooed. "I just love the bow in your hair."

Piper did a twirl. "Thank you."

I bent down. "Hey, Pip, why don't you go find my mom? I bet she made some of your favorite cookies for today."

"Ooh, yay. Thanks, Everly." She ran off on her new mission.

I reined in my emotions as I stood, dragging my eyes from Bree's arm around Ty, and meeting her glare. I tried to think of a polite way to ask Ty what he was doing with Bree, but Molly beat me to it.

"Uh, Ty, you feel like explaining what you're doing with her?"

Ty fidgeted, his dark brows knitted together as he sensed the hostility hovering between the women. When he scooted slightly from Bree's grasp, she pulled him closer and whispered something in his ear, eliciting a laugh. Ty relaxed and replied, "Molls, Ev, this is Bree—my girlfriend."

Well, that explains Ty's drastic change in attire, but like Molly said, WTF?

Molly's mouth fell open. "How's that possible? Bree only just came to town. We had the displeasure of meeting her yesterday when she interrupted our yoga class before she flirted with Darion." Molly glared at Bree, challenging her to deny the accusation.

Bree didn't miss a beat. "She misunderstood. I was only inviting Everly's brother to see my new studio as a potential new student."

Ty nodded as if that all made complete sense to him.

Acid bubbled in the back of my throat. Bree had Ty wrapped around her finger.

"How did you meet?" I asked in a casual tone, hoping to defuse the heat while I scanned Bree's aura.

Before Ty could answer, Bree jumped in. "Ty was the sweetest thing. I was unloading supplies into my studio a couple of weeks ago when he saw me struggling and offered to help. And fast-forward to now, and here we are." She waved her free hand in the air, nearly swatting a passerby.

The tips of my ears burned. Bree's explanation sounded perfectly reasonable, and nothing in her energy indicated she wasn't being honest. Ty nodded along while he watched Bree speak with goo-goo eyes. But I couldn't shake the feeling that something didn't seem right between these two. Maybe Jasper had rubbed off on me, and I was just being an overprotective friend. But overprotective or not, Bree was an obsessive flirt who craved attention, and Ty deserved better.

Green glitter reflected in Bree's eyes as she stared behind me like a panther stalking her prey.

"Cool alien costume, Jasper." Ty seemed more like himself as he gave Jasper and Lucas details of his own costume he planned to wear for tonight's performance.

I noticed Bree's arm drop from Ty's waist as she ogled Jasper and Lucas.

I wanted to shake Ty and tell him he was too good for Bree, but we didn't have that kind of friendship anymore, and crossing that line might end the small thread that remained.

Darion sidled up next to Molly. Her tight-lipped expression faded as she peeled her attention away from Ty and Bree, and accepted the plate of food Darion handed her, which he'd loaded with all of her favorites.

Darion scanned the scene, rolling his eyes when they landed on Jasper. "An alien. How … original." He popped a bite of something into his mouth, then nodded sideways at Molly to follow him.

Molly edged toward Ty. "We're going to talk later." She spun on her heel and slipped her hand into Darion's.

I didn't like the way Bree stalked Molly as she walked away with Darion. This time, *prey* took on a whole new meaning. I shook myself. I was probably reading too much into Bree's behavior. She was new in town. Sure, she only seemed interested in getting to know the guys, and she had returned my gift basket, but maybe Ty saw something the rest of us didn't.

"Bree …?" The question I'd planned to ask flitted from my mind as the floor spun away. A buzzing vibrated deep inside my ears as I locked onto the familiar thread of energy.

Every nerve in my body sizzled with electricity as I felt him move through the room. I recognized his aura on instinct. Heat torched my skin, and before I could stop myself, I turned in search of him, my feet moving with a will of their own.

Lucas's and Jasper's voices faded into the distance as they called my name, drowned out by the buzzing that now vibrated within my entire body.

Our eyes locked, and a shudder ran through me as a rush of vivid memories flooded my mind: the earthy scent of the dark woods, the rough texture of the ancient oak tree against my back, the lingering sensation of fiery lips on my skin. Since the night we'd said goodbye, and he'd vanished through the portal, taking him back to his home and duty as commander of the Vitarian army, Arden had possessed my dreams.

My breath caught in my throat as he strode toward me, closing the last few feet between us.

Despite not seeing him for a year, the same familiar feelings rushed back at the sight of him. I felt a sudden wave of panic.

What do I say? I'd been so angry when I'd read his letter. *Did he still feel the same way I did, or had he moved on?*

I swallowed hard, trying to rein in my emotions. It was probably already too late. He would know exactly how I felt with his own empath abilities. My cheeks burned hot as I thought of how he'd smiled at me while I'd stared at him like a silly love-struck teenager and dropped his menu to the floor that first time we met here at the café. And here I was, having the same reaction, only a million times worse. And there he was, standing tall with that same confident stance and knowing look in his eyes. The panic intensified, and I could feel the room spinning around me.

Damn it, Everly. Breathe. Just take a breath and fill your lungs with air.

Too late. My heart thrummed against my chest as I lost myself in a sea of blue-green.

Arden took another step, while his gaze drifted to my lips. We stood staring at each other as the room and everyone in it spun out of existence. Arden's lips curved into a delicious grin as his hand grazed my cheek. Just as he was about to say something, he paused and glanced over my shoulder, and an icy wave hit me as his hand fell away from me and he took a step back.

As soon as I felt fingers interlacing with my own, I understood the reason behind Arden's sudden change.

Lucas.

Arden's eyes flicked down to the hand that Lucas had

claimed. A flash of understanding and a bolt of pain disintegrated the outer blue ring that circled his green iris, giving away what he kept hidden behind the wall he'd resurrected between us.

Guilt coursed through me, making my skin feel like it was on fire, as I couldn't bring myself to look away from Arden's intense gaze. I knew it was irrational. Arden had been the one to end things between us. And yet ... The gentle squeeze of my hand jolted me back to reality, making the room and everyone in it come into focus once again. I tore my eyes away from Arden's and glanced to the side, meeting Lucas's questioning stare. In that instant, he knew that the obstacle that had been keeping our relationship stagnant was now right in front of me, causing me to shiver with a simple look.

Turning back to the man who had captured my heart, a dryness settled in my throat, giving it the texture of leather. "Hi," I managed to croak out, my voice cracking with embarrassment.

"Hi," he responded, sending traitorous tingles shooting down to my toes.

"What are you doing here?"

"It looks like he's brought you a birthday gift," said Darion, coming into view while giving me a knowing smirk before positioning himself at my side and settling his glare on Arden. "Arden" was all he said.

The two had a history, and it wasn't good.

Tension stirred as Arden shot Darion a matching glare. Then his expression softened as he returned his attention to me.

"Happy birthday, Everly." He held out a small rectangular package.

Uncontrollable butterflies raced in my stomach as his hand brushed mine, and a charge of electricity rippled between us.

Arden guarded his emotions, but the crease of his brow and the slight quiver that shuddered through him told me he felt it, too.

He dropped his hand, and an icy cold filled the air once again.

I stared down at the neatly wrapped box, feeling unsure of what to do. I untangled my clasped hand from Lucas's.

"You can open it later," Arden suggested.

An arm slid around my waist, and without thinking, I nearly shrugged Lucas away.

"Aren't you going to introduce Arden to your *boyfriend*?" Darion questioned with a ridiculous smile. He enjoyed using the situation to torture Arden, even at my discomfort.

I never explicitly mentioned Arden to Lucas, assuming they would never meet because of living in separate galaxies. And after receiving Arden's letter, I never imagined him unexpectedly appearing like this. But thankfully, both Lucas and Arden had more tact than Darion. They shook hands casually as I introduced them.

"How do you two know each other?" While Lucas maintained a friendly composure, I could sense his uncertainty as he shifted his gaze between Arden and me, piecing together the answer to his unasked question that had always lingered between us.

Darion opened his mouth, ready to add more fuel to the fire, but my silent plea shut him up. He pressed his lips together tight while I answered Lucas.

"Arden is ..." The guilt of keeping the truth from Lucas tore at my heart. But what could I say? This is the love of my life who broke my heart and now that he's back, all I want is to feel his lips on mine while his arms crush me against him. I felt my cheeks and chest flush as the image filled my mind.

"I'm a friend of the family," Arden jumped in and saved me.

I nodded my thanks as I tried to get hold of myself.

"You should open your gift." Lucas stepped back, giving me space.

"Oh—I—" I glanced at my hand, realizing I had completely forgotten about the gift I held. I glanced back up at Arden, unsure of what to do.

"Yeah, Ev. It's rude not to open a gift in front of the person who gave it to you." Darion shrugged when I glared at him.

Irritation gnawed at me. If I hadn't been afraid of losing control of my magic, I'd have sent Darion a jolt or two that would keep him quiet. Instead, I had no other choice but to open Arden's gift now in front of Lucas.

My fingers hesitated with a slight tremble before I peeled the wrapping paper off to reveal a long and narrow wooden box. Intricately carved flowers decorated the top. As I touched the wood, a familiar energy hummed beneath my fingertips, confirming its origin from the legendary ever tree. Carefully, I lifted the lid on its tiny hinges, my eyes drawn to the engraving beneath it. Elegantly scrolled in the Vitarian language was a message meant for my eyes only. I kept the lid low to escape Lucas's view.

I stared speechlessly at a sparkling bracelet. It wasn't gold or silver; it had an unfamiliar, ethereal quality. Ever flowers adorned the bracelet, sparkling like jewels. The hues shimmered and gleamed, creating a dazzling display.

"Arden, this is stunning. Thank you."

"May I?" he asked, indicating the clasp.

I handed him the bracelet and held out my wrist.

The air warmed as his hands brushed across my skin. Sweat beaded on the back of my neck as I tried to calm the erratic flutter of my heart.

"It fits perfectly," Arden admired. As his fingers trailed

across mine, a surge of energy pulsed between us before he abruptly withdrew his hand.

"That's quite the gift," Lucas remarked with a slight furrow to his brow as he studied me.

"I'm glad you like it." Arden glanced around him, looking at anything but me. "I should go," he said, "and give others a chance to wish you a happy birthday."

My throat clenched at the thought of Arden disappearing again. "I'll walk you out."

I kissed Lucas on the cheek. "I'll be right back."

His aura grew murky as he offered me a strained smile.

I rushed through the crowd, thanking people along the way who wished me a happy birthday, and followed Arden around the corner of the building.

His long legs strode quickly. "Arden! Wait!"

He stopped, and I ran to him. His arms wrapped around me in an instant, and we clung to each other with the same fierceness as we had that night in the woods.

"I need to explain about Lucas."

"It's okay," he whispered in my ear. "I understand. You are living your life, just as I wanted you to. You don't have to explain anything." He lifted his head, and a blaze of green stared down at me. The world slipped away, and our lips crashed together.

The kiss was brief, but said everything.

I took a couple of steps back. The wind swirled through my hair and cooled the sting of my skin, but not the heat I felt from the anger building inside me. "Why? I know what you said in your letter. But you still feel the same way I do? So why would you end things?"

Arden sighed, reaching for my hand. "Because you've sacrificed so much already. You deserve to live a normal life while you can here on Earth. You're a young woman, Everly, and you deserve to have all the experiences that come with that, not saving yourself for someone galaxies away who can't put you before his duty."

"Why a letter? Why didn't you come to tell me in person? You owed me that."

He lifted his free hand and cupped my cheek. "Because one look at you, and I would have lost the courage to let you go."

I shook his hand away. "Why come back now? After all this time."

Arden smoothed the honeyed five-o'clock shadow growing along his jawline. "Felix received a message from your mother."

I nodded. I knew about the message she'd sent. My mom trusted Felix, and she often sought his advice. He had been her guardian as a child and had accompanied her to Earth when Siobhan exiled her. He'd only returned to Aenoas-Vita with Arden at our request. We needed someone we could trust unquestionably to preside over the council in my absence.

"Is that the only reason?" I glanced down at the bracelet adorning my wrist, trying to hold on to the anger I felt.

Arden lifted my chin with his finger, his eyes squinting from the sun as his lips curved into a smile. "No. It just gave me a reason to get past my fear of seeing you."

"Why would you be afraid?"

His forehead rested on mine. "Because you're all I've thought about every day this past year. And I was afraid you wouldn't feel the same way after—"

"After you broke my heart," I finished for him.

"Yes." He breathed in my hair and traced the tip of his nose down the side of my face until his lips brushed mine.

I put my hand on his chest. "Lucas is an incredibly great guy, and he has really been there for me this past year."

Arden nodded and released me from his grasp and stepped back.

I shielded my eyes with my hand to block the intense sunlight reflecting off the building's side windows. "Are you going back?" I held my breath, waiting for his answer.

He shook his head. "I'm staying at the cabin for now."

Felix's cabin sat nestled in the woods near a mountain peak. He'd spelled it with powerful magic. The cabin and its surrounding forest were impenetrable to anyone the spell didn't recognize.

The cabin was also where Arden had trained me, and where we'd shared our first kiss.

Arden's intense gaze sent another chill rippling down my spine. He was thinking of that night, the same as I, and the memory sparked another charge of energy that drew us closer. We each took a step, our fingers interlacing of their own accord.

"I have to get back." I told myself to turn and get back to the café—back to Lucas. But my feet wouldn't budge; they stayed cemented in place as my face instinctively lifted.

"I've missed you," he breathed, his lips moving closer to mine.

The ache that grew deep inside me felt explosive. Just as I couldn't take it anymore and dug my nails into Arden's shoulders, and his mouth touched mine, voices boomed around the corner.

I breathed a sigh of relief when I didn't recognize any of the people strutting past us. They paid us no attention as they weaved around our bodies and continued down the block toward the river.

I peeled myself away from Arden, quickly changing the subject. "Did you leave Rheya in charge?" Rheya was the obvious choice as Arden's second-in-command, but I needed a distraction to cool down and get my thoughts off the feeling of Arden's lips on mine.

His taut muscles vibrated with soft laughter. "And she's loving every second. Rhal and Malakai will make sure she doesn't torture the guards too much."

I almost felt bad for the new guard members in training. But Arden trusted Rheya, and after everything we'd all been through together, so did I. She was hardheaded and strong-willed and sarcastic as hell, but she was also a fierce warrior and loyal to the core.

Arden gently combed his fingers through my long hair.

My scalp tingled, and goose bumps raced down the back of my neck. I cupped his hand with mine and drew it down. "I better go before someone comes looking for me. Are you sure you don't want to stay and have some food or cake?"

The corner of Arden's mouth turned up in a partial smile. "I don't think that's a good idea."

"Yeah," I agreed. "Probably not. We'll talk more later?"

"We will." Arden stepped back, and I felt the familiar chill that wrapped around me every time he left.

I turned and raced back to the café and bumped into the sheriff as I flew through the entrance. He quickly caught hold of my arms to help us maintain our balance. "Oh, sorry, Sheriff. I should've been paying better attention."

His brisk nod and heightened energy immediately put me on edge. "Is everything okay, Sheriff?"

"I'm sorry, Everly. I'm needed at the station. Enjoy the rest of your party." He sidestepped past me and sprinted to his vehicle.

As the sheriff sped away, a sense of gloom cast an invisible shadow over the otherwise bright blue sky.

I pushed into the café, thrown off by the upbeat acoustics rocking the speakers. Everyone chatted gaily, as they had before I'd followed Arden out, but something dark now lingered in the air that no one but me seemed to notice. I scanned the crowd, searching for my mom, and spotted Piper coloring happily at a table.

Darion and my mom stood off to the side in a huddled whisper. I searched for Lucas but found no sight of him. Molly, Ty, and Jasper hovered near the buffet table, grazing on snacks with no signs of concern. Bree wasn't with them. I could only hope she'd gotten bored and left.

My gaze swept across individuals adorned in costumes for the upcoming ball, while others were dressed in their usual attire, as I searched the room once more. Maybe Lucas had gone to the bathroom. I made eye contact with Jasper and mouthed, "Lucas?"

Jasper shrugged and shook his head, then stuffed something from his plate into his mouth.

I shimmied over to my mom and Darion. "Has something happened?" I kept my voice low so as not to worry Piper, who was still consumed with her coloring sheet. "I bumped into the sheriff, who left in a hurry."

My mom motioned me closer. "There was a body discovered, and the sheriff was called away. Darion caught snippets of the conversation and heard the mention of a symbol being etched onto someone's forehead."

"What?" My stomach dropped.

Darion handed me a folded piece of paper. "I glimpsed the picture sent to the sheriff's phone as I passed him."

I unfolded the paper and stared at the dotted symbol. Something about the formations of the dots seemed familiar, but I couldn't place it. I quickly folded the paper and shoved it back at Darion. I forced myself to swallow, trying to suppress the feeling of nausea bubbling up. "How could someone do that to another person?" My voice shook. "Why?" I mumbled, thinking of the loved ones who were about to find out about their loss.

"It has to be Vitarian." Darion talked in such a hushed whisper I could barely hear him. "But I don't recognize the symbol. Most likely a rune of dark magic."

The three of us shared a look as if the same thought ran through our minds. "The Spider Witch," I breathed.

Death, destruction, and chaos. *It's started.*

∼

*T*he remainder of the party continued in a mechanical blur. I accepted gifts, offered thanks, and we cut the cake, though Darion, my mom, and I had no appetite for cake or any other food.

My mom quietly updated Calista and Selkie about the call the sheriff had received, and they each took a turn studying the symbol Darion had sketched. No one was certain about the significance of the symbol, but Darion was convinced it had the markings of dark magic.

Lucas was still nowhere to be seen. I tried his cell again with no answer and typed a quick text.

U ok? Where are u?

Finally, I spotted him through the sliding glass doors that someone had rolled open.

What were you doing, Lucas?

He walked toward the café from the waterfront park. He stood out in the sea of other costumed people moving along the street, since *Crocodile Dundee* hadn't been mainstream in a couple of decades. A gust of wind blew his cowboy hat off his head, but he caught it in midair and dangled it in one hand instead of putting it back on.

I rushed outside. "Hey, where'd you go?" My breath hitched when Lucas avoided eye contact with me, something he'd never done before.

"Just for a walk to get some air." His tone was unusually cool.

I thought to reach for his hand, but stopped myself. Arden's arrival had changed things between me and Lucas, and we both felt it. "Do you—"

Before I could get the rest of my words out, someone bumped into me from behind, shoving me forward into Lucas's arms. He caught me but held me at a distance. When his eyes locked on mine, I knew he'd seen me with Arden outside the café. My insides twisted as if someone were wringing them out. I struggled to find the right words to explain, but all that echoed in my mind were the ominous words of the witch: death, chaos, destruction.

I shook myself. "Lucas, I—"

He dropped his hands from me. "I need to find Jasper. I'm supposed to practice with him and Ty before we play the show tonight."

Crap! I'd nearly forgotten all about the annual Halloween ball and our meeting with Freya Moon tonight. This day had really taken a nosedive.

"Lucas," I tried again, but Jasper and Ty came up behind him.

A neon-green hand clapped Lucas on the back. "Let's go, buddy," Jasper announced. "It's time to jam."

"Woo-hoo!" Ty hollered as he and Jasper dragged Lucas away into the parking lot. They were nearly at Jasper's mom's car, which he routinely borrowed when he drove more than himself.

"Wait!" I called, and caught up to Lucas. "Can we talk later? I need to explain."

An awkward silence hung between us. Lucas turned away, but stopped. He spun back and pulled me into his arms, warming my body against his.

"I'm sorry," I whispered. "I should have told you about Arden. It's just—"

"Later," he said, then took off to catch up with Jasper and Ty.

"Complicated," I whispered to the wind as I watched Lucas go with a pang of guilt and confusion. Now that Arden was back ... everything had changed in an instant. After being in Arden's arms today, I knew that even when he returns to Aenoas-Vita, I couldn't pretend with Lucas anymore. I cared for Lucas, but I could never truly give my heart to him, no matter how hard I tried, not when it still belonged to Arden. I trudged back inside, my shoulders slouched and a sense of foreboding weighing me down, knowing that this day would inevitably bring pain.

As the party finally came to an end, I could feel the tension in my lips ease as I let go of the forced smile. Darion stayed behind to help Molly and Selkie's catering crew clean up, while I left with my mom. She'd agreed to drop Piper with her grandparents and dropped me off at home on her way. A few hours remained before our planned meeting with Freya at her shop, and there was someone I wanted to see.

I barely remembered the drive when I pulled up to the warehouse that appeared to be abandoned to anyone who wasn't Vitarian. My body jostled in my seat as my car bounced over the bumpy ground until I found a spot to park in the grassy field. The music never stopped at the club. Whether they arrived through portals or by other means, there was always a steady stream of partygoers at any hour, and Neil was dedicated to keeping them entertained. Windows rattled in the vehicles as I walked past, and the ground practically vibrated with the bass coming from the club.

I paused inside the foyer and glanced around.

Where is the front-desk attendant?

Neil never left the entrance unguarded. If he wasn't perched behind the counter himself, hired help would sit in his place. I walked through the red velvet curtain leading into the main part of the club, and a blast of bass vibrated across my skin like an indoor breeze. I scanned the space for Neil, but it was impossible to make out a single person in the wave of bodies moving on the dance floor in such low light.

Hmm ... Neil could be upstairs in his flat, where he lived above his club. I turned to head in that direction when a voice echoed in my mind: "My queen."

I spun around. "Neil!" I threw my arms around his neck and bumped his glasses out of place.

His shoulders shook with laughter. He ignored his lopsided glasses, which he wore for effect and not necessity, and hugged me back. "Darling! What are you doing here? Shouldn't you be getting ready for the ball with your hunk of a date? And please"—he leaned back and waved his arm all diva-like—"tell me I'm not a matchmaker made in heaven," he joked.

When I looked down at my feet, he said, "Ahh ... I see." He scratched his chin. "Do you want to talk about it?"

I shrugged.

"Come on, sweet thing. Let's go upstairs."

Neil's flat was a full one-eighty from the club downstairs. Bright and cheery, with white and soft gray tones. Sleek modern furniture decorated the open, airy space, which Neil kept extremely tidy. The only thing that ever littered the room was stacks of books.

Since not everyone possessed Neil's ability to mentally block out external noise, he had the flat designed with incredible soundproofing to ensure that you couldn't hear a peep of the music bouncing off the walls below.

I plopped down on the white couch, which was more

comfortable than it looked, and leaned back into the cushion with my eyes closed.

As Neil sat down next to me, I could feel the warmth radiating from his body. He waited quietly until he was sure I was ready to talk. When I finally cracked open an eye and sighed, he said, "Has the Aussie done something untoward? If he has, the glasses are coming off," Neil joked, or maybe he wasn't joking. His expression was pretty serious when I opened both eyes and looked over at him.

I covered my face with my hands, not caring if I smudged my mascara. "Lucas did nothing wrong. He's perfect. It's me. I've done something. I'm so terrible. Argh!" I moaned and scooted farther back on the cushion. I kicked off my shoes and tucked my legs up in a cross-legged position. "Arden's back."

"Oh."

"Yeah, and I'm sure Lucas saw me kiss him today." I grabbed a cushion and buried my face in it.

"Double oh."

"I'm a horrible person, Neil." The cushion muffled my voice.

Neil slipped the cushion from my grasp. "Come here." He pulled me over to him, and I laid my head on his shoulder while we both leaned back against the stuffed cushions. "You're not a horrible person." He smoothed my hair.

"If you had seen the look on Lucas's face, you'd think otherwise. I hurt him. And the worst part is I can't say I wouldn't do it again. When I'm near Arden, it's like every-thing else vanishes, and it's just the two of us. Lucas is such a good person, and I care about him a lot. He's been my rock this past year. And the last thing I want to do is hurt him. But I haven't stopped loving Arden, and today proved that I'm not ready to let him go even if we can't be together because we're galaxies apart."

Neil mussed my hair. "I've known Lucas a few years now. He's a good guy. He's honest and understanding and level-headed, which is why I trust him to manage one of my bars. I think the best thing you can do is to be honest with him about your feelings. He loves you, and yes, he'll be hurt, but he deserves the truth." Neil gave it to me straight.

I nodded into Neil's shoulder. "You're right. I'll talk to Lucas tonight, after the ball." My eyes burned at the thought of causing Lucas pain, but I forced the tears back as a lump settled in my chest. Although I didn't want to hurt Lucas, ending things now would prevent more pain for him in the future.

We sat quietly for a moment. Outside Neil's tall windows, a lush expanse of towering trees stretched as far as the eye could see, teeming with creatures leading uncomplicated lives, oblivious to the troubles that burdened mankind. I remembered the exhilarating sensation of soaring through the sky as my mind wandered back to the memory of Malakai sharing his gift with me.

Neil's breath brushed the top of my hair. "Why did Arden come back?"

Neil's question reminded me of the meeting with Freya tonight. I reached for my bag and checked the time on my phone. *Shoot!* I sat up. If I didn't leave soon, I wouldn't have time to get ready.

I uncrossed my legs and tapped my feet around the floor in search of my shoes. "My mom sent a letter to Felix. Some things have happened in the last couple of days, and they're not good."

Neil quirked a brow and waited.

I ran my hands through my hair, smoothing the frizz I felt floating above my head.

"Long story short, Calista went to Bali under the guise of taking a vacation while attending some rare markets. But she was actually searching for someone who might have knowledge about the curse linking Darion and me."

Neil nodded like he was following along.

"She met a witch called the Spider Witch." I paused to see if that name meant anything to Neil. No signs of recognition crossed his face, so I continued. "This witch practices all types of ancient Earth magic. Calista found her, or rather, the Spider Witch found Calista. She gave Cal a tarot reading, and —" I shuddered at the memory of the Spider Witch's warning and reached for my cheek, remembering the raw power of her cool touch.

Neil's eyes narrowed. "Go on," he urged.

"The Spider Witch warned of a grave threat that will bring with it devastation."

Neil sat erect. "Anything else?"

I nodded. Neil deserved to know everything. "My mom used her power to retrieve the memory of the reading. Only the Spider Witch expected this. She gave Calista the cards from the reading, but Cal didn't know the witch had spelled them. While Calista was in her trance, the witch channeled through her. She warned not to 'give him what he wants.' Then the rest was all riddles: dark will consume light, and the stars hold the answer." I threw up my hands.

"Then Lucas showed up with new photos of the man from the pictures you gave me last year."

Neil tilted his head.

"The ones Lucas brought were taken recently, just this past week. We're positive it's the same man who sat with Creagan in the original photo."

"Did Lucas get his name or remember what he looks like?"

I got up and went to the window. Leaves the color of apricot and pumpkin swirled in the air as they fell from branches above.

"Someone wiped his memory."

Neil joined me at the window. "I have more bad news. It may be a coincidence."

My stomach twisted. "What is it?"

"Well, the reason I wasn't able to make it to your party today, and you know I wouldn't have missed it for anything less than an emergency." He ran his hands through his short black hair, causing strands to stand straight up, and for the first time since I'd known Neil, he actually seemed stressed.

I put my hand on his shoulder and released my magic. The lines smoothed around his eyes as he relaxed.

He smiled and placed a hand on top of mine. "Someone intercepted my delivery of the ever leaves. It was a substantial delivery, and I'm out loads of dollars and favors on that shipment, and nearly out of current stock for the club."

"What would anybody want with an enormous shipment of ever leaves?" I knew the ever trees embodied magic and that the oils from the leaves contained hallucinogens, but my knowledge of the magic of Aenoas-Vita was still sparse.

Neil answered patiently. "The leaves in that quantity could create massive spells. Ones that aren't good." His dark eyes settled on me. "When Arden finds out about this, he'll shut me down. You barely persuaded him last time to cut me a break."

Neil was right. Arden had been ready to pack Neil's operations up and haul him back to Aenoas-Vita for his illegal smuggling. If he found about this, Neil would be done for.

"I won't say anything to Arden."

Neil's posture relaxed.

"For now," I added.

"I understand, my queen."

"Neil, I've told you not to address me that way. You're my

S. L. WATSON

friend, and you know I only accepted the title out of obligation. It's not what I want."

Neil glanced around his flat like he was about to lose it all, then shook himself and folded his hands around mine. "Well, you'd better get used to it, because you are a queen. And whether or not you want it, you were born to rule."

I kissed Neil on the cheek. "I have to go. And don't worry about Arden. If he finds out, I'll talk to him. I am queen, after all." I winked at Neil and hurried out, feeling more ominous than when I arrived. First, someone marked a corpse with a dark magic symbol, and now someone has hijacked Neil's shipment of ever leaves capable of powering huge spells. It could just be a coincidence, but my gut felt otherwise.

CHAPTER 4

*M*y mom, Darion, and I left the house dressed in our costumes. Our moods lacked the usual excitement that came with attending the Halloween ball, and a bleak silence filled the car as we drove to Freya's.

I fiddled with the fringing at the hem of my dress. Three months ago, I'd been in love with the sequined black flapper getup that now just felt cumbersome and itchy. I adjusted the black feathered headband that pressed at my temples. A tension headache brewed as I wondered why I thought this outfit had ever been a good idea.

I cracked the window, letting in a wisp of cool October breeze, and tried to relax. I had no idea what to expect when we got to Freya's and just hoped she'd have some answers about the Spider Witch, at least. Or maybe recognize the symbol Darion had sketched.

Darion reached over from the back seat and squeezed the top of my shoulder. Of course, he sensed my unease. The curse made it impossible for either of us not to know certain things about each other, which we determined was how Siobhan had always stayed one step ahead of him.

He hadn't known then that Siobhan had linked him to her through a curse she had conjured when she had stolen him from our mother's womb. She'd created a barrier, so the benefits were one-sided.

Darion and I hadn't been so lucky with such an attempt. We assumed that the fact that we were twins had something to do with the magic, creating a stronger bond between us than it had between him and Siobhan. The spell we'd concocted helped minimally while in each other's presence. At a distance, it worked much better.

We turned onto Freya's block, but cars lined the street. It was no surprise, since the town blocked off the major downtown streets to vehicles every year for Halloween festivities.

After circling the block a few times, we found a spot and parked. Hundreds of costumed bodies crowded the streets, making our short trek take longer than it should have. Kids ran back and forth carrying plastic pumpkins and bags filled with candy as they went to the next house or business for more. The residents along the downtown strip went all out with decorating for Halloween. There wasn't a bare porch or storefront in sight.

I jumped, and a scream tore from me when one prop we walked past suddenly came to life and darted toward us, holding a bloodied butcher's knife. Darion pulled me behind him and blocked the creepy character from coming any closer.

"Sorry, man." The mask muffled the man's words. "It's Halloween. Chill."

I pulled on Darion's arm. "Come on, Darion. I overreacted. I'm fine. Sorry!" I waved at the man dressed in blue overalls and a hockey mask. "Your costume is great. You really freaked me out."

He shook his head and went to torture the next wave of people heading his way.

Dried leaves crunched under our feet as we continued down the block in a flock of black. We had chosen our color theme completely by coincidence. Darion looked slick in his black Gomez suit, with his raven hair combed back with some type of product that gave it that wet gel look while holding it in place.

My mom, who seldom wore makeup except for special occasions, had her sapphire eyes lined in kohl, and the surrounding eyelids dusted in gold. She'd flattened her new haircut straight and decorated the top of her head in a metallic gold headband with a red jewel adorning the center, which was a replica of the belt wrapped around the waist of her sparkling black Egyptian dress.

Moans echoed from the haunted house hosted by a town building. We weaved through the line that spanned several blocks. If you liked haunted houses, it was worth the wait. The time Jasper persuaded me to go inside with him was the one and only time I'd ever done it. I'd had nightmares for a week after.

We stopped in front of a huge three-story Victorian home renovated for dual residential and commercial use, like many on the downtown strip had been.

A mock witch sat propped at a table with a set of tarot cards spread in front of her, and a bright crystal ball. As we neared, a mechanical voice came from the dressed-up mannequin: "Sit and receive a reading you'll never forget." A low cackle vibrated from the witch's plastic lips.

Melodic chimes jingled as Darion pulled the front door to Freya's shop open. My mom walked through, but I lingered, staring at the table of tarot cards laid out and wondered what menace lay ahead of us.

"Ev," Darion urged.

I met his silver eyes and hesitated at the door, unable to shake the ominous feeling that rocked my core. Something was coming for us, just as the Spider Witch had predicted. I could feel it in my bones. I searched the shadows as they played their tricks.

"Come on."

Darion's voice yanked me from my thoughts, and I followed him inside.

The crystal shop was as mesmerizing as the last time I'd visited with Molly, when she'd been looking for a heart-shaped pink quartz, which I now suspected had something to do with Darion.

Shelves of crystals of all shapes, colors and sizes lined the walls, and baskets of them sat atop tables throughout the open space. Dried herbs, tarot cards, and books on tarot and crystal healing were also scattered on shelves and tables, along with candles, miniature statues, and crystal singing bowls. Bracelets, necklaces, and rings adorned with all sorts of gemstones filled a glass case. Several lit candles placed strategically throughout created a peaceful ambiance and added a hint of cinnamon to the air. The space felt both welcoming and magical, as soft hymns played from hidden speakers.

A girl about my age greeted us from behind the register. Her rich bronze arms shimmered under the glow of the light. She was the same girl who'd helped Molly find her crystal. Besides having blue eyes that were hard to look away from, she had a unique energy field that I couldn't make sense of. Since honing my magic, I'd become sensitive to the differences between Vitarian and human energy. Hers was neither human nor Vitarian, but something in between.

"Hello." Long curls cascaded down from the mass of thick ringlets she'd wrapped atop her head, and framed her heart-shaped face. "Welcome. Please let me know if there's anything I can help you find." Her friendliness was genuine, and her warm, melodic tone made me think of Selkie, and some of the tension knotted in my shoulders eased.

My mom smiled in return. "We're here to see Freya."

The girl's eyes scanned us more thoroughly this time. "Is my mother expecting you?"

Her mother? But Freya was Vitarian. Did that mean that humans and Vitarians could procreate? If so, then that explained both the human aspects and the magic I sensed in this girl's energy.

The clatter of beads clinking in the doorway behind the register distracted my closer examination of the girl. A woman of much darker mahogany skin came into view. Her onyx eyes landed on me. "I'm expecting them, Anya." She held back the beads, revealing a hall that led to other rooms. "Come."

My mom went first. Darion and I followed her lead while Freya whispered something to her daughter before I heard the beads clink, followed by Freya's footsteps behind us.

"Straight ahead," Freya instructed when I paused at a staircase.

We came to a landing just past the staircase and took the few steps down into a living room. Furniture and tapestries of earthy tones made the space feel just as tranquil as the shop upfront.

A rug with frayed ends accented the center of the hard-wood floor where we entered. Placed in the middle of the rug was a tray holding teacups, a cast-iron teapot, and a bowl filled with loose tea leaves.

"Please, sit in a circle." Freya motioned to the setting on the floor, where four plush round cushions lay.

"What's this?" Darion kicked a corner of the rug, revealing a large circle painted on the floor underneath.

"A protection spell. No evil may enter this space, nor may any other witch use magic to cross this threshold."

81

My mom reached out her hand. Her fingers locked around Darion's. "It's okay, son. I've been here before, and I'm aware of the spell. It is what Freya says."

Darion kicked the corner of the rug back in place and glanced warily toward Freya as the three of us lowered ourselves down onto the cushions.

It wasn't the easiest or most comfortable position to be sitting in while wearing a knee-length flapper dress. I folded my knees and shifted my legs to my side while wishing I'd chosen an ankle-length dress, like my mom's, or better yet, a costume that included pants.

"Please pick up your teacup and place a scoop of tea inside to steep. You may sip throughout our session, and I'll read your leaves before you go."

Darion humphed, earning a peaked eyebrow from Freya.

We each added tea leaves and hot water to our cups as Freya moved about the room, collecting items and setting them within our circle. She brought a bowl of stones, a large quartz crystal, and a deck of tarot cards, then arranged several tall white candles along the edge of the circle. They sparked to life as Freya chanted.

Freya joined us in the circle and scooped up the deck of tarot cards. She fanned them out, blowing on their edges. Then she packed the cards back together in a neat deck and knocked on them.

"What's she doing?" Darion glanced sideways at our mom.

Freya answered, "I'm cleansing the deck of old energy that may have clung to the cards from a previous reading. I perform the cleansing ritual after and before each use as a precaution." She held the freshly stacked deck out to me. "Take these in your right hand," she instructed. "Close your eyes and breathe over the cards. Keep doing it until you sense a warm energy surrounding you. When that happens, you'll know you've established a connection with the cards, and you can pass them back to me."

I did as Freya said.

Clutching the cards tightly, I inhaled deeply and let out a slow breath. With a few more breaths, a jolt of energy shot through my fingertips as my heart started racing. The cards buzzed with vitality, while another surge of energy enveloped me like a snug blanket, causing a warm flush to spread across my skin.

"Good." Freya's fingers curled around my wrists. "You've created a strong connection with the cards." Her grasp loosened as she clasped her fingers over the cards. "You can release them to me now."

My fingers felt stuck to the cards and clung to them even as I tried to pry them away. My eyes snapped open as my heart fluttered.

"Relax, Everly. The spirit realm is on the cusp of life and death tonight. You've drawn a great deal of energy, but you are safe." Freya blew over my hands and chanted as a bright violet hue bloomed within her own energy field.

A tingle spread through me as my body cooled and the invisible blanket peeled away, leaving my skin feeling sticky with residue. I shook as Freya took the deck from me and laid out three cards in the center of our circle.

"Past, present, and future." She breathed heavily as she flipped each from left to right, revealing the Devil, the Tower, and the Moon.

My shoulders trembled as I looked down at the winged creature with clawed feet and horns sprouting from his head.

Freya sat directly in front of me, holding the remaining deck in her right hand while her left kept contact with the cards that lay on the rug. "The Devil can have multiple repre-

S. L. WATSON

sentations. As an element of the past, he is tethered to resentment, vengeance, and greed. The individual this card beholds has sighted you as a piece in the puzzle to achieve an ultimate goal." Freya flattened her left palm down over the Devil's face, revealing symbols tattooed on top of each of her fingers. "He has waited patiently for his revenge, building his strength and power." Freya's onyx eyes pierced mine. "The Devil is cunning and manipulative. Don't let his glamor fool you."

The candles flickered as Freya's fingers trailed from the Devil's face to the next card. A chill hovered over our circle, and flames shot up from the candles as if they were torches.

Darion stiffened as he searched the darkened room for a threat.

"It is only the wind of the spirits," Freya assured him without a hint of worry in her voice.

My left hand warmed as my mom covered it with her own.

"No," said Freya. "If your energies cross, it will interfere with the reading."

My mom snatched her hand away. "Of course, Freya. I apologize."

Freya inclined her head and directed her attention back to the cards. "The Tower is your present. It represents challenges that have yet to come. When the walls collapse, you will be forced to surrender to the power of the Tower."

"What does that mean? To what will she be forced to surrender?" My mom's voice shook as she dug her fingernails into the sides of the cushion.

Candlelight danced across Freya's eyes as she shifted her gaze to my mom. "You know as well as I, Cacsha of the Ever bloodline, that the messages that travel the spirit realm are fragments and metaphors. We can only learn their true meaning as events unfold."

A blotchy haze shrouded my mom's aura as her concern grew. We both knew that what Freya had said was true.

As Freya's fingers walked to the third card, the future, an eerie calmness washed over me. Whatever was to come would come, regardless of resistance. My only option was to face it head-on. Freya's fingers stopped on the Moon. The luminous circle glowed between two towers, shining down over a dog and a howling wolf.

"Internal and emotional turmoil has already begun, but soon you will choose a direction." She reached out and clasped my wrist. "Let the wolf guide you past your fear and into the unknown. Your path into the darkness of the soul will be your family's salvation." Freya released her grip on my arm.

More candles hissed to life, and the room brightened.

My mom wrung her hands in her lap. "There must be something we can do to stop this."

Freya took my mom's hands in her own. "There are always choices. Here." She picked up my mom's teacup. "Drink this. The leaves will reveal the secrets."

What Freya said reminded me of the Spider Witch's message.

"The Spider Witch told me the stars hold the answer. Do you know what she meant?"

Freya thought and shook her head. "I'm sorry. The Spider Witch practices many types of Earth magic. Maybe if I knew the source of the magic she used, I could decipher the meaning."

Darion spoke up. "From what I've learned about her and her kin, they guard their practices well and are not likely to share their methods. We'd need to speak to her directly, and she's disappeared."

I glanced up. "What do you mean, she's disappeared? How do you know that?"

Darion shifted his body on his cushion to face my mom and me. "I've tried locating her since what happened last night, but she's covered her tracks well. Better than I'd expect of a human."

Darion's news didn't surprise me. Of course, he'd searched for the Spider Witch.

"Why would she vanish?" I thought aloud.

Darion rocked his hips on his cushion as he adjusted his long legs. "She never remains in one place very long, and when she departs, she takes all signs of her existence with her."

"Perhaps the witch will make herself known when she's ready." Freya held the bowl of stones out to Darion. "Take one. And hold it in your hand while you drink your tea." Freya extended the bowl to each of us. "Don't look at it," she instructed Darion. "Tuck it into your palm and wait."

Darion pinched his brows together, but he followed Freya's instructions. The three of us quietly drank our tea at Freya's urging.

As I sipped my tea, I glanced about the room. A protective energy vibrated around the entire space. It reminded me of the spell surrounding Felix's place.

Crystals adorned every corner. And Freya had an abundance of plants. Everywhere I looked, there were green foliage or colorful succulents. A female statue stood tall near an altar, with her hands held in prayer.

Peeking over my shoulder, I saw giant windows faced north and overlooked the Columbia River and Sand Island. I imagined a spectacular view throughout the day.

Glass rattled, drawing my attention back to the present. I gulped down the last of my tea and flipped my cup over on its saucer, as Darion and my mom had.

Freya started with Darion. Her eyes narrowed at his cup. "You care for someone deeply, but you guard your feelings from yourself as much as her." She glanced at Darion over the teacup. "But you've trusted her with a great secret."

Darion glanced nervously at both my mom and me and pinched his lips together.

Was Freya talking about Molly? And what secret had Darion shared?

Freya's fingers traced a line of tea leaves leading to the rim of Darion's cup. Her neck muscles strained, and energy whirled around her as she lowered her face closer to the leaves so that her nose practically touched them. "I see a shadow hovering over the girl you love. She's in danger. The shadow is stalking her this night."

Darion jumped up so abruptly that Freya swayed backward, dropping the teacup to the floor. The fragile glass cracked apart, splattering Freya's rug with wet tea leaves.

"What are you talking about? What's going to happen to her?" Darion's panic latched onto me, and my legs trembled as I stood. My mom swooped an arm around my waist to steady me.

Freya snatched Darion's cupped hand and took the stone he'd been squeezing. "The dream stone." She stood on tiptoe and whispered something to Darion in Vitarian, then pressed the stone back into his hand. "Keep this with you." She led him to a side door that led directly outside, and Darion raced away without looking back.

"Thank you, Freya," said my mom as we rushed out to follow Darion, but he'd already vanished at inhuman speed.

"Good luck," Freya said, and the two women clasped hands. Freya went back inside and closed the door.

"My cell phone's in your car, and we need to call Molly," I said.

"I've got mine." We ran as my mom whipped out her phone from her purse mid-stride.

Running in heels was a lot harder than the movies made it look.

The Old School of Music, where the ball was already in full swing, was only a few blocks from Freya's, so we didn't bother going back to my mom's car.

"No luck. She's not answering." My mom held the phone at her side as we kept moving.

"Damn it! Try Jasper."

After a few seconds of holding her phone to her ear, she shook her head. "Cal and Selk aren't picking up either."

I could only think of one other person. "Mom, call Sam."

She shot me a questioning look. "He'll wonder how I know to warn him."

We were still a block away from the school where the ball was being held, and where I knew Molly would be. "We'll worry about that later. Just call him. Now!" I picked up the pace while my mom stopped to dial Sam's number. If we hadn't been nearly there, I'd have kicked these ridiculous shoes off and run barefoot.

Darion wasn't anywhere in sight as I plowed past the line waiting to get inside the school. Thank the lucky stars I'd remembered to put on the VIP pass Jasper had given me. As a faculty member of the school, they allowed him a certain number of passes for family and friends, which meant no line, and we'd all gotten one.

I whipped out the pass I'd secured around my neck and tucked inside my dress earlier and flashed it at the security guard as he waved for me to stop. He ushered me inside, and I ran straight into a billowing patch of fog filling the room from hidden dry-ice machines.

Overhead, rainbow spotlights made the fog appear in a stream of colors. I pressed through the crowd filtering up the stairs, trying not to push anyone over. It was almost impossible with how many bodies filled the stairway and how hard it was to see.

Inside the ballroom was even worse. Black lights flashed down on the crowd, making it impossible to recognize anyone, especially in costume. The heat in the room felt suffocating as I squinted into the mass of glowing dancers. I fanned the back of my neck with my hair.

Where are you, Molly?

I used my other ability and sifted through the vibrations, but between the sea of people and the vibrations coming from the instruments onstage, I couldn't tell whose energy was whose.

Jasper's voice boomed over the speakers as he, Ty, and Lucas rocked the crowd with spooky cover songs. Ty beat the drums, while Lucas ripped on the bass, and Jasper tore up the electric guitar while covering vocals the crowd sang along with.

My heart raced as I spun in all directions. Twisting and turning bodies bumped into me as I searched for the Morticia character Molly had chosen as her costume.

I spotted Selkie directing her catering staff near the buffet table, where purple lighting shone down over the food. I kept my eyes on her crisp white shirt while I edged her way and swiped at the trickles of sweat beading down from my temples.

A hard body bumped into the back of mine, and an icy chill tickled my scalp. I spun to apologize, but breathed a sigh of relief when I saw Darion standing behind me.

"Thank God. I've been searching everywhere. Did you find Molly? Is she okay?"

Darion stared down at me with a twisted scowl, not responding to my question. A shudder rippled through my body as a chilling sensation slowly crept up my spine.

"Where's Oria's ring?"

His question threw me. I met his hard stare, and pins and needles prickled everywhere, warning me. Sapphire eyes the color of my own narrowed with agitation.

"Did you put colored contacts in?"

"The ring," he growled.

"What the hell, Darion? Stop acting like a jackass. Did you find Molly or not? And what's with the contacts and weird question?"

A tingle of apprehension crept over me as I scanned … *Wait …*

Not only were Darion's eyes a different color, but age lines caressed the skin under his bottom lashes, around his mouth, and across his forehead.

I reached into his aura and took a step back. Whoever stood in front of me resembled Darion, but this person wasn't my brother.

A hammer slammed against my chest as his lips curved up. I had turned when he whispered something in Vitarian. The room spun, and I swayed on my feet. By the time I regained my balance, he was gone, and a bloodcurdling scream rang out from across the room.

My ears filled with the pounding of my heart. Lights flicked on, and bodies pressed all around me as everyone tried to find the source of the scream. I forced my legs to move when a crowd near the stage backed away in a frenzy.

I shoved past anyone blocking my way, this time not caring who I bumped into. People fanned out in confusion. I heard paramedics barking orders behind me.

Sam. Thank God! He had wasted no time.

My knees buckled when I saw Darion hovering over a limp body on the floor. He pumped Molly's chest frantically while checking her pulse. Blood dripped from her nose and trickled down the side of her cheek.

We're too late.

My eyes burned, and I choked on the air trapped in my throat. "Is … is she …?" I couldn't bring myself to say the words. Molly had to be okay.

Darion kept his attention on Molly as he continued to pump her chest and breathe into her mouth.

"Out of the way!" paramedics barked at the people gathered around us.

A man crouched at Darion's side. "You did good, son. Now it's our turn." Another paramedic coaxed Darion and me out of the way, then lifted Molly onto a stretcher, while another placed an oxygen mask over her face. "She's got a pulse. Let's move."

The paramedic that'd first arrived nodded to Darion as he passed.

Darion had kept Molly alive, but his expression wasn't one of relief; it was deadly.

I placed a shaky hand on his shoulder. "She'll be okay, Darion. Molly's too tough not to be."

"Whoever did this to her is going to pay with their life." Darion clenched his jaw. "I need to get to the hospital." He shrugged my hand off his shoulder.

"Wait!" I grabbed Darion by both arms and looked into his eyes. Silver.

Who was I talking to? And how did he look so much like you?

"What is it?" Darion tensed.

I bit my lip. He had enough to worry about.

"Darion!" Our mom rushed to our side, with Sam close behind. She pulled Darion into her arms. "I'm so sorry, son. Molly is a fighter." She squeezed him tight.

Sam's sharp eyes studied me. "Do you know what happened?"

I shook my head. "I didn't see anything. By the time I reached her, Darion was already giving her CPR."

Sam shifted his attention toward Darion, but my mom

halted him with a look. He nodded with an unspoken under-standing and went to question the onlookers.

"I'm driving Darion to the hospital. Are you coming with us, honey?"

I shook my head. "You two go on. I'll meet you there. I need to find Lucas."

The music had stopped with all the commotion. I searched and found the band members being questioned by one of Sam's officers.

Instead of heading toward them, I turned for the exit. The dry ice cloyed in my lungs, and I needed air.

I searched the ballroom as I moved, looking for Darion's look-alike. If he was still here, he kept himself hidden.

Who was he? And why did he want Oria's ring? What the hell happened to Molly?

"Apparently, karma does exist."

I glanced up to find Bree blocking my path. "What are you babbling about?"

Her bare shoulders rolled back, and she pursed her perfectly red-stained lips. "Your friend wasn't very welcoming when I came to your studio, and she tried to turn my boyfriend against me at your party." Her fake lashes drooped, and green eyes watched me through slits as she clicked her fire-engine nails.

"I don't have time for your games. Move it, Barbie." I shoved past her, but she stepped in my way again.

"Do you think Molly will mind if I comfort Darion?" She bounced on her hip, wearing a self-satisfied smirk.

My hand flew out and whacked Bree across the cheek, leaving a bright red handprint to match the rest of her attire. "I mind. Stay away from my brother. And Ty too! He's too good for you."

Shocked whispers echoed around us.

Bree's face twisted with fury as she cradled her cheek, but

she moved aside. When I finally got out of the room, I sucked in a deep breath, then slid down onto the top step of the staircase and buried my face in my hands.

Oh, Molly. Please be okay.

No wounds or attack marks had been visible. Besides the blood dripping from her nose, Molly looked to have collapsed. But I knew better. Someone had done something to her, and in my gut, I knew it had to do with the Spider Witch's warning.

The weight of responsibility pressed on me as I realized that my ignorance had put my friends in jeopardy from a malevolent entity. The longer I remained on this planet, the more danger I brought to those I loved. Oria had warned me there would be repercussions if I hadn't upheld my end of our deal before I'd taken off her ring and stashed it away. Was she somehow responsible for everything happening? That couldn't be right. She was dead and in the spirit realm, and besides, why would she hurt Molly?

As I sat on the stair, memories of laughter echoed in my ears, transporting me back to past years. It seems like just yesterday when Jasper, Molly, Ty, and I would race up these stairs, excited to put on our costumes and immerse ourselves in the enchantment of Halloween. Jasper and Ty used to dream about playing gigs in this ballroom when they were kids, and now their dream has not only come true, but Jasper is now a music instructor here. Holding onto the railing, I thought about everything Jasper was willing to sacrifice for me, even after I had freed him from his promise to my father.

Jasper wasn't just my sworn Shield; he was my best friend, and stubborn, and overprotective. He made it perfectly clear that his commitment to accompany me back to Aenoas-Vita and support my ascension to the throne was unwavering. And nothing I said could change his mind. "It's not because of an oath," he'd told me. "It's because you're my best friend, and I love you. Protecting you for as long as I live is both my duty and honor."

My hands balled into fists. Whoever had attacked Molly could go after Jasper next, or Ty. I had to find out who was after us. The timing of someone impersonating Darion and inquiring about Oria's ring right before Molly's attack couldn't be a coincidence.

I pulled myself up and took each step on autopilot as I replayed every detail in my mind, beginning with the Spider Witch's warning and the photos Lucas had brought. The two had to be connected, but how?

Loud cheers brought me out of my thoughts. A rambunctious crowd thronged the streets for the after-hours dance party in front of the school. The town allowed the annual tradition to go on until midnight each year. Then the sheriff and his team would usher everyone out of the streets to return home or to their hotels.

I stayed on the outside of the ropes bordering the designated dance area, taking in the rowdy atmosphere while avoiding getting caught up in the commotion. As I made my way through the park in front of the town courthouse, I noticed a much calmer crowd of families wandering around the Halloween-movie-themed settings.

A family dressed as wizards and witches pointed excitedly at the mechanical "Whomping Willow" tree that swung its limbs when it sensed motion nearby. Most onlookers were careful not to walk too close to the swinging branches, though there was usually at least one genius every year who thought it'd be funny to climb the twisting tree.

The family currently pointing at the tree laughed at this year's winner as he dangled and cried out for help from a thrashing limb. A pack of teens sitting atop a yellow cab prop howled with laughter as the tree's captive lost his werewolf mask to the ground. The security heading his way didn't find the situation funny.

The teens turned their howls up toward the sky. One girl in the group caught my attention. Pink stripes streaked her blond hair, like Molly's.

Heat flared in my belly, and an overhead streetlight popped, eliciting another wave of cackles from the teens.

Crap! I took a breath to calm myself. I had to get my powers under control.

"Excuse me." A woman approached. "Would you mind taking our photo?"

It was the family dressed as witches and wizards. "Sure." I took the woman's phone, glad to have a distraction.

The family huddled in the orange glow in front of the gigantic artificial pumpkin. I adjusted the phone to capture them all in the image at different angles. "Say happy Halloween." I snapped a few more photos and passed the phone back to the mom, whose kids had already run off toward Jack the skeleton and crew from *The Nightmare Before Christmas*.

If Darion had been here, he'd have been whispering in my ear about how ridiculous humans were. But I was seeing through his gibes. He envied humans and their freedom to be silly and appreciate mundane things, like dressing up in costumes and howling at the stars.

Stars. I craned my head back and surveyed the sky, looking for some clue to the Spider Witch's words.

What answer do you hold?

The Big Dipper and Little Dipper twinkled above. I searched each handle and pot for something out of the ordinary. Nothing. I spotted the zigzag lines of Cassiopeia and still found nothing unusual. This was pointless and wasting time.

I hurried through the park and down the next couple of

blocks back to Freya's place. She'd known about Molly's attack. She had to have more answers.

When I got to the door, I stopped to catch my breath and glanced through the window. Freya sat behind the counter, staring into a teacup. Lifting her gaze, she set the cup aside and moved towards the door to unlock it.

"I knew you'd come back." She stepped aside as I pulled the door open and nudged in.

A gush of chilly breeze trailed in behind me before the door swung closed.

Freya's long braids fell down past her shoulders, free from the wrap she'd worn them in earlier.

"What else do you know?"

Her dark eyes sparked with magic. "That you can't beat this threat without sacrificing yourself."

Frustration churned inside me. "I don't care about myself. I'll do whatever I have to. If you know something, please just tell me."

She walked back to the counter and retrieved the teacup she'd been examining. "Does this mean anything to you?"

I stared into the delicate glass. "Are these my leaves?"

She nodded.

My eyes widened with recognition. "I've seen this shape before. Darion sketched this symbol earlier today after seeing it on the sheriff's phone when he got a message about a dead body. But why did my leaves take this shape?"

Freya surveyed her shelves. "I only sense glimpses of things, receive hints from the spirits. It's never complete answers, only fragments. All I sense when I read your leaves is a warning. Something is coming for you. Whatever it is, it's menacing and powerful, and will eliminate anything in its path. Do you still have the stone you selected from the bowl?"

I'd forgotten about the stone. I had carefully hidden it in the small square pocket, a decorative detail on the front of the dress. With a gentle touch, I pushed my finger against the silky fabric, guiding the stone towards the top. I hadn't examined it before, hastily shoving it inside my pocket as we'd been running. One side of it had a painted swirly-looking S. I passed it to Freya.

She made a *tsk* sound through her teeth.

"What does the S mean?" I wrinkled my nose at her reaction.

"It's not an S, child." She cupped the stone in her hand as if to keep it hidden, then went to one shelf and took a small white pouch from a stack. She whispered over her tightly clutched fist until her skin emanated a soft glow. After depositing the stone inside the pouch, she opened a jar of ivory-colored sand and added a scoop with the stone.

I jumped when an audible hiss escaped the pouch.

Freya quickly cinched the strings tight, while the glow pulsing within her skin traveled to her fingertips and disappeared inside the pouch, just before she tied it closed with a triple knot. When she saw my startled expression, she explained. "The marking on this stone is a coiled serpent. It's a warning of a masked enemy. It could be someone close to you, maybe a friend or a loved one."

Masked enemy. Darion's image flashed before my eyes, only it wasn't Darion. That had to be the masked enemy the stone represented. *Who are you?*

"Take this." Freya pressed the pouch into my hand. "I've spelled this pouch with a protection spell. The knot acts as an additional binding. Don't untie it"—she clasped my hands —"for any reason. As long as you keep the serpent trapped within the spell, it will offer some protection against your enemy. It may not be much, but it will help."

"Thank you, Freya."

Her eyes softened. "I'm sorry I can't be of more help. The spirits are never as forthcoming as we'd like them to be."

I nodded. After dealing with Oria in the spirit realm, I understood how frustrating spirits could be. "Wait. There might be something else you can help with," I said, my fingers tightly clutching the top of the serpent's pouch. "I encountered a man tonight at the ball. I thought he was my brother at first, but he was hostile and demanded to know something that Darion wouldn't have asked me about. He was nearly identical to Darion, but his eyes were a different shade. At first, I thought Darion had put contacts in, but then I noticed he had age lines in places Darion didn't, and his energy and aura definitely weren't Darion's."

"Hmm …" Freya twisted her long braids over her shoulder, revealing a tattoo of symbols that led down the back of her neck and disappeared beneath her shirt. Her hair bounced back in place when she noticed my attention drawn to the ink marking her skin.

I glanced away, hoping my curiosity didn't offend her.

"There are others," she continued, "from another planet, where denizens can shape-shift. But it's not like a shifter to leave out such distinguishable characteristics, especially if he was trying to gain knowledge from you. What was he asking about?"

I hesitated. As queen, it was my responsibility to protect Oria's ancestral ring, and there was still so much about Freya Moon I didn't know.

A collection of deity statues snagged my attention, some I recognized and others I'd never seen. I remembered the life-size statue at Freya's personal altar, Guan Yin, the goddess of mercy and compassion. I tuned in to Freya's aura and decided.

"He wanted something that belonged to my ancestor." I saw no reason to explain further.

Freya peaked a brow. "I see." She wandered through her shop, searching through her stones until she plucked a translucent pear-shaped one from a shelf and brought it to me. "A truth stone. Keep it with you. It will turn black in the presence of anyone who means you harm." She added the stone to another pouch and handed it over.

"What do you know of these shape-shifters?" I asked. "Why would they want something that belonged to my ancestor?"

"The shifters have always envied our long lives. Before Oria's time, we were at war with them. They demanded we share our secret to longevity, not understanding that it is a part of our genetics. But we have been at peace with them for centuries, so I cannot say what the intention of this individual was, if it was a shifter."

"It had to have been," I added. "What other explanation could there be for his resemblance to Darion?"

"Mom?" Anya's voice sounded from the hall. The beads hanging from the doorframe clicked together as she pressed them to the side and walked through.

"It's okay, Anya, honey. I was just finishing up with Everly." She smiled warmly back at her daughter.

Once again I found myself puzzled by Anya's unique energy and stared for too long.

"Anya's father was human." Freya answered my unspoken question.

"I'm sorry. I didn't mean to—"

Freya held up a hand. "You are an Empath. Not using your gift would be like not breathing. It's okay. But please keep your knowledge between us. Anya's life could be in danger if certain individuals found out about her."

"What do you mean?"

Before Freya could say more, the door swung open, and an icy blast of air rippled in and sent a shiver up my back.

I turned to see who'd come in. "Jasper. What are you doing here?"

"Looking for you." He glanced around the shop, his amber eyes landing for a moment on Anya. I didn't miss the instant wave of heat generated between the two before Jasper pulled his gaze from Anya and back to me. "Your mom and Darion followed the ambulance to the hospital. Your mom thought you might have come back here and sent me after you. Let's go."

I glanced out the door. Jasper's mom's car idled out front, with Lucas and Ty waiting in the back seat.

Freya dashed behind the register and came back with a larger bag to fit the two smaller pouches inside.

"Thank you, Freya," I said.

She nodded, and the door clicked as she locked it behind us.

∽

J found my mom in the emergency waiting room. A sea of worried faces and crying children packed the area, waiting either to be seen by a doctor or to find out about their loved ones. My mom's creamy skin had turned pasty pale, and black smudges from wet Kohl rimmed her eyes. When she saw me coming, she jumped up from her chair, and I ran into her arms.

She explained Molly was in some kind of coma and that the doctors couldn't find any external injuries but were running other tests to find an internal cause to determine the treatment for Molly's condition.

"Mom, we both know Molly's condition has nothing to do with—" I glanced around, but nobody was paying us any attention "—natural causes. Magic caused her coma, and only magic can fix it."

My mom sighed and blotted her eyes and cheeks with a rumpled-up tissue she held onto. "You're right, honey. But at least the doctors can keep her comfortable while we figure out what to do next."

"This is all my fault." The overhead lights flickered. I pulled the stupid feathered band off my head and tossed it onto an empty seat. "Whoever is coming for me did this to Molly. It's a message. But why? Is this happening because I haven't returned to Aenoas-Vita like Oria demanded? She warned me, and I didn't listen, and now there's someone pretending to be Darion, looking for Oria's ring."

"What?" My mom scrunched up her brows, her face filled with concern, and she tightly gripped my shoulders. "What do you mean someone is pretending to be Darion?"

I quietly told her about what happened at the ball just before Molly's attack and my visit with Freya afterward.

"That doesn't make sense. Why would the shifters be after Oria's ring? And why would they hurt Molly? These actions would directly violate the treaty Oria brokered with them when she lived. I need to speak to Felix immediately. But first, listen to me, Everly. You are not to blame for this. Okay?" She cupped my cheeks and made me look at her. "You didn't cause this. We don't know why this is happening, but I think you have no other choice but to put the ring on."

I sighed. "You're right. But what if Oria won't respond?"

"Then she's not the queen we all thought she was." My mom pulled her buzzing phone from her purse. "Cal's in the parking lot, waiting for me. We're heading to Selkie's to scour our grimoires for anything that might help Molly. Will you be okay?"

I nodded. "Go."

"Be careful." She kissed my forehead. "The shifters can look like anyone," she warned. "But they can't mask their aura. We still don't know if it's them, but there's no other explanation."

"What about you?" I asked. "You can't read auras. We have to warn everyone else. Here comes Lucas."

"Don't worry about me," she said, just as Lucas came up to us. "I'll send out a warning spell," she whispered in my ear as she hugged me, and then hurried out to the parking lot.

The doctors had asked that only two visitors go into Molly's room at a time, so Jasper, Ty, and Lucas stayed behind in the waiting room, while I went to find Molly's room. Molly's grandparents had raised her, but they recently passed away. The only other relatives I knew of lived out of town, and they weren't close. We were Molly's family.

The lights throughout the entire hall leading to Molly's room dimmed low, then buzzed bright, and it wasn't me this time. Nurses spoke in rushed whispers about the cause, but I already knew. Darion's energy seeped through the entire fifth floor. I had to pause and steady myself. The curse raged through my veins as I drew nearer to my brother.

I swallowed a dry bubble as my hand hesitated on the doorknob leading into Molly's room. Machines beeped from the other side of the door, and whispers came from Darion. I didn't want to eavesdrop, so I pushed the door open and went inside.

Molly lay face-up on the hospital bed with closed eyes. Darion sat at her side with his face pressed sideways on her bare arm and her hand cradled in his.

Be strong for Darion. I refused to let the hot tears spring loose. I steeled myself as I tiptoed to the sink and found a clean washcloth, and ran it under warm water. The black wig Molly had been wearing had been discarded, but she still wore the heavy makeup she'd applied for her Morticia costume. Molly was a stickler for a clean face, and she'd be furious if someone let her sleep with all that goop clogging her pores.

I maneuvered carefully around the heart monitor, which beeped a steady rhythm, and made sure not to disturb the tube taped down the length of Molly's arm, which was connected to a needle on the back of her hand, delivering a constant source of fluid. I smoothed the pink strip of hair back so it blended with Molly's natural blond and began gently cleansing her skin.

"What are you doing?" Darion looked up, and I felt my gut twist, like someone had kicked me hard. His strained eyes were silver pits of worry.

I spoke quietly even though I knew the volume of our voices couldn't wake her. "Molly will be furious if we let her sleep with makeup on."

Darion placed a soft kiss on the top of Molly's hand that he held folded between his. "She's such a feisty little thing. I've never met anyone like her. I—" He broke off, and his forehead fell back down to lie on her arm. His voice came out in a harsh muffle. "I should have told her how much she means to me. I should have been there to protect her."

Fire burned in my chest. I crumpled the washcloth in my hand. "I'm so sorry, Darion. Molly is going to wake up."

"When I find who did this to her, I'm going to make them pay." The sudden rage surging from Darion's aura put me on edge. When Darion got angry, he got reckless. And what he was feeling now was explosive.

I teetered on whether I should tell him about his impersonator. The gray storm brewing in his eyes nearly held me back. But he deserved to know that someone was masquerading around, looking like him. As I was about to speak, I noticed a shining object with red and orange sparks as Darion placed Molly's hand on her abdomen.

I recognized the stone Calista had brought him from Bali.

He'd tucked it in Molly's hand. Calista had said it enhanced determination and willpower. Darion had a stone of a different kind in his hand. He rubbed his thumb over the image painted atop the dream stone he'd drawn from Freya's bowl.

"Darion. What did Freya say to you before you ran out?"

He glanced up from the stone and stared past me as if lost in thought. His hair stuck up in all directions. I'd never seen Darion so disheveled.

My heart ached for both him and Molly, and I decided he didn't need anything else to worry about tonight. "We'll talk about it tomorrow. Come home with me and get some rest. There's nothing we can do until we figure out what's causing Molly's coma."

His attention snapped to. "I'm not leaving."

Rather than engaging in a futile argument, I quickly scanned the room and my eyes landed on the spacious cushioned area beside the window, perfectly suitable for someone as long as Darion. A folded blanket and an extra pillow were lying there, ready to be used.

"I'll bring you clean clothes in the morning. But please at least try to get some rest." I patted the pillow and lifted the blanket. "Molly needs you to be strong for her. If you stay up all night worrying, you won't be much help to any of us. Now come on."

Darion tucked Molly's arms under her blanket.

I turned away to give him privacy while he whispered in her ear.

He plopped down on the narrow cot and kicked off his shoes, while I shook out the blanket and tossed it over him.

"She said it's the toll to cross the barrier."

I'd already forgotten about my question, so it took me a second to register what Darion was talking about, but then I remembered the dream stone. "What does that mean?"

"I don't know yet." Darion's head turned so his eyes fell on Molly's motionless body. "But I'm going to figure it out."

I smoothed his hair back. "Get some sleep first." I turned away, but Darion's hand reached for mine, and the curse buzzed between us. We didn't need to speak. Thanks to the mysterious spell that bound the curse, our emotions vibrated as a single thread when we made contact. I squeezed his hand back. "I'll see you in the morning."

I dimmed the lights in the room before I slipped back out into the hall. As soon as the door clicked shut, tears that I'd held back in front of Darion flooded out. My body shook as I slid down to the floor.

Onlookers averted their gaze, accustomed to witnessing visitors of patients deteriorating in the hallways, out of sight from the room's occupant. A caring nurse, who hadn't layered herself with cold emotional barriers, crouched down and softly placed her hand on my shoulder.

"Is there someone I can call for you?" Kind brown eyes squinted over me.

I shook my head and mumbled, "Thank you." Then I pushed myself back to standing.

When I got back to the waiting room, Lucas sat alone with a duffel bag on the floor next to his feet. He'd changed from his Halloween getup into jeans and a T-shirt, which made me even more aware of how uncomfortable my costume felt.

"What happened to Ty and Jasper?" I glanced around the still-full waiting room.

Lucas stood and pulled me into his chest. "They thought we might like some time alone, so Jasper left me his mom's car, and they both got a ride with your mom when she came back in to give me your purse you'd left in her car. They're coming back in the morning to see Molly."

"Oh." I nestled against Lucas's chest, and his arms snuggled tighter around me.

His fingers kneaded the tight muscles in my neck. "Do the doctors know anything yet?" he asked.

I shook my head, not wanting to make up any more lies.

"Don't worry." He smoothed my cheek. "I'm sure they'll know more by the morning."

I wished I could tell Lucas that he was wrong, that there was no way the doctors could fix Molly, since what was wrong with her had nothing to do with human anatomy, but I just nodded. "Take me home."

Lucas swung his duffel bag over one arm and tucked me into the other as we left the hospital. Neither of us spoke during the drive. I noticed Lucas stealing glances at me multiple times, as if he had something on his mind, but he stayed quiet.

I checked my phone for messages. The most recent text was from my mom, letting me know she'd taken Luna with her to Selkie's. I released a grateful breath. Luna had been alone most of the day, and going on a car ride would have thrilled her.

When we got inside my apartment, I kicked off my shoes and set the bag of stones Freya had given me on an end table. Then I sank onto the couch, too exhausted to even go change out of the uncomfortable flapper dress.

Lucas stood by the door, watching me with a careful expression. The overhead kitchen light reflected in his eyes as they trailed my body with a hard intensity. The corded muscles in his arms tensed as he bent down and tore off the cowboy boots he'd worn as a part of his earlier costume. He ran his hand through his sandy waves as he came over and sank down next to me. He stretched my legs atop his and massaged my calves and feet. My eyes wanted to drift closed, but I took a deep breath and plunged forward before I lost my nerve. "Lucas, I—"

"Shh … not tonight." He slid his hands underneath my body and pulled me onto his lap. His fingers massaged up the back of my neck and tickled my ears before he unclipped my hair.

My scalp tingled with instant release as my long black hair fell down over my shoulders in loose waves. I trailed my fingers across Lucas's forehead and circled his almond-shaped eyes, dreading the words that I could no longer put off.

With a gentle touch, his hand slid into my hair as he guided my head down to meet his lips. His lips softly caressed mine in a delicate and uncertain kiss. I responded briefly before pulling away. "Lucas, we need to talk."

I could see the hunger in his eyes as he stared at me. With a fierce intensity, he pressed his lips against mine as he maneuvered me beneath him in one quick movement. My body went rigid as my hands pressed against his chest.

Lucas froze and lifted himself off of me.

I sat up and adjusted my dress back over my legs.

"You can't be with me because of him." His jawline hardened. "All this time, I thought you just weren't ready, but it's been him all along."

I sucked in a breath. I couldn't deny the truth. And if I did, I'd just be lying to both Lucas and myself.

"It all makes sense now," Lucas went on when I didn't answer. "Why you've always kept a part of yourself from me." His words weren't angry, just sad and disappointed. "I think a part of me has always known that you had to be in love with someone else, but why didn't you just tell me?"

As the tears welled up, I struggled to keep them down, feeling a lump forming in my throat. "I guess I thought if I could pretend Arden didn't exist, then I could move on, but I was wrong. I'm so sorry, Lucas. I care about you so much." I reached across the couch and grasped his hand. "I never meant to hurt you."

He threaded his fingers through mine. "I saw the way you looked at each other. And when I saw you in his arms, I knew …" His hand separated from mine.

Lucas wiped the burning tears from my cheeks with the back of his finger and tilted my chin up. "Do I even have a chance for you to feel that way about me?"

The spark of hope faded from Lucas's eyes when I looked at him. He nodded, then stood and pulled on his boots.

My thoughts spun, and I scrambled to explain. "I have a complicated relationship with Arden. I don't want to lose you, Lucas. Our friendship means so much to me."

Lucas stopped at the door and smiled half-heartedly. "I love you, Ev. And I want you to be happy, but friendship isn't enough for me. I want to be with you. I want you to look at me the way you looked at him: like there was nothing else in the world but the two of us. But that's never going to happen, and I can't settle for just your friendship. At least not right now. I need some time."

I crossed the room and stood in front of him. He opened his arms, and I squeezed my own around him. I didn't want to lose Lucas's friendship, but he deserved to be with someone who could give him the love he deserved, even if it meant I couldn't be a part of his life anymore. We held each other with a desperate grip, as if we knew it might be our last embrace.

His chest rumbled against mine when he said, "I'll come see you tomorrow before I head out of town, okay?"

I nodded into his chest and sniffled as my tears soaked into his T-shirt.

He kissed the top of my head and then gently backed out of my arms and left.

I crumpled to the floor and buried my face in my hands. Letting Lucas go had been the right thing to do for us both. But it still felt like everything was falling apart ... again. Molly, poor thing, lay motionless in a coma, her body trapped in a spell-induced slumber that we had no clue how to break. And a malevolent darkness we knew nothing about was closing in on us.

I didn't know how long I'd been on the floor, but when the knock came at the door, my back and legs ached as I uncoiled myself to stand.

When I opened the door, a sea of blue-green washed over me. Arden took in my appearance, and I shrugged, not needing to explain. The connection I shared with Arden went beyond words. He reached a supportive arm toward me, and when I didn't object, he scooped me off my feet and into his arms. My body relished the weightlessness and melted in his warm, protective energy as he carried me in a comfortable silence to my room and laid me on my bed.

"Will you stay?" I whispered, exhaustion pulling my head down onto the pillow.

He nodded and tucked the covers over me, cocooning me in a blanket of warmth. My eyes drifted as the weight of his muscled arm settled across my body.

～

The fragrant smells of garlic, rosemary, and strong coffee enveloped the air, coaxing my senses to life. Opening my eyes felt like lifting weights as my eyelids stubbornly clung together. I carefully removed the crust that sealed them shut, knowing that my eyes would appear swollen when I glanced at my reflection in the mirror. My legs felt constricted when I tried stretching. *Oh, I slept in my dress.*

Memories of last night came rushing back, and I quickly checked the other side of the bed. It was empty, and then I smelled the scent of herbs again. Arden must be *cooking.*

I darted up out of the bed. I couldn't let him see me like this. Silently, I opened my bedroom door and quickly made my way to the bathroom across the hall. I took a shower in record time, using my best-scented washes, brushed my teeth, hair, and threw on some yoga pants and a tank top.

My stomach growled with the anticipation of food. I hadn't eaten since the birthday party, and I was starving. When I walked into the kitchen, my hunger pains morphed from painful knots into a twist of flutters.

Arden stood over the stove, barefoot in a pair of jeans and a dark gray T-shirt that stretched against the taut muscles of his upper body. His golden hair had a slightly mussed look, but in a good way. He gave the "just rolled out of bed" look a whole new meaning. Using tongs, he flipped the bacon, causing it to sizzle and fill the room with a delightful, savory aroma.

My cheeks flushed when Arden caught me watching him. He grabbed a mug from the cabinet and filled it with coffee and a splash of coconut milk from the fridge. "I hope you don't mind me taking over your kitchen." He smiled, handing me my coffee.

I took a long sip and then another, while my eyes traced the honeyed stubble covering his strong jawline. "Not at all." A crackle from the stove and the snap of grease popping forced Arden to turn away. "I could get used to waking up like this," I teased.

Arden glanced sideways with a look that sent shivers racing across my skin. "Me too." The words were so quiet I wasn't sure if he'd said anything at all, or if I was just making words from the hissing of the oil cooking.

I leaned against the kitchen island, admiring the sight of

an army commander cooking in my kitchen. It seemed such a natural task for him that I wondered about his life on Aenoas-Vita. "Do you cook much when you're back home?"

He retrieved two plates from a cabinet and piled them high with an egg-and-herb scramble and slices of bacon. "Not as much as I'd like to. I mostly eat at the royal palace, but I enjoy cooking for myself when I can." He carried our plates over to the kitchen table, which overlooked the field of wildflowers, and pulled a chair out for me.

"Thank you."

Arden watched me dig in with a look of satisfaction. The buttery eggs and savory bacon settled my stomach.

After we'd both eaten every bit of food on our plates, we leaned back in our chairs. I gripped my coffee mug.

"Do you want to talk about what happened?" Arden asked, signaling for me to hand him my cup. He refilled it and brought it back to me.

I sipped the warm, earthy brew. The thought of discussing Lucas with Arden left me feeling uneasy and unsure of what to say. I decided to begin at the start, detailing the chilling reading by the Spider Witch, and then recounting all the events that had taken place at the ball and before, finally revealing that I had broken things off with Lucas.

Arden's entire demeanor changed, and his muscles tensed. The cerulean vanished from his eyes as they became a pool of green algae.

"I'm sorry about Lucas," he said. "But can you describe exactly what happened at the ball?"

"You didn't already know? I thought that's why you came last night," I said.

His answer came out as a low growl. "No." He got up and cleared our plates. He moved quietly, deep in thought, while I explained everything, including my conversation with Freya after the paramedics had taken away Molly.

"Who are the shape-shifters, and what would they want with Oria's ring?"

He rinsed the plates and added them to the built-in dishwasher. "The shifters are from a planet near to ours. Oria brokered a treaty with them when she still ruled, and we've coexisted since with minimum conflict. I don't know what they are doing here or why they want Oria's ring, if it was them. But I'm going to find out. I need you to be careful. I'll have guards sent immediately with Rheya."

I stood up. "You're going back?" I walked over and gripped the edge of the countertop.

Given that Arden's entire life revolved around safeguarding Aenoas-Vita, I knew it would be irrational to expect him to stay. But he'd only just got here, and I wasn't ready to lose him again so soon.

Arden closed the dishwasher and then came over to stand in front of me. He gathered my hands in his. "I'm sorry about your friend. I won't be gone long, I promise, but after everything you've told me, this threat is more dangerous than Felix presumed."

"Why did you come last night?" I had to know before he left.

His intense stare bore into me as his hands glided up my arms, leaving a trail of goosebumps in their wake. "I never should have let you go," he breathed as his head moved towards mine.

I threw my arms around his neck, and when our lips met, fire ignited. He tightened his grip and pressed me into him. Our bodies molded together like a lock and a key. Every touch and stroke of his tongue sent flames rippling between us. He lifted my legs around his waist, while his lips never left contact with mine. I wanted nothing more than to let go completely and be with him.

His mouth tasted my neck as he sat me on the countertop and pulled my shirt over my head. "Beautiful," he whispered.

I brushed my fingertips under his shirt, gathering the fabric, and lifted it upward. His muscles tensed under my lips as I kissed the Vitarian symbol tattooed over his heart. My tongue trailed the tip of the V and followed the thick line to the top, where it crested to a tightened fist on either side.

Arden's breath quickened, and he slipped a finger under my bra strap and slid it down as he kissed the top of my shoulder.

My entire body quivered, and I clasped my legs tighter around his waist. His lips found mine again when a sudden knock at the door broke the moment.

"Ignore it," Arden moaned.

I nearly lost all restraint just as another knock came, and I heard Luna yelp outside the door. I pulled my woozy head back, feeling as though I'd just woken from a dream I never wanted to end.

"Everly—should I get the door?"

"Huh," I blinked, realizing we still had our shirts on and Arden held my hands. "Oh …" I turned with dizzying disappointment, wishing everything I'd just imagined had been real. "It's my mom."

"Wait," Arden whispered and pulled me back. He cupped my face, and my stomach somersaulted as he touched his lips to mine. Our lips parted, and he kissed me like the world was about to end. "That's why I came last night. Letting you go was a mistake I won't make again."

"Did that just happen?" I pinched my arm just to make sure I wasn't imagining things again.

Arden smiled at me like he'd done the first time we'd met,

like I was some conundrum he was trying to make sense of. Then he kissed me again. "I'll never let you go again."

"Why is our timing always off?" I groaned and kissed him once more before I hurried to the door and pulled it open. Luna bolted in and bounced around for pets.

"Hey, girl." I bent down and smoothed her black and auburn fur, while still trying to get my wits about me. Her fur had a fresh sheen and smelled of lavender. She sprinted toward Arden, who was pulling on his shoes and grabbing his jacket.

"The girls gave Luna a doggy spa treatment last night." My mom glanced past me. Her brow furrowed with an unspoken question as Arden headed our way.

"Commander," she said, glancing back at me with a shadow of concern.

"Queen Mother." He inclined his head.

My mom flicked her hand. "Enough of that. It makes me sound ancient, and you know I prefer Cacsha."

Arden grinned. "It's good to see you well, Cacsha."

"And you." A knowing look flashed across my mom's eyes.

I couldn't help but smile when the commander of Aenoas-Vita shifted nervously.

Arden switched his attention to me. "I'll return as soon as I can."

I could tell by his body language that he was unsure of whether to kiss me goodbye in front of my mom, so I wrapped my arms around him and hugged him tight. "Don't be gone long," I whispered in his ear.

When he released me, his look said he didn't want to go, but we both knew his duty took priority.

"Cacsha." Arden inclined his head once more and then left the two of us.

I kneaded the ache in my chest as I watched him go.

"I know that look." My mom's voice brought me back

from my thoughts. "It's the same look I had for your father. But I worry about you, honey. Arden will never leave Aenoas-Vita for good, and you aren't ready to leave Earth. And what about Lucas?"

I sighed and walked to the porch railing. A soft breeze brought relief to my flushed skin. My mom settled beside me, with her arms folded atop the railing as she leaned forward, lifting her face to the sun.

A faint shimmer danced across my skin as I stretched my arms under the warm rays. As my powers increased, so did other subtle changes. Luckily, the faint shimmer resembled a hint of glitter in body lotion to the human eye. I glanced over at my mom, noticing the sparkle in her skin as well, since she'd been using magic more often.

"I don't mean to pry." My mom's words floated between us. "I want you to be happy, sweetie. Arden's a good man, and it's obvious he cares deeply for you, but you two have been down this road before, and I don't want to see you get hurt again. And Lucas adores you."

"I know," I exhaled. "Lucas is important to me, and I never intended to cause him any pain. Our relationship should never have gone beyond friendship when my feelings for Arden were still unresolved. It was a mistake to believe that I could make myself feel something that wasn't genuine. I'm an Empath. I should know better. When Arden appeared at my party, it was as if a meteor crashed into me, causing all my pent-up feelings to explode, and I realized I hadn't moved on at all." My hand instinctively reached for my heart, and I could feel its steady beat as I rubbed it. "I don't want to be apart from him anymore, even if the distance between us spans across two different planets." I touched my lips, still feeling the tingle from Arden's kiss. "His duty as commander will always take precedence over our relationship, and I accept that, just as he must accept my choice to remain on

Earth. Someday we'll live on the same planet, but until then, we can make it work."

"And Lucas?" asked my mom.

My gaze drifted over the field of wildflowers as I drew in a deep breath of the sweet-scented air. "I ended things with Lucas last night. He's supposed to come by later today on his way out of town. He's been so good to me, Mom. All I want is for him to find someone who loves him the way he deserves." I wiped at an escaped tear. "The way he looked at me last night, it was heartbreaking to see him so hurt. I wish things could have turned out differently."

"Oh, honey." My mom smoothed a lock of hair behind my ear. "You've put other people's happiness before your own for too long. If Lucas isn't the one, then the best thing you can do for him is let him go. Over time, he'll realize it's for the best."

My mom's phone buzzed. "It's Cal. She's found a spell she wants me to look at." She squeezed my arm. "Are you going to be okay?"

I rubbed my eyes. "Yeah, I'll be fine. I'm going to take Darion some food and clothes, and check on Molly."

She sighed. "I spoke with your brother this morning. My poor boy is suffering, and it just breaks my heart to think of sweet little Molly, but all we can do is stay focused on finding a way to help her." Her phone lit up again. "Cal's getting impatient. I better go. Love you, Ev, and be careful."

"Love you too, Mom, and you be careful too. We don't know what we're dealing with. I still haven't told Darion about his look-alike at the ball, and after seeing him last night, I'm not sure I should."

Her keys jingled as she pulled them from her purse. "I know you're worried about his response, but he deserves to know what you saw." Luna barked and bounded onto the porch, looking up at my mom expectantly.

"Looks like somebody wants to go for another joyride." I laughed. "And you're right," I said, giving Luna's belly a scratch. "I'll tell him today. Arden's going back to see what he can find out, and he's planning to send Rheya with guards."

My mom nodded and patted Luna's side. "That's good." Her phone buzzed again. "Selkie's at Cal's." She glanced up from her phone. "I better head over there. Come on, girl. Let's go see what spell Cal dug up."

I went back inside the apartment and found my phone and sent Darion a quick text: *On my way! Bringing clean clothes and edible food.*

∼

*M*y shoes squeaked against the shining hospital floor, catching the attention of a group of nurses dressed in blue and light-pink uniforms. They smiled as I passed, then continued their chat with coffee cups in hand.

I held on tight to the two paper mugs and the bag of pastries in my hands as I pushed through the door to Molly's room.

Molly's body lay the same as last night, only now she had a stone sitting in the center of her forehead, and her eyelids twitched rapidly. I nearly dropped the loot in my arms in my rush to get to her bedside.

"Darion! Did you see that?" I set the coffee cups and pastries down and slipped the strap from my shoulder, dropping Darion's duffel bag to the floor.

Darion didn't respond. He sat at Molly's side, holding her hands. His closed eyelids twitched the same as Molly's.

My breath hitched. *What's going on here?*

I snatched the stone from Molly's forehead, and Darion's eyes snapped open. He wasn't glad to see me.

"What the hell, Ev? Why did you do that?"

"Seriously, Darion. What if I'd been the nurse? What would they have thought coming in here and finding a rock on Molly's head and you in a trance?"

"Ev," he intoned like I was a child. "You own a yoga studio that is always full. People love this New Age woo-woo." He waved his hands sarcastically. "They would just assume I'm practicing some kind of trendy meditative healing."

I picked up a hot cup and handed Darion his coffee and a bag of pastries. "What were you really doing?" I shot a glance at the door to make sure we were still alone.

Darion sat up straight, stretching and twisting his back.

"Did you even get any sleep?" I noted the shadows under his eyes.

He gulped his coffee and inhaled a pastry, ignoring my interrogation.

I glared down at him. "Darion. I'm serious. Tell me what you're doing."

He held up a hand. "Okay. But promise you won't freak out first." His eyes became more alert with the infusion of sugar and caffeine.

I huffed and pulled a chair over on the opposite side of Molly. "I'll do my best. As long as whatever you're up to is not putting Molly in more danger."

He winced and clenched his jaw. "So, we're back to you not trusting me? Do you really think I'd do anything to hurt Molly?" He kissed the top of her hand, his expression softening.

My chest tightened. "That came out wrong. I'm sorry." Gently placing my hand on top of his and Molly's, I said, "I know you would never intentionally do anything to hurt Molly." Just then, I remembered what Freya had said when we'd been to see her with our mom.

"Darion, I need to know." I paused. He met my stare and waited for me to finish. "Did you tell Molly about us?"

His shoulders tensed, and I wasn't sure if he'd answer me, but then he nodded. "Yes, but I didn't tell her everything, just that we aren't human and come from another planet. She doesn't know that you're our queen or anything else."

I pulled my ponytail slightly loose to relieve some of the tension in my scalp. Darion had every right to share his life the way he chose, but that didn't change the danger involved.

Darion sensed the direction of my thoughts. "Molly didn't even get upset. She'd suspected something was different about us, and said she was glad I'd told her. She would never tell anyone, Ev. We can trust her."

I shook my head. "That's not what I'm worried about. This knowledge could very well have put Molly in danger."

Darion's eyes flashed wide, and the air tensed as his energy vibrated. "Are you saying this is my fault?" His voice cracked.

"Of course not, Darion. That's not what I meant. I just think—" I stopped. Anything I said would just make Darion feel worse. This wasn't his fault. It was mine. Someone was after me. The Spider Witch's warning and Freya's reading had made that clear, and I knew in my gut that what they had done to Molly was a message for me to comply. "Something happened last night that I need to tell you about."

Darion listened intently while I recounted my encounter with his impersonator at the ball. When I finished, Molly's heart monitor beeped erratically.

"Darion!"

He snatched his hand from Molly's, realizing that his magic was affecting her. His chair fell backward as he stood abruptly, squeezing his fists into balls. He said through gritted teeth, "If he did this to Molly, then the last person she saw was me. She'll think I did this to her." Darion fell to his knees. His hands shot into his messy hair.

This was exactly the response I'd been worried Darion would have. I went to him and reached a tentative hand toward his folded torso. "Molly would have known it wasn't you. I've seen the connection between you two."

Darion shook, his emotions going wild, and without stopping to think, I felt for the dark spots materializing in his energy field and drew them into me. I couldn't let Darion lose himself in the darkness again. He'd worked too hard to come this far. His body relaxed in my arms.

"I felt that," he said. "You can't keep taking in everyone else's dark energy. It's going to consume you."

"Don't worry about me. I know what I'm doing. Come on." I ushered him up. "You're stronger than this, Darion. Don't let the shadows prey on you, and I won't have to take them from you."

Darion roused himself, and we both went back to our chairs. A fury still vibrated within his aura, but he controlled it.

"Now, tell me what you were doing before I got here."

A knock sounded at the door, and a nurse popped her head in. "Everything okay in here? I thought I heard a thump." It was the same nurse, with the kind brown eyes, who'd checked on me last night when I'd broken down in the hall.

"Oh, sorry," I said. "I just tripped over a chair, but I'm fine."

She glanced around the room and studied the heart monitor. "Okay, then. You two let me know if you need anything."

"We will."

The nurse popped her head back out and closed the door.

I looked back at Darion and waited.

"Okay," he said. "Well, you know I can dream walk."

I wasn't sure I liked the direction Darion was heading in with this, but I nodded as I was following along.

He continued, "I thought if I could get inside of Molly's dreams, I could find out what happened or get her to wake up." He stopped, grinding his teeth. "But something is blocking me from getting in. I think it's a part of the spell keeping her asleep, and a safeguard against someone with my ability breaking through the spell."

"What about this?" I picked up the dream stone from Molly's blanket and handed it to him.

He rubbed his thumb over the mark on the smooth midnight stone. "Freya told me it was the toll to break through the barrier."

A jitter of excitement took hold of my hands as what Darion said sank in. "Did it work? Were you able to get inside her mind?" I tried hard not to remember a darker time, when Darion had used his ability to trespass in my mind, but this was different. This time, he'd be using his magic for good.

He lifted his shoulders. "I don't know. Just as I thought I felt something happening and saw a glimmer of images, you came in and broke my connection."

My chest deflated. I cracked my knuckles.

If Darion could get inside Molly's head, then maybe we might have a chance of waking her up.

My pulse raced. "This could work, Darion. Try again."

My enthusiasm infused Darion with confidence. He settled the stone back on Molly's forehead and took her hand. I watched anxiously as both sets of eyelids flickered with rapid movement. His free hand gripped Molly's blanket, and he gasped. His eyes flew open.

"What happened?"

Wrinkles creased across his forehead. "I got pushed out—

121

more like slammed out." His mouth turned down as he studied Molly's face.

"Did you see anything?"

Darion pushed up from his chair and paced. Muddy blue-gray tones shrouded his aura.

I held my stomach and breathed as Darion's pain passed through me.

He returned to Molly's bedside and smoothed his hand over her cheek. "Her mind is stuck in a loop of her dancing with me at the ball, only it's not me." His words came out hoarse. "She's stuck in there, Ev, with someone she thinks is me." He reached over and latched onto my wrist. "What if I can't get her back?"

"No!" I refused to accept the thought. "Try again, but this time, we go together, and we're bringing this." I snatched the stone from Molly's forehead.

Darion's eyes widened. We both knew that once we linked our magic, it allowed the other to end the curse that bound our lives in the only way we knew possible: by absorbing it in its entirety and becoming the sole keeper of the spell and all the life force attached to it.

"You trust me that much?" Darion asked in a stunned whisper.

My answer came in my action. I latched onto his hand with mine and held on tight. "Let's get Molly back."

I closed my eyes, along with Darion. My stomach flipped as I lurched out of my body. We maintained contact with our clasped hands to keep our magic connected, and Darion brought me into Molly's dream.

"Don't let go of my hand," Darion instructed as a thick fog pressed against our skin like a damp blanket.

It was hard to breathe, and every movement felt motion-less, like we were moving but staying still at the same time. Shadows formed around us. They twisted and swayed as if moving to music only they heard. Sinister laughter echoed overhead, which made my skin crawl. I choked on the cloying air, trying to fill my lungs.

"Look at me," Darion demanded through the fog. His silver eyes bored into mine as he shook me to focus on him. "Remember where your body is. Don't lose your connection to it. Let your body breathe for you."

I pictured my body sitting back in Molly's hospital room, my lungs pumping with air, and suddenly the choking stopped, and I took a deep breath.

"Better?" Darion asked.

I nodded, ignoring the taunting shadows as we kept pushing forward. Two bodies materialized through the evaporating fog. Molly stood in her costume with the man pretending to be Darion.

"Molly!" My voice echoed, unheard by Molly's ears.

Darion's heartbeat raced, causing mine to speed up through our link.

It was impossible to hurry through the thick, sticky air. The harder we tried to drag ourselves forward, the more it seemed to resist our movement.

"Darion, let's see if we can do something about this fog."

We stood in place. I wasn't sure how my magic would work in this dreamworld, but I felt its presence within me, as always. I reached out my mind to the elements, and a force rippled out and away from us. The fog dissipated, taking the dancing shadows along with it.

We continued with less resistance, and as we got closer to Molly, we could see Darion's doppelgänger whispering in her ear. She listened intently with cheeks pale and shoulders tensed, and that was when I noticed the symbol cut into her forehead, and so did Darion. His face twisted with the same rage I felt.

The impersonator glanced up at us like he knew we were

there, and the smile he gave us was so evil that I faltered and nearly dropped Darion's hand, but Darion tightened his grasp and snarled at the impostor in return.

"Let Molly go!" Darion edged us closer, but we slammed into an invisible wall.

The man grabbed Molly roughly by the arms. He twirled, twisted, and lifted her off her feet as they danced to soundless music, as the shadows had. The void stare on Molly's face tore at me; she was a prisoner of her own mind.

"Darion! Darion!" I shook him, trying to get his attention.

Darion's lips moved, but he stayed locked on the two twisting forms. "He's marked her." The anguish in his voice ripped into my chest.

"We'll fix it, I promise, but right now, you need to get Molly to see the real you so she'll wake up. Take this." I shoved the dream stone into his hand.

Darion closed his fingers over it. "Do you think it'll work?"

"Yes. I think only you can cross the barrier of his magic with the stone. Freya referred to it as the 'toll.' You drew the stone. The magic was meant for this moment, but you need to work quickly. I'm going to get his attention, and as soon as he comes for me, let go of my hand and go to Molly."

Worry etched his brow. "You're not a dream walker. If I let you go, you—"

"I trust you, Darion. Wake Molly up, and then come back for me."

"Okay," he agreed with a torn expression as he glanced at me, then back at Molly. "But if this works, and she wakes up, you won't be in Molly's dream anymore; you'll be stuck in between ..."

Molly and her captor faded farther and farther away. If we didn't act now, we might not get another chance. "Just follow my lead."

"Hey! You! You want Oria's ring?" The dancing halted, and the forms shimmered and materialized in front of us.

"Where is it?" the voice that wasn't Darion's snarled at me.

I cocked an eyebrow. "It's here." I tapped my pocket and released Darion's hand. Then I turned and ran, pumping my arms. The shadows that had appeared as just empty figments only moments ago re-formed with menacing hisses. Their forms solidified as they knocked into me, shoving me sideways and blocking my path. My fists flew out in front of me, but they found nothing but empty air, as the shadows disappeared as swiftly as they appeared. I ground my feet into the surface and propelled myself forward. Sweat trickled down my face, and I hurriedly checked behind me to confirm that my plan had worked.

Thank God.

Darion had Molly, and the shape-shifter chased behind me. With renewed hope, I ignored the pain locking up my leg muscles and ran faster. A hand clawed my shoulder from behind, tripping me up. My head whipped sideways for an instant, and I glimpsed a silver ring engraved with an E as the fingers raked across my skin.

"Ahh!" I screamed as my shoulder burned with fire. I gagged, trying to force air into my lungs, and pressed on harder and faster. My feet went out from under me, and I stumbled forward.

"No!" My gut coiled with fear.

I expected him to be on me any second, but when my body spun, everything from Molly's dream had disintegrated, along with my pursuer.

I wasn't sure how much time had passed, but my legs burned like I'd been running for miles, and my shoulder throbbed. As I twisted my head to examine the wound, the lack of light in my surroundings made it impossible to see anything clearly. I ran my fingers over the area instead and winced at the torn flesh. Then panic set in when I realized that my body floated in infinite black nothingness.

Did this mean Molly was awake, and I was somewhere in between, like Darion had warned?

I forced the panic aside and focused on calming my heart rate. Darion would come back for me.

As time went on, plumes of color exploded in the black, and I was suddenly swimming in sparkling swirls of magenta and clouds of violet, yellow, and gold. Sparks of light sprang to life all around, millions of twinkles everywhere. Some pulses of light made formations in the sky. I spun, realizing constellations surrounded me.

Where am I?

My body floated toward a cluster of pulsing blue-white and red stars that formed into a round shape, the size of a head with two long antennae. Or were they supposed to be horns on a head? It was hard to tell. But with a rush of alarm, I realized I floated straight toward a bright, burning light. I was going to collide with the stars. I pumped my arms, trying to get my body to float in the opposite direction, but I kept spinning the wrong way, like it was reeling me in.

I screamed into the darkness as the body of stars appeared to move together in a menacing way. A bow took shape, and long stretches of stars making arms pulled the string back on the bow and aimed it at me. I flailed and cried out for Darion to find me.

"Everly!"

"I'm here! Help me!"

Darion materialized and snatched me in his arms.

Bright florescent lights burned my eyes. I squinted, trying to make out the silhouette hovering over me. With a heart-shaped face similar to mine, she stood out with her unique hairstyle-blond hair with a bold streak of pink. Wide brown eyes the color of an aged oak roamed over my face.

I sprang up, only to fall back with a dizzy head.

Molly's cool fingers pressed against my cheeks and forehead. "She's burning up." Concern strained her usual sassy tone. "I'll get a cold washcloth."

"Wait," I groaned, struggling to keep my eyes open despite the dizziness that intensified with every blink, but I needed to see Molly's face and reassure myself that she was really okay.

"You're awake." My lips turned up into a smile. Then my eyelids drifted closed.

Darion knelt beside me and handed me a plastic cup filled with water. "I'm sorry, Ev. I came right back for you, but you'd vanished. It took me several tries to follow your energy trail. Are you okay?"

A year ago, I never would have imagined seeing Darion so worried for me, or hearing the shaken edge to his voice over my well-being. I pushed myself up and leaned against the wall and clenched my teeth. My hand flew to my shoulder, now covered with a bandage, drawing Darion's attention to it.

"I'm sorry you were hurt. Whoever did this is stronger than me. I should've been able to protect you in there, but I couldn't." The guilt in his voice caused an ache in my chest.

I shifted to find a position that didn't hurt as much. "All that matters is you found me, and we saved Molly."

Darion cast his eyes down.

"What?" I asked. "What's wrong?"

Molly came back with the cold cloth. I tried shooing it away, but she maneuvered around me and drooped it over my head, folding the edge back at my forehead so I could see. I couldn't deny that the cool temperature felt nice and helped steady my dizzy head.

"What am I missing?" I glanced between the two faces hovering over me.

Molly sat next to me and shared a worried look with Darion. Then she pointed to her forehead. "The man who attacked me gave me a message. He said I have his mark."

The bloodied mark I'd seen in her dream was no longer visible, but I knew its ugliness lay beneath her skin. The slight hum of its magic leached into Molly's aura.

Molly continued in an eerie calm. "And unless you give him what he wants, he'll put me back to sleep." She paused and then finished. "For good."

I squeezed the pillow that lay at my side and forced back the scream that welled at the back of my throat. I threw my arms around Molly and held her tight.

"I'm so sorry, Molly. You must hate me for what's happened to you and for not telling you the truth about what I am."

Molly shook her head. "I could never hate you, Ev. You're my best friend. And I understand why you were scared to tell me that you're an *alien*."

We both laughed, and the mood eased slightly.

Molly sat up. "Jokes aside …" She adjusted the cloth on my head. "I get it. I can't say I'd have done it any differently. But I hope you can figure out how to get this creepy invisible carving out of my head."

Darion still knelt beside me, and Molly reached out her arms and brought our heads together so they all three touched. "Thank you both for getting me out of that nightmare. I don't know who that guy was, but he was real scary. His act didn't fool me for one second, and it made him angrier that I resisted him. I think he wanted to kill me, and it was hard for him not to, and I don't want to go back there with him." Her body shuddered at the memory.

Darion sat up and lifted Molly in his arms. "I won't let him get anywhere near you again."

What Darion didn't say, but what I suspected—and he most likely did too—was that the shifter didn't need to be near Molly to activate the mark. There was something different about this magic and the way the rune had been absorbed beneath her skin, but there was no reason to frighten Molly further if this was the case. She'd been through enough.

"You're awake!" a voice exclaimed from the door. "She's awake," the nurse announced again, this time to someone in the hall.

Two nurses came barreling in, followed by a skinny man with copper skin and an East India accent. He pulled a penlight from the front pocket of his crisp white doctor's jacket.

"You gave us quite the scare, young lady. Do you mind if we check you over?" He patted the hospital bed.

The nurses ushered Molly onto the bed, wrapping her arm to test her blood pressure, and popping a disposable thermometer under her tongue, while the doctor flashed his light in her pupils. He checked her temperature and read the blood pressure reading. "Everything appears normal, but we'll need to run some blood work and schedule another brain scan now that you're awake."

Molly shrugged. "I'm fine. I feel great. Good as new and ready to go home."

The doctor wrinkled his nose. "I know you're eager to be in the comfort of your own home, but we still don't know the cause of your coma, and we need to be sure everything checks out before we can release you."

Molly huffed, but went off with the nurses like a good patient to get her blood drawn.

The room fell silent once the doctor and nurses took

Molly away. I was attempting to stand to go use the bathroom when Darion shot up to help me. "Darion, I'm fine, I promise." I shooed away his help.

"Now you sound like Molly, and we both know she's not out of the woods yet." He slammed his fist into the hospital mattress.

"I'm sorry. We'll find a way to remove the mark for good, but at least she's awake now. And there's something I need to tell you about when I was trapped inside wherever I was." I leaned against Molly's hospital bed for support.

Darion bent forward in his chair. "What is it?"

"Your impersonator had a ring on. When he clawed my back, I turned just enough to see it before he disappeared. It was the same ring from the photo Lucas brought."

Silence hung between us as the implication of this news took root.

"It's him."

"Yeah," I agreed. "It has to be. But if he's after Oria's ring, why would he have killed our father? I didn't even know about the ring then."

Darion breathed hard. "Argh!" he growled as he jumped up and kicked back the chair he'd sat in. "I'm going to kill him!"

"We need to find out who and what we're dealing with." My legs wobbled as I took a step forward.

Darion sprang forward and caught my arms.

"It was just a dizzy spell, but I'm fine now. See?" I steadied myself as I took a step toward the bathroom. "All better." I hurried into the bathroom and closed the door before Darion saw the strain on my face. He had enough to worry about. He didn't need to add me to the list.

Several splashes of cold water on my face calmed the headache brewing at my temples, but the helpless feeling of floating in infinite blackness lingered. And the fear of nearly colliding with stars still clung to my skin. I shuddered to think what would have happened if I'd died while stuck in nothingness. Would my body have died too, or would my mind have stayed asleep indefinitely?

Thank goodness Darion found me in time.

I patted my face dry with a clean towel and looked up into the mirror above the sink. My breath caught when a pair of sapphire eyes that weren't my own stared over my head. I spun around, heart pounding, but no one stood behind me.

Ouch!

The metal towel rack met my elbow with a sharp thud. I rubbed at my tingling funny bone, feeling a slight jolt of electricity shoot up my arm, and checked the mirror again. This time, only my pale reflection stared back. Examining my sapphire eyes, I wondered why the shifter's eyes mirrored the exact same shade instead of Darion's, the person he was trying to imitate. None of it made sense, just like everything else happening.

"Everything okay in there?" Darion's voice called from the other side of the door. "I heard a noise."

"If you call losing my mind being okay." I hung up the hand towel and opened the door. "I thought I saw your impersonator standing behind me, and I whacked my elbow. Being trapped in a black hole really messed with my head."

"Huh," Darion looked me over. "He can dream walk, Ev. Maybe being trapped in there with him created some kind of psychic connection. We don't know what he's capable of, but he could reject me from Molly's mind when I tried entering alone, and that's never happened. Something is different about this shifter. He has magic most shifters don't have."

An icy flush came over me. *We need to take this creeper down before he attacks again.*

"You sure you're okay?" Darion wrinkled his nose. "You look a little clammy."

"Thanks, brother." I faked agitation. In truth, I felt like I'd been turned inside out. "I just need to get out of here and get some air." I glanced around for my purse.

"Um, no. You're not going anywhere alone in your state." Darion challenged me with a hard stare.

My hand flew to my hip. "Damn it, Darion. Don't pull a Jasper on me. You're becoming as overprotective as he is, and I can take care of myself."

"Where are you going?" he demanded.

There was no point in hiding my intention. "I'm going to Felix's."

"Oria?" He tilted his head, and I nodded.

Darion lifted a black-booted foot onto the chair he'd picked up from the floor. "I'd feel better if you called Jasper, but I know you're too stubborn. Promise you'll call me as soon as you get there."

I rolled my eyes. "I promise."

"It's been a while since you put the ring on." Darion bent over his propped leg and smoothed a scuff from his leather boot. "Oria helped you because you agreed to return to—" He paused and checked the door and lowered his voice. "You agreed to go back to Aenoas-Vita and rule, but you haven't lived up to your part, and the last time you tried to communicate with her didn't go so well. She warned you. What if—"

"I know. The thought has definitely crossed my mind." I fumbled in my purse for my keys. "The shifter wants her ring. She had dealings with them when she was alive. If she's not behind it, then she must have some idea why they would come after it. Wait …"

"What?" Darion asked.

"Maybe that's it. Freya told me they think we're hiding some secret to our youth, so maybe they think the ring is the answer. It's our link to …"

Darion froze. "The ring holds a piece of life force from

every Ever ruler that ever lived, and with it, their knowledge. If they've found a way ..." He broke off.

"But it only works for the chosen member of the Ever bloodline," I reminded him. "And we're the last. What good would it do them?"

A quiet moment passed before Darion said, "I don't know. Maybe they figured out a way to extract and use the auras inside. The shifters have always hated us. If they gain access to the magic ... We can't let them have it, not when the lives of everyone on Aenoas-Vita are at stake. We have to find another way to save Molly without handing over the ring."

My finger brushed a key loop, and I snagged it, pulling my keys from my purse. "I'm glad you agree. And maybe Oria can help figure out why a shifter is wearing a royal Vitarian signet ring with an E. Tell Molly we'll talk later, and I'll call you when I've gotten to the cabin."

Darion looked like he was about to argue again about me going alone, but just then, a nurse came in to change Molly's bedding.

"Talk later, brother." I darted out of the room while I had the chance.

CHAPTER 5

*T*he bumpy ride up to Felix's cabin made every pothole and uneven surface painfully noticeable. Taking the turns at a snail's pace in my hybrid, I cringed with every bone-rattling impact of the enormous potholes.

Felix had the right idea by leaving the road unmaintained. Most people would have turned around by now if they didn't have a reason to ignore the dangerous driving conditions. But the cabin at the top of the mountain was my destination, so I continued on my crawl uphill, keeping as far from the cliffside as possible. I hadn't been back here since hiding the ring in the same place where Felix had kept it safely for many years. I figured the hiding place had worked so far, so why not keep using it? We'd had new wards placed around the area, and this time we warded against portals after Siobhan's clever attack.

I finally pulled up near the cabin. The new ward recognized specific energy fields, so I could move straight through it reciting no spell. I parked and took in the view of snowy mountaintops just visible through the clearing Felix had cut directly in front of the cabin entrance. Brisk air tickled my nose as I breathed in clean scents of fresh pine and wood, and walked around to the back of the cabin to the chicken coop.

As the wind picked up, my ponytail came alive, swaying and bouncing with each gust. With a swift motion, I caught it before the thick hair could whip me in the eyes and held it over to one side, stealing a quick glimpse into the enchanting forest. My eyes lingered on the path that led to an active portal used to travel between planets. Arden had taken that path only hours ago to return to Aenoas-Vita. Early as it was, I clung to the hope he'd find something crucial in time.

The aluminum roof rattled atop the vacant chicken coop, bringing my attention back to the task at hand. I waved the cobwebs aside as I stepped into the dimly lit coop and removed the empty hay nests from atop a long wooden bench. With the bench top raised, I delved my hands into the chicken feed, reaching towards the bottom to locate the two hidden boxes. One was a small square, while the other boasted a longer, rectangular form. I clenched my hands around the boxes and exerted force to lift them out of the feed. As I closed the bench top and sat down, memories of the first time I was offered the items flooded back. Initially, I resisted accepting Oria's ring and the responsibilities it entailed, but I had to give in to the fate she had prophesied because of the circumstances. I had every intention of keeping my end of the bargain when the time was right. But Oria had been angry when I hadn't complied immediately, and she shut me out of the spirit realm. Right now, all I can do is hope that I can reach her. Molly's life and Aenoas-Vita's survival were at stake.

Searching the woods for energy signals, ensuring I was alone, I quickly made my way to the cabin. Locks weren't necessary, since no one could enter but those the ward recognized. I didn't bother turning on any lights. None of the windows in the cabin had coverings, and the natural light was enough to see by.

Traces of spicy cedar and sandalwood lingered, and I closed my eyes and imagined Arden standing near me, his warm breath on my neck. A flutter trembled through me at the memory of his lips on mine. I passed the kitchen on my left, and a smile danced across my lips at the thought of Arden cooking, barefoot in jeans. I shrugged off the image and proceeded to the living room. The antique furniture shone bright, and the air smelled of fresh orange-scented wax. I had a hard time imagining Arden doing common housework, but he'd left the place spotless.

Interior design wasn't one of Felix's strong suits. He'd furnished his cabin with basic essentials, but since he'd returned to Aenoas-Vita, my mom, Calista, and Selkie had been keeping up on routine maintenance for Vitarian visitors, and they'd livened the place up a bit with Felix's blessing. A new lamp sat atop an end table. It kept with the rustic theme but added a hint of modernity to the space. I switched the lamp on, and the tapered drum shade brightened with a luminous white glow.

I propped the box with Oria's sword down on a cushion and opened the smaller box. The only difference in it from the first time I'd set my eyes upon this ring was now it contained a piece of my aura.

A mesmerizing swirl of colors merged inside the opaque orb. The sparkling silver band hummed with energy as I held it between my fingers. So much history and knowledge bound within such a tiny space. My fingers curled, and I popped my knuckles. I had no choice but to seek Oria's help.

I stretched out my fingers and hesitated, but then slipped the ring onto my left index finger. Nothing happened. A sharp twist of fear shot through me. I didn't feel the connection to my ancestors, as I had before. Oria was still angry.

My pulse quickened as I anxiously called out: *Oria.* My thoughts raced when no answer came. *Damn it!*

I repeatedly reached out mentally. No voices or visions answered my call, like before.

A wave of anxiety washed over me, causing my chest to tighten, and I instinctively closed my eyes. Giving up was not an option. Molly's life depended on me.

I sat up straight, ignoring the hopeless thoughts creeping into my subconscious, and tried again.

Oria! I need your help.

Silence. I slumped back against the cushions and gazed at the forest on the other side of the floor-to-ceiling windows. A splash of sunlight filled the room with a soft glow.

I twisted the ring around my finger, watching the prisms of light from the sun dance off the globe, and thought of the hidden mark carved into Molly's forehead. Without banishing it, she would never be safe. I scanned the room, considering ways to elicit a response from Oria. I spotted a bow hanging on the wall and shuddered at the reminder of being trapped in infinite black space. The image of stars took shape in my mind as the hunter trained its bow on me. My heart thumped. I took a deep breath, trying to forget the fear I'd felt in that moment before Darion had found me.

"Everly!"

I bolted upright at the sound of Oria's voice in my head. *Oria!*

"Tell me about the mark you were just thinking of."

One thing that bothered me about wearing the royal ring was the intrusive presence of the ancestors' spirits, who could delve into my thoughts. However, I didn't bother questioning Oria about her curiosity regarding the mark. This was my opening to ask for her help.

My mind formed thoughts and images of everything that'd happened, beginning with the Spider Witch's reading, the man in the photos Lucas had brought, and the ring he wore. The image Darion had sketched from the sheriff's phone, and then the same image burned beneath Molly's skin.

Can you help me remove the mark from my friend?

"Yes." Her voice seemed distant and off, her usual authoritative tone gone and replaced with an emotion I hadn't sensed in her before—fear. "I've seen this mark before," she added, then paused.

My knee bounced as I waited, eager to hear more.

"Long ago, when I was still among the living, my twin brother crafted a spell that left that very mark. He proudly named it after himself. It's the Mark of Orien." Her voice shook with an edge.

But Orien's dead! You took his life yourself.

"Yes, that's true, but I've not had contact with his spirit in the afterlife. I've always assumed his spirit went someplace different from me."

Maybe someone found his spell, or he told someone about it before he died.

"Orien never shared his spells with anyone but me. His greed for magic consumed him. After his punishment, I gathered all of his grimoires and hid them in the palace. I told no one of this. I should have destroyed them." Anger dripped from her words.

What did Orien look like? A fresh suspicion grew in my mind.

All went quiet. Then Oria spoke with nostalgia. "Orien was very handsome. His hair was black as midnight, and his eyes blue as the deepest ocean. He was tall and strong, and never without a lady trailing close at his side, hoping to gain his favor."

My stomach dropped as I pictured the haunting sapphire eyes of Darion's look-alike.

Oria. Your description matches the man trying to get your ring. The one who looks just like my brother, only his eyes weren't silver, like Darion's; they were sapphire, like mine, and he wears the royal Ever signet. It's too much of a coincidence. We suspected a shifter was pretending to be Darion, but what if it's not a shifter? Let me show you.

As I conjured the image of the man holding Molly hostage in her dream, the Spider Witch's words came back to me: "The stars hold the answer."

The constellation I'd seen in the in-between that aimed its bow at me was Orion. I realized why the markings on Molly's forehead and the body found by the police seemed familiar. Both mirrored the Orion constellation. The answer was Orien!

Oria's aura drifted as the silence stretched. I stood and paced the room. The runes carved into the stone wall bordering the fireplace drew me nearer. I traced a swirling image cut into the grainy stone. There was so much I didn't know about my heritage and the planet I came from.

I squatted and checked the contents of the fireplace. A crisp black log from a previous fire remained inside. I threw a blast of energy into it, and it sparked to life. The charred log crackled and sizzled as the flame consumed it.

Growing impatient, I called out with my thoughts as I stood and turned my back to the blazing heat. *Oria! How do I save my friend from your crazy brother's mark?*

After more silence, her aura grew stronger, and she finally responded. "Orien and I both possessed the gift of crafting our own spells, but he believed it was clever to bind them to his blood, making them impossible to undo for anyone outside our bloodline."

A large air bubble lodged in my throat. I went to the kitchen and retrieved a glass, filling it with tap water, then gulped it down. *But what does that mean? There has to be a way to save my friend.*

Oria continued. "The spell attached to Orien's mark is blood magic that is tied to the Ever bloodline—my bloodline. You and your mother and brother are the last descendants of my blood. If you want to save your friend, one of you will need to mix your blood with the list of ingredients I tell you. Your friend will need to drink every drop. She is human, and I don't know how her body will respond to Vitarian blood, but this is the only remedy I know. And if this is Orien, he'll sense when he's lost connection to the mark and know that you've healed your friend."

You had no part in sending this man after me for refusing you?

"Is that what you thought? Dear child. Yes, I want you on my throne, but I would never harm you or my people."

I felt her aura fade slightly. *Oria.*

"The ancestors grow weary. We need to hurry before the connection is lost. If you want to save your friend, this is what you need."

I fumbled through my purse, looking for something to write with, and quickly jotted down Oria's instructions.

Thank you, Oria.

"Everly, you must be very careful. Orien is dangerous. I do not know how he could have survived unless traitors lived within my walls. And if it is him, he's done something unnatural to sustain his youth. Vitarians age slowly and live long lives, but a natural death should have come to Orien by now, even if he survived my punishment."

And if it's not Orien but a shifter, why impersonate Orien and come after your ring?

"The shifters have always envied our youth. Their race has a degenerative disease. Once they grow to adulthood, their aging accelerates in a most unflattering and painful way. We tried to help them with our own spells and herbs, but the effects were short-lived. To avoid a war, I agreed with their leader that we would continue to provide the tonic if they stopped their attacks on my people. The treaty was fragile at best, but the attacks ceased. If the shifters are seeking my ring, then they must have learned something about its magic that they think can help them. You must protect the ring—at any cost." Her last three words rang heavy with intention. "If they've found a way to access the magic inside the ring, they'll have knowledge that could end the Vitarian race."

My neck tensed, and the familiar heat stirred in my belly, warning me of the restrained magic that burned to be released. Trying hard to separate from the Vitarian world only pushed me deeper into it.

I won't let them have it. I slipped the ring over my knuckle and secured it back inside its box.

Relieved to have my thoughts as my own again, I scanned the long list of ingredients, hopeful Felix would have some of the items. I opened the kitchen cabinet where I'd seen Felix's stash of dried remedies when I'd stayed here. He'd left his cabin as is when he went back to Aenoas-Vita with plans to return to Earth.

I reached for my cell phone from my back pocket and dialed Darion. I activated the speaker function and placed my phone on the counter while I searched the cupboards for labels that corresponded to my list.

Darion's voice boomed through the speaker. "Does she know how to remove it?"

"Yes," I answered, pulling out jars of nettle, charcoal, agrimony, turkey tail, reishi, red clover, ashwagandha, and black cohosh. "But it might be risky."

"Risky how?" Darion's words cracked over the speaker, and I adjusted the volume down.

I found a bag under the sink and started loading in the jars. The remainder of the list I had at home.

"Are you going to answer me?" Darion said impatiently.

"Sorry. I'm gathering most of the ingredients from Felix's place now." I tied the handles on the cloth bag and leaned against the counter. "It turns out Oria's twin brother, Orien, designed this spell. It's a blood spell tied to the Ever bloodline." I paused, giving Darion a moment for what I was saying to sink in. An audible hiss sounded over the speaker.

"I'll tell her," he said.

"It can be yours or mine. As long as it's Ever blood, it should work."

"There could be side effects," Darion seethed. "But it should be mine."

I grabbed the bag of jars and my phone, along with both boxes holding the ring and sword. "Are you both still at the hospital?"

Voices echoed in the background on Darion's end of the line. "Yeah. I'm outside Molly's room. The nurses are inside, fiddling with her machines and checking her blood pressure again."

Taking one last glance around the cabin, I yanked the door shut behind me and headed for my car. The mountain wind had sped up since I'd been inside the cabin. My foot hit a stick, and I nearly dropped the bag of jars as it propelled my body forward.

Calm. My silent command stretched across the forest, and the tree branches settled as the wind subsided. I tried not to use my magic to change the pace of nature, but sometimes it was necessary.

"Hmm … We can't do this at the hospital and risk someone coming in. Can you sneak Molly out and bring her to my place?"

"Uh-huh," Darion answered with a hint of excitement.

"Good. I'll meet you there. And, Darion—"

"Yeah?"

"We might be dealing with more than a shifter imperson-ating you." I opened the back passenger door and placed everything safely in the back seat.

"What does that mean?" Darion asked, the earlier excite-ment gone.

The engine purred to life as I turned on the ignition, then clicked on the front and back defrosters. "Oria described Orien to me. And based on her description, you look just like him—only his eyes aren't silver; they're blue like mine. That would also explain why he wears the royal signet. It's his ring. And Freya thought it unusual that a shifter wouldn't change their eye color to match the one they're mimicking, and then there were the signs of aging. Why would a shifter leave out both eye color and wrinkles?"

Darion went quiet, absorbing the implication of what I'd told him. I could hear shuffling on the other end, like Darion was walking, and the background voices faded away. "So, our ancient ancestor, who's crazy as hell, might be back from the dead and wants to destroy us all? And I *look* like him. Well, that's just great. Oh, the nurses are leaving Molly's room. This is my chance to get her out of here. I have to go." He hung up.

The fog cleared from the windows. I tossed my phone onto the passenger seat and put the car in gear, but before releasing my foot from the brake to back up, I reached out my mind once more, searching the forest for a sign of Arden's or Rheya's return. A frustrated breath coated the windshield in a fresh layer of fog. Using the sleeve of my jacket, I cleared the window and started for the bottom of the mountain.

*T*here was no sign of Molly and Darion when I arrived at my apartment, so I got to work on the spell. Everything simmered except the final, crucial ingredient.

While I waited, I blended together a protection spell I remembered from my mom's grimoire. Spell magic was still new to me, and my mom had warned that mixing even one ingredient incorrectly could drastically alter the spell. I triple-checked that I had all the right herbs and spices, then ground them together. I wrote Molly's name on a piece of paper, rolled it up, and nested it beneath the blend of ground clove, cinnamon, sage, juniper, and cedar. Carefully, I sprinkled the top with dried orange and lemon zest, each sprinkle releasing a burst of citrus aroma as I recited the incantation. I lit the end of a white palo santo stick heavy with tree resin and laid it over the mixture.

Tires crunched over gravel outside my apartment, and seconds later, footsteps rushed up to the door.

"It's open," I called.

Molly burst through the door, looking freshly showered and dressed in regular clothes. But the skin under her eyes remained a shade of light violet, as though she hadn't slept in days, even though she'd spent hours in a coma.

An intricate braid at the top of her head with her single pink strip woven throughout caught my eye.

"Darion did my hair." She spun so I could see it from all angles. "He calls it my battle braid."

"Fit for a warrior," Darion added as he came up behind Molly, his expression pinched and his eyes hard. He rubbed Molly's shoulders. "Are you sure you want to do this?"

Molly's gaze settled on the pot simmering on the stove. She pushed her chest out. "I'd rather take my chances with your blood than go one more second with this mark burned inside my head."

Darion lowered his forehead to the top of Molly's head before letting her go.

I pulled Molly into a hug. "This will work," I said, to reassure myself as much as her.

She squeezed me back and sniffled in my ear.

Darion went to the pot and discreetly did his part.

Molly sat on the sofa, wringing her hands together, while I retrieved the incense with her name buried inside. I carried the bowl around the room, filling every corner with powerful smoke. Then I settled the contents on an end table near Molly.

Darion brought the brew over in a ceramic mug and handed it to Molly.

"What about Mom?" I asked him.

"I left her a message. Maybe we should wait."

"No." Molly wrinkled her nose. Her eyes lingered on the bandage wrapped around Darion's hand. "I just want to get this over with." She glanced up at Darion.

They exchanged a meaningful look. Then he nodded and sat beside her. A shadow of doubt clung to his aura as he stretched his lips in a reassuring smile and settled his hand on her leg.

Molly lifted the mug. Her skin paled when she looked inside at the contents.

A vein bulged in Darion's neck as he restrained himself from stopping her.

"Bottoms up." Molly squeezed her eyes closed and sucked in a deep breath before bringing the mug to her lips.

I teetered on the edge of my seat as she drank. Despite gagging, she forced herself to finish the mug after a few gulps.

"That wasn't so ..." Molly began to say when the mug

slipped from her hands to the floor, and she slumped forward.

Darion threw his arms around Molly and gently leaned her back against the sofa. He scooped up her legs and stretched them onto the cushions.

"Is this supposed to happen?" My voice shook.

Before Darion could answer, Molly's body started convulsing.

Darion dropped to his knees. "Molly!" He touched her forehead. His hands trembled. "She's burning up! Ev, get some ice!"

I rushed to the kitchen and forcefully pulled open the drawer filled with sealable bags. In a hurry, I grabbed one and swiftly filled it with ice before tossing it to Darion. "What do we do?"

Darion pressed the ice to Molly's forehead and cheeks. "I … I don't know. Maybe her body's rejecting the blood."

Molly's body stilled, and her eyelids fluttered. She moaned something incoherent and fell silent.

"Molly …" Darion's back quivered as he arched over her. He reached behind and searched his back pockets. "Damn it! I left my phone in the car. Where's yours?"

He didn't wait for my answer. "Call Mom again. I have to get something." He bolted for the door. His footsteps pounded against the gravel outside.

My fingers shot into my hair as I thought of what to do. Molly's energy was weak but still present. An idea occurred to me. My heart raced as I leaned over Molly's motionless form and placed a hand on either side of her head and connected with her vibrations. Slipping past the outer biofield of Molly's aura, I released my own energy and poured out everything I had until my body wobbled from depletion. My head dropped onto her chest, but I refused to let go until I heard a soft murmur below me.

"Ev …"

Fingers trembled over mine.

A hoarse cry burst from my lips when I lifted my head to find Molly's big brown eyes staring up at me, wide and teary.

She pulled her legs toward her and tucked them under her chin, making room for me to collapse next to her.

"Are you okay?" she asked, her voice growing stronger.

I nodded, still too exhausted to talk.

Molly squeezed my hand. "I felt what you did. Darion didn't reveal much about your abilities, but I could feel you strengthening me. Thank you."

"I'm so glad you're okay." My voice sounded weak and gravelly, and keeping my eyelids from closing felt like a chore.

Cushions shifted as Molly got up. She filled a glass with water and brought it back and carefully tilted it to my lips. She looked around in a daze. "Where's Darion?"

The cold water soothed my achy throat. I took the glass from Molly and drained it. "You gave us quite a scare. We thought your body might be rejecting Darion's blood. You went into convulsions and weren't responding. Darion rushed out in a panic to get something. He should be back any minute."

Molly's hand flew to her forehead.

"Do you feel any different?" I asked her.

Her fingers crawled across her forehead, massaging the skin this way and that. "The mark, it's gone. And … I don't know how to describe it, but I feel stronger than I did before I had the mark, like I could jump off the top of a roof or run a marathon."

I laughed. "No roof jumping, please. Let me take a look."

Molly sat beside me and tilted her head to the side, causing the end of her braid to fall over her shoulder. A high frequency vibrated all around her, and there was no trace of the dark magic that clung to her aura.

"I don't sense the mark anymore. The spell worked." I slumped back and flung my arm across my forehead. *Thank God.*

"When the mark was there"—Molly wrinkled her forehead—"I felt the weight of it inside of me. It was like something foreign and threatening coiled in my head. But now ... it feels empty. Well, not empty." She laughed, and so did I. "Just light and normal again."

"I get it," I said, sitting up and leaning forward, my strength coming back.

Molly shot up and grabbed her bag. "I'm going to go brush my teeth and get rid of this blood breath." She started down the hall. "Wow!" She stopped and turned back. "That's not something I ever thought I'd say."

"Me either," I agreed.

Molly made a sour face. "Yuck!" Her tongue shot out of her mouth. "I actually drank blood. How disgusting!" Her sour expression turned serious. "But at least it worked." She swiveled on her heel and headed back toward the hall for the bathroom.

Yeah, I thought. *At least it worked.*

I leaned back against the cushion, sighing with relief, and shook out my arms and legs, letting the tension fall away as I stared through the open blinds at the red sky.

What's taking Darion so long? I rose and glanced outside, surveying the area from the house to my apartment. "Huh."

Something didn't feel right. He wouldn't have left Molly for so long. The hairs on my neck raised. "Darion!" I stepped out onto the porch. "Darion!"

A loud thump, like something heavy hitting the floor, came from the back of the apartment.

"Molly!"

I tore down the hall, flying into the bathroom, only to find it empty. My bedroom door creaked, and I bolted from the bathroom and burst through my bedroom door, searching the room. Feet on the floor stuck out from around the other side of my bed. I rushed over and stopped, stunned to see Molly lying on the floor, tape wrapped around her ankles and wrists.

What the hell?

I spun, searching the room, then dropped to my knees and peeled the tape from Molly's mouth as gently as I could. The duct tape clung stubbornly to her skin like glue, so I gave it a quick yank and winced at the raw skin around her mouth.

Molly's eyes flew open, and she started to struggle.

"It's okay. It's just me. What happened?"

Her eyes widened. "Behind you!" she cried.

"Hey, beautiful."

I whipped around, but instantly relaxed. "Lucas. Thank God you're here. Someone snuck in and attacked Molly. I don't know how—" I glanced up to see that my bedroom window was open, and the screen popped out.

"Shit. Whoever it was must've broken in through my window. Did you see anyone?"

Lucas leaned into the bedroom doorframe and slowly shook his head. His expression gave me pause, but I ignored the strange tingle of warning.

"Help me with this tape."

When he didn't move to help, I knew something was off.

His lips turned up in a sneer I'd never seen on Lucas before. "I like her better taped up."

My nerves buzzed as I shielded Molly's body with mine and tried to make sense of the Lucas who glowered at me. A black glow caught my eye from the bedside table. *The truth stone!* But where was the pouch that held the serpent stone?

Lucas followed my eyes to the bedside table. The corner of his lip curled up as he sniggered and pushed away from the doorframe and snatched the stone.

A pang shot through my chest. The stone worked exactly as Freya had said.

"Don't worry," Lucas drawled. "Before I borrowed your boyfriend's skinsuit, I had him get rid of that pesky stone bound with the protection spell. Won't do you any good now."

I struggled to match the Lucas I knew with the one who stood in front of me. "You're not Lucas." Magic hummed at my fingertips.

He laughed with a note of mockery. "Ding-dong." The laughter died on his lips. "Took you long enough, but I guess you're not as powerful as your ancestors. I snuck in, right under your nose." His nostrils flared, and then he chuckled, as though he amused himself.

"What did you do to Lucas?"

He leaned casually against the doorway again and rolled the black truth stone over his knuckles. "I'm the one making demands here. Now, be a good girl and give me what I want, and I'll let your little friend live." His eyes flicked toward Molly. "And maybe your boyfriend, too."

"Where's Lucas?"

His silence mocked me, but it was the cruel grin that sent fear twisting through my veins. What had he done to Lucas?

When the heat burned inside me this time, I welcomed it. "Forget it, shifter. I'm not giving you anything." I lifted my hands, and a blast of energy sent him flying backward. The force knocked him off his feet, and he slid on his back down the hall.

I slammed the bedroom door and locked it, then yanked open my bedside drawer and took out a pair of scissors and cut the tape that secured Molly's limbs.

"Climb out of the window." I held onto Molly's trembling hands as I pulled her to her feet and ushered her to the window.

She rubbed at the red rings on her wrists left by the tightly wrapped duct tape. "I'm not leaving without you." Her voice cracked.

The shifter was up and thumping back toward my bedroom door. He jiggled the handle, then kicked at the door.

"There's no time to argue. I'll be fine, I promise." I shoved her toward the window.

The door burst open just as Molly jumped and vanished outside. Before I could react, the shifter leaped through the air and knocked me to the ground. He landed on top of me and wrapped his hands around my neck with inhuman strength. He squeezed the air from my lungs until my vision blurred. My head thrashed back and forth as I struggled to get free, but he only squeezed tighter, until I felt my consciousness slipping away. My arms stretched to either side of my body, and my fingers clawed against the carpet in search of the scissors I'd tossed aside after cutting Molly's tape. I arched my back, trying to knock him off, but my strength waned. A loud ringing filled my ears as panic seized me.

"I see why the bartender likes you." The shifter licked the side of my face while I squirmed underneath him with every bit of energy I could muster. "You've got spunk." He bit my lip.

I tried to scream, but nothing came out. The taste of blood filled my mouth, and I choked on it as it pooled at the back of my throat. Everything faded; my arms and legs tingled as they fell limp.

The shifter's laugh echoed in my ears as his hot breath hovered over my face. With no air left in my lungs, my eyes drifted closed. Then I heard a loud thunk, and my attacker fell sideways.

I frantically gulped for air. As my breathing steadied, my vision returned, and so did the feeling in my arms and legs.

Molly stood over us, poised with a cast-iron skillet. Her hair frizzed from her braid, and her eyes stared, wild and sharp, at the body sprawled across me. She tightened her grip on the cast-iron handle. Then she propelled her arms forward.

"Stop!"

The skillet halted in midair, inches from the shifter's head. I exhaled a sigh of relief.

"He's done something to Lucas. I need to question him. Then we'll decide what to do. Let's bind him before he wakes up."

I wanted to take this monster out as much as Molly did, but he knew where Lucas was, and I planned to make him talk.

Molly heaved the skillet onto the bed and helped roll the shifter off me. We found the tape he'd used on Molly and wrapped his hands and feet together.

"Payback's a bitch." Molly kicked the shifter in the side.

I always knew Molly was a badass, but this was a new side of her. Darion would be proud.

Darion!

"The shifter must have also done something to Darion. He's been gone too long. I need to go look for him."

"Oh my God," Molly said. "While taping me up, this asswipe laughed and congratulated himself for fooling the renowned Vitarian Tracker. Darion avoids discussing his past, but he once mentioned he was good at finding people." Her entire body trembled when she asked, "Is Darion a Tracker?"

"Yes!"

Molly bolted for the door. "Molly! Wait!"

She didn't turn back.

Shit!

I left the shifter on the floor and took off after Molly.

Tires crunched over gravel, and headlights flashed into view as I tore across the porch. *Mom! Thank God!*

She parked and got out of her car and ran toward me when I waved my arms.

"What's going on, honey? I got Darion's message about Molly and the spell, and came straight home."

"I have to find Molly. She's looking for Darion. A shifter attacked us, but he's bound up in my apartment. Can you make sure he doesn't escape while I find Molly and search for Darion?"

My mom radiated a mix of emotions. "Is Darion okay?"

"I don't know. He left the apartment but never came back. Then the shifter attacked us."

Blotches of red sprang from my mom's aura as she opened the passenger door of her car and Luna sprang free. "You look for your brother. I'll deal with this shifter."

"Oh, and, Mom …"

She turned.

"He's taken Lucas's form."

Her mouth twisted with disgust as she ran up the porch with Luna at her side.

I sprinted toward the sound of Molly's cries. Not much natural light remained, and it was even darker within the forest.

"Molly!" I followed the trace of energy she'd left behind and searched between the trees for signs of both Molly and Darion.

The greenhouse.

I latched onto Molly's vibrations and hurried toward the greenhouse. Sheets of stars and a bright gibbous moon replaced the fading crimson sky and made me wish I'd thought to bring a flashlight.

Fear gripped me as I realized that no trace of Darion's energy was near.

I darted up the path behind the greenhouse and heard Molly's whimper inside.

Broken pots and shredded plants lay across the floor.

Molly clung to a piece of black fabric. "He was in here. They must have snuck up on him."

A pile of black ash on the floor caught my attention. *Activated charcoal.* That was what Darion had been getting. He'd planned to flush his blood from Molly's system.

"The shifter must have had an accomplice. They took Darion. I don't sense him anywhere, but we'll find him, I promise." I tucked my arms under Molly's armpits and lifted. "Come on, Molls. Let's go get some answers."

"If he's hurt Darion, he's going to wish I'd put him out of his misery." She wiped her eyes with the torn fabric from Darion's shirt and locked her arm around mine.

We walked arm in arm back to my apartment in silence. Luna's growl vibrated on the other side of the partially open front door. She circled the bound shifter, who sat perched in a wooden chair in the kitchen with multiple layers of duct tape securing his body to the chair. He stood no chance of escape.

"Molly, dear." My mom held her arms open. She caressed Molly's hair back. "I'm so glad to see you awake and safe." She glanced over the top of Molly's head. "Tell me everything."

I started at the beginning, from the time I'd arrived at the hospital that morning.

She shook her head when I gave her the recap of what had happened after we'd entered Molly's dream. "Absolutely reckless," she scolded, which made me hesitate to tell her about the blood potion that Molly had drunk, but I didn't want to leave anything out.

"Everly." She leaned against the kitchen island and ran a hand through her hair. "You, of all people, should know how dangerous blood spells can be, after last year."

I pulled a barstool out from under the kitchen island and hopped onto the wooden seat. "I know, Mom, but we had no choice. Oria said it was the only way to save Molly. We did what was necessary, just like the last time I used this kind of magic."

"All that matters now is Molly's safe, so let's focus on finding your brother and Lucas." Her brows knitted together as she narrowed her gaze on the shifter. "I need something from the house."

She left and returned within minutes, carrying a long, thick rope, which I knew wasn't just any rope. It was spelled to restrain magic.

"It's time we wake this monster up." She ran her hands across the twisted rope. "Molly, honey, I know Darion explained some things about us, but this creature is not Vitarian. He comes from another planet altogether. What I'm going to do may seem grotesque and cruel, but it's the only way to deal with him. If you want to go over to the house and wait, that's okay. Darion wouldn't want you to see this."

Molly straightened her spine and shook her head, her brown eyes wide and stubborn. "No. I'm not going anywhere until Darion is safe and back home."

Satisfied, my mom turned back toward the shifter.

Luna's hackles rose as her growls grew more aggressive.

"She smells the Shimera," my mom explained. "Come here, girl." She called Luna to her. "I've got this," she whispered, and brushed her finger across Luna's brow to calm her.

Luna hung back, giving my mom space as she stretched a

length of rope from the bundle in her arms and wrapped an end around our prisoner's exposed neck. Smoke hissed as the skin melted away.

"What's happening?" I asked my mom, who seemed to have expected this result.

"The spelled rope restrains magic. Well, the Shimera—that's the name of their race," she explained when my brows shot up at her reference, "only have one kind of magic, and that's hiding behind their false skin. They hate their appearance. Just wait," she said as the rope burned through what looked like Lucas's flesh.

My stomach recoiled at the smell, and Molly stared wide-eyed at the sizzling flesh.

The room echoed with a scream as the shifter abruptly woke up.

"Stop!" he cried. "Please take it off."

I grimaced. Underneath the disintegrating skin appeared red and pus-filled flesh. Molly bent over, gagging at the smell. I pinched my nose, afraid I might barf if I breathed one more whiff of the decaying odor. I didn't know how my mom tolerated being so close to him.

When he caught me gawking at his skin, he wailed and thrashed against his bindings. His effort was of no use. He wasn't going anywhere.

"Tell me where my son is." The cold, harsh tone of my mom's words left no room for misinterpretation as she slowly reeled in the piece of rope.

Fear painted the face that mirrored Lucas's as he stared at the rope hanging from my mom's hand. He growled and stubbornly continued his fight against the tape. Luna darted in and bit his leg, eliciting a painful howl from the shifter. "I'm going to roast that beast when I get free."

Luna barked triumphantly.

My mom loosed more of the rope from her hands and drooped it over his shoulders.

The acrid smell of burnt flesh sizzled at the contact, exposing more of his rotting flesh. The nauseating odor permeated the room.

Molly dashed over to the kitchen cupboard where I kept candles and incense. She chose a long incense stick and lit the tip, waving the smoke around us. It helped, but not much.

The shifter remained tight-lipped, earning himself a twist of the rope around his face. I wanted to turn away, but he knew where Darion and Lucas were, and if he thought we were weak, he wouldn't talk. I hardened my resolve, and my eyes bored into his. *What kind of monster hides under someone else's skin?*

"Where's Lucas?" I demanded. "Where's my brother?" I scanned his fingers for the royal Ever signet, but it wasn't there. Either he'd taken it off when he'd changed form, or this wasn't the man from Molly's dream or the photo with my father.

When the soft skin melted off his grotesque cheekbone, he relented. "Okay!" he cried out. "Take the rope off, and I'll talk."

My mom unwound the rope from his body and wrapped it back around her wrist. "If you don't tell us everything we want to know, I won't go so easy on you again, and we'll see that face you're so afraid of revealing."

He sneered at my mom. If he could get loose, he'd try to kill her; I was sure of it. We wouldn't be able to let him go.

I watched in horror as his skin repaired itself, with fresh skin forming over the gaping holes, masking the sickening odor that came from his exposed flesh.

"Why did you make yourself look like my brother and attack Molly at the ball? Did you have something to do with my father's murder?"

My mom's attention shot toward me. "What are you talking about?"

"The ring from the photo that Lucas brought. I saw it again on the man who attacked Molly."

The shifter flinched when a dark scowl formed on my mom's face, and she approached him. "Did you kill Creagan?" She bared her teeth as the rope twisted in her grasp.

The shifter tilted his head, lips twitching into a smirk. He may have looked like Lucas, but he resembled him less and less, making expressions Lucas never would.

"I never made myself into your brother," he answered me, while keeping his eye on the rope dangling in front of him. "And I never attacked her," he nodded at Molly, "before today."

"What about the king?" My mom growled.

The shifter shook his head furiously. "It wasn't me, I swear."

"Is Darion being impersonated by another shifter?"

"So many questions," he jeered. "You're all just little fish in a bowl with nowhere to go."

My mom lashed him with the rope.

The sound of his sharp hiss revealed the intensity of his anger. "He's no shifter! He's Orien of the Ever bloodline, and he's going to kill you all."

His answer didn't surprise me. The man who had approached me at the ball and tormented Molly in her dreams had been Orien, and now I had confirmation.

The rope flew out and grazed his face, sending up a blast of smoke. The shifter writhed in the chair.

"Orien's been dead for centuries. Tell me the truth, or I'll flay every inch of you," warned my mom.

"It's true, you Vitarian bitch," he spat.

More rope twisted around his face, and I jumped in. "Mom, wait, let's hear him out. He's telling the truth."

The shifter's head bobbed up and down. "Listen to your daughter. She's got good sense."

I spun on the shifter. "Tell us about Orien."

The rope receded as he spoke. "Orien made a deal with our leader, but we weren't able to get him off his planet until after Oria had drained him of his magic. Her punishment created the perfect ruse. We sacrificed one of our own and switched the bodies. We took Orien back to our planet, where he's spent centuries rebuilding his strength so he can honor his part of the deal."

"Which is?" my mom asked, but I already knew.

"They want the secret to youth," I answered for the shifter.

He nodded that I was right. "We want bodies that don't rot and stink of decay. Orien promised to make us magic that allows us to keep our appearance indefinitely." He motioned at the false skin he wore. "And when he gets what he wants, he'll have everything he needs to fulfill his end of the bargain."

I winced at the thought of this creature continuing to look like Lucas, and he smiled at my unease.

"There is no secret to our youth, and Orien knows that," I told him. "We don't use magic to stay young. We age slowly because it's a part of our genetics, just like our magic is. Orien wants the ring for his own reasons, so he lied to get your people to help him."

He laughed at me like I was an ignorant child. "Orien found a way. He will help us, as we helped him. And thanks to your boyfriend, we know the magic works."

I stepped back. "What are you talking about?" My shoulders shook.

The shifter gloated at my confusion. Eyes the color of the bluest sky that should only belong to Lucas narrowed at me, and I fought the urge to look away from him.

"Humph," he grunted. "Orien used your boyfriend to test his spell. This skinsuit belongs to me for as long as I want it."

I leaned forward and gripped both of the shifter's bound arms. "And what does that mean for Lucas?"

He shrugged with a glint in his eye. "Sorry. That's for me to know and you to find out."

My grip tightened.

"Such a pretty face your boyfriend has, don't you think?"

My fingernails cut into his skin, and he just smirked. I lifted my chin and slammed my forehead into his nose, breaking it. "Not so pretty now." I smiled and backed up.

"You bitch!" He groaned, shaking his head. "Argh!" he growled. "I'm going to slice you to pieces when I get free."

Luna barked and leaped through the air, landing atop the shifter, and crunched his shoulder.

"Argh! Get this beast off of me!"

"Tell us where Orien's holding Lucas and Darion."

He shook his head. "If I tell you that, he'll kill me."

Luna bit deeper. Then the shifter twisted his neck and sank his teeth into her neck.

"No!" I screamed, and Luna yelped, falling backward off the shifter. I swooped over her and checked her wound. She whimpered at my touch. "It's okay, girl."

"Here." Molly handed me a warm, wet towel.

I wiped the blood away. A large gash appeared under the fur, but it wasn't life-threatening. Molly took over while I stood.

My mom looped the rope around the shifter's neck in a flash. "If you don't tell us what we want to know, we'll kill you."

His eyes darted beyond us, toward the window. "I'm already dead," he mumbled, wide-eyed, as my kitchen window exploded with an arrow that punctured straight through the side of the shifter's neck.

The room filled with Molly's scream. I jumped to cover her body with mine. My mom crouched beside us, protecting Luna. I scanned the window. There was no one, and no more arrows came. I crawled toward the door.

"Wait," the shifter gurgled, and coughed out a clot of blood. "He's gone, and there's not … much time. Orien … betrayed me." Blood dribbled from his mouth. "Cut open my chest."

I balked. "What? Why?"

His head drooped forward.

"Is … he dead?" Molly whispered.

The shifter's head bobbed as he coughed a spray of blood over his chest. "If you want to save your boyfriend, you need what Orien put inside of me. It's in the center." This time, his head fell forward with finality.

My mom crawled near him and reached to check his pulse. "He's gone."

"Holy shit!" Molly's voice shook, and Luna whimpered. She cradled Luna's head in her lap and gently smoothed her ears.

I met my mom's stare. Lines creased across her forehead. "I think we should do what he said."

"Okay." I stayed low to the ground. "Let me just make sure whoever shot the arrow really is gone." I crawled the rest of the way to the door, then carefully stood and cracked the door an inch to peek out. It was too dark to see beyond the porch, but I searched with my other senses. I turned back toward Molly and my mom. "There's no one out there. They did what they came to do and fled. But why only attack him and not us too?"

I went to the kitchen and grabbed the sharpest blade I could find.

My mom stood up. "Your guess is as good as mine, but

maybe we're about to find an answer." She grabbed the sides of the chair the shifter was bound to and paused.

"Molly, honey, will you grab a plastic garbage bag and lay it out?" She nodded toward the floor.

Molly fumbled through the utility cabinet and grabbed the box of garbage bags and a roll of duct tape. She shook out several large plastic bags and layered them to cover a wide area. Then she quickly taped the edges together to make one large plastic sheet.

"That's perfect," said my mom, as she leaned the chair down next to the plastic bags. She cut the tape that bound the shifter to the chair, and we rolled him onto the plastic.

My hand trembled as we all stared at the sharp tip of the blade.

"Honey, I'll do this." My mom reached for the knife handle, but I gripped it tighter.

"No, Mom. It has to be me. Whatever it is inside of him has to do with Lucas. It should be me."

She squeezed my shoulder, lifted the shifter's shirt, and then scooted back with Molly. I could practically taste the tension oozing from them both as their eyes followed the blade as I lifted it in the air and tilted the tip straight toward the shifter's chest.

I steeled my mental shield and sucked in a deep breath as I stared at the face that resembled Lucas's.

It's not Lucas. He's a monster. Lucas and Darion are depending on me.

The blade plunged down and slid straight through his chest cavity. I yanked down with all my strength to open a long enough cut to fit my fingers into. Vomit bubbled up the back of my throat at the crunching sound, and I gagged, forcing myself to swallow the burning liquid.

My mom's hand wrapped over mine. "That should be enough, honey."

The knife made a sticky sound as I pulled it out of his body and set it on the plastic. I shoved my fingers inside the wound, eager to be done with this task.

Either Molly or my mom passed me a hand towel to cover my face with my free hand. The decaying odor rising from his open chest was worse than when his skin had melted away.

My fingers dug through the wet interior of his chest, brushing against bone and tendon until they touched something smooth and hard that felt out of place.

"I think I found something." I curled my fingertips around the object and slid it toward the open wound, then used the towel I held to wipe it clean.

"Whoa," Molly breathed.

I smoothed my finger over the opalesque surface, thinking of how similar it was to the Ever ring. Tiny thunderbolts flickered within the stone. An energy gripped me, and my muscles seized as a sensation of being separated from my body overcame me. A rush of images filled my mind: hundreds of Shimera marched through a land of lush and colorful plant life. They slaughtered everything and everyone in their path. Another image of them invading a stone palace, and Felix on his knees. Blood covered his face, and bodies lay all around. He gazed up as a sword descended upon him.

I choked at the bloodbath in my mind. My torso crouched over, and I gasped for air. The stone slipped from my grasp, making a clunk and a clang as it hit the floor and rolled away.

My mom hunched over me, gripping my shoulders. "Everly! What happened? Are you okay?"

"I don't know." I straightened and scooted away to press my back against the wall for support, waiting for the knots in my stomach to subside.

"It's okay." My mom stood. "Take a minute to breathe. I'll find a cover for him." She left the kitchen and came back carrying an old sheet and tossed it over the shifter.

Molly handed me a glass of water. After a long drink, I said, "When I touched the stone"—I squeezed my eyes shut at the memory—"I saw images. I think they were of the Shimera, and they were invading Aenoas-Vita. I'm sure of it. There was so much blood and so many bodies, and Felix …" I couldn't bring myself to say it.

"Shh." My mom sat beside me and rested my head on her shoulder.

"There's living energy held inside the stone. It feels familiar to me, but I don't know how."

My mom snatched the rock from the floor and examined it. "This is from Aenoas-Vita. It comes from a cave in the Ever Forest, but it's forbidden to enter." She rubbed her hand over it as I had, her brow furrowed deeply. "Your premonitions have started. We need to alert Felix immediately, and warn him of Orien's return and the Shimera."

I pressed my head against the wall, wishing my mom was wrong, but the vision could only have been a premonition. I'd hoped this part of Oria's prophecy would never come true. But Felix had been sure that one day this facet of my magic would eventually present itself, and now I knew that no matter how much I wished for things to be different, I was the heir Oria had prophesied to return her bloodline to the throne. She had warned me if I didn't comply with her demands, there would be consequences. Had she foreseen the catastrophic outcome that would befall her planet and its population as a result of my refusal?

Suddenly, my lungs felt like they were on fire, and I let out a breath I hadn't even realized I was holding. The burden of knowing the future weighed heavily on my soul. With every discovery about my true identity, the anchor that bound me became more powerful, dragging me deeper beneath the surface.

"If this was my first premonition, then that means Orien will win and destroy our planet."

My mom held my cheeks. "Look at me, baby. Not all premonitions are definite. They're interpretations of possibilities. Events can alter the future. If we can stop Orien now, we can change this."

"But how? We don't even know …" I grabbed my mom's hands from my face and pulled her into a hug. "I have an idea."

Excitement coursed through my veins, and my heart raced. "I know how to find Darion and Lucas. It worked before, when Siobhan held you captive. You take care of alerting Felix and Arden and keep Molly safe with you. I'm going to Neil's."

"Okay," my mom agreed, even though I could sense her uncertainty. "But please don't go after Orien on your own. Find out what you can and then hurry back here so we can go together. Be safe." She kissed me on the forehead. "I'll take care of him." She motioned toward the body.

Molly quirked her brow. "Well … I guess today's the day for firsts: woke up from a magic-induced coma, drank alien blood, and now I'll be helping your mom move a dead shifter. Wonder what tomorrow has in store for me." She barked out a choked laugh, then sobered. "Bring him back to me, Ev." She threw her arms around me.

"I will. I promise. And, Molls …" I pried her arms from my neck and lifted the end of her braid. "Darion's right. This braid is fit for a warrior. You are a serious badass. I'll never underestimate the use of a cast-iron pan again."

Molly's lips cracked into a partial smile as her shoulders

rolled back. "Does this mean you approve of me and Darion?" She bit her bottom lip.

"You're like a sister to me, Molls. You make Darion happy, and he's crazy about you. And I have no doubt that you'll keep him in line."

Molly laughed as her confidence returned.

"I couldn't agree with my daughter more." My mom wrapped her arm around Molly's shoulders. "Seeing you and Darion together makes me the happiest mom of all the planets." She kissed Molly's forehead.

"But," I added, handing Molly a tissue to wipe her eyes as happy tears sprang free. "Don't try anything heroic while I'm gone. Stay with my mom and stay safe. Darion will never forgive me if I let anything happen to you."

She nodded and sniffled into her tissue.

I bent down to a waiting Luna and gave her a kiss between the ears. "How's my girl doing, huh?" I gently spread the auburn fur apart on her neck and checked where the shifter had bitten her. The bleeding had stopped, but the wound had yellow pus festering in the center. "Mom?"

"Don't worry, honey. I'll take care of that. When you come back, she'll be good as new."

Luna barked, as if she agreed with my mom. I ran my finger down her long snout and smoothed her tall ears, then grabbed my bag, keys, and the stone, and hurried to my car.

It has to work; I told myself as I pumped the gas, and my tires screeched out of the driveway, leaving tread marks in my wake.

I turned on the car stereo system and accessed the Bluetooth function. "Call, Neil."

After a few rings, Neil answered, "Hello, my darling." The club's music blared in the background.

"I need your help, Neil. I'm on my way now."

He responded without hesitation. "Yes, my queen."

I hung up and pressed the gas harder, and my car practically caught air as it flew over the train tracks to the back road that led to Neil's club.

My phone rang over the speakers. Jasper's name popped up on the screen. *Damn it!* My mom must have called him. I didn't want Jasper involved again. He deserved to have a normal life.

I answered with a casual tone in case he didn't know anything. "What's up, Jasp?"

"What's going on, Ev?" His tone wasn't casual at all.

"Did my mom call you?"

"No. I'm at Freya's shop, and she was giving me a reading. You need my help."

I breathed out a sigh. "I can handle this, Jasper. It's better if you don't get involved. And what are you doing at Freya's, anyway? You've never been into that sort of thing." And then I remembered the look Jasper and Anya had shared, and realization dawned on me. Jasper was finally moving on. I couldn't pull him back into more of my family drama.

Jasper ignored the second part of my question. "Freya says everything is ready and to bring Neil to her shop tonight. I'll be waiting for you."

Before I could argue, he added, "I'm your Shield. It's my duty to protect you. And that's final, Your Majesty."

Nothing would change Jasper's mind, not when it came to his role as my protector. This was one area he would not flex on, and I'd only be wasting my breath if I tried.

"Fine! I'm getting Neil, and then I'm coming straight there."

I was so distracted I nearly missed the turn to Neil's club. The smell of burnt rubber filtered through the air vents as I slammed on the brake pedal and yanked the steering wheel right. At this rate, my tires would be bald by the end of the day.

Neil stood gaping as he watched my erratic turn down his road. I plowed through the field and skidded to a stop so he could get in. "Sorry about the grass." I glanced in my rearview mirror at the missing clumps that were probably still stuck to my tires.

"Oh, pish," he said. "Grass smash, easily replaced. But that's some fancy driving." He winked, and I couldn't help but laugh.

"Thanks for coming, Neil. I'm sorry to ask for your help again, but something terrible is going to happen if I can't stop it."

Neil put his hand on my arm. "I'm always here for you, my little queen. Let's go kick some butt. And by that," he added, "you know I mean that you'll be doing the actual butt kicking."

Neil arched his brow. His ability to lighten the mood in any situation was a gift, but he was no fighter.

"I love you, Neil." I hit the gas pedal and peeled back up to the road.

"I know, darling." He gripped the door rest and held on tight.

I'm coming for you, Orien.

❦

I turned down the main strip, heading toward Freya's shop. My foot let off the gas as I neared my yoga studio. It was late and dark, and the building was vacant. In a few hours, students would fill the classes led by my part-time instructor, who ran the studio on my days off.

My grip tightened on the steering wheel. The studio and my students were a part of my life—a life that I'd have to give up to follow through with my promise to return to Aenoas-Vita, a promise that I wasn't ready to fulfill. I blew out a frustrated breath and was about to pull away when a flashing light caught the corner of my eye.

"Oh, darling," Neil drawled, glancing across the street. "How tacky."

I flinched at the bright pink neon sign that flashed BREE'S YOGA & SPIRITS. At the end of the sign, there was a distinctive pink martini glass outline. The monstrosity hadn't been up two days ago. Bree must have just had it done.

"I'm confused," Neil mused. "Is that a bar or a yoga studio?"

I shook my head and pressed the gas pedal. "Your guess is as good as mine."

Now that the Halloween Town festivities had ended, parking was no longer an issue. I pulled up to the strip of historic Victorian homes with slate roofs and expansive porches, most of which now doubled as home and business, and slipped right into a spot in front of Freya's, where Jasper stood waiting with Anya under the glow of a streetlight.

Neil softly whistled and said, "Tell me those two weren't meant for each other."

He was right. Both Jasper and Anya exuded beauty individually, but together, they were breathtaking. The two were nearly equal in height, with bronzed and copper skin and dark hair. Their eyes made you feel watched, and now Jasper's tiger eyes settled on me with a scowl.

Anya stepped forward as Neil and I exited my car. "My mother is waiting for you." Her words were friendly. She glanced curiously over my shoulder at Neil.

"Thank you, Anya. And this is my friend, Neil. He's here to help."

Anya smiled graciously at Neil when he took her hand and placed a kiss on top of it. "It's a pleasure, Anya." Then

Neil beamed up at Jasper. "Jasper, my friend." The two embraced, and Anya raced toward me.

"I need to speak with you privately before you leave." She brushed past my shoulder as she held open the door to the shop.

"How have I never been in here? This place is incredible." Neil perused the shelves like a kid in a candy shop.

Energy permeated the room, and Freya's familiar vibrations caught my attention.

"I'm glad you think so." She parted the beads that led to the front of the home where she and her daughter lived. Runes painted in black and gold covered every visible part of her dark skin, and the magic vibrating around her was palpable.

Neil sucked in an audible breath, and the rock he'd been examining thunked onto the shelf as he turned. "Freya Moon of the Moon Star clan. Great Seer of earth and stone."

"You know each other?" I asked.

Neil scanned Freya from head to toe like he couldn't believe his eyes. "Freya is a legend among many on our planet, and she saved my life as a child."

"You have grown into a fine man, young Neithropolis, as I knew you would." Freya's tone held a hint of pride.

"*Neithropolis?*" Jasper said, lifting his brow, and he teasingly punched Neil's shoulder.

Neil's cheeks blushed. "It's my given name, but I shortened it to Neil when I came to Earth."

"And a strong name it is." Freya cupped Neil's face and kissed each cheek. "I'm glad to see you well. Now, please, if you'll all follow me," Freya instructed. "Anya, please lock the door. We can't have any interruptions."

Anya obeyed her mother's request, and we trailed behind Freya, passing through the beads and into her living room.

Neil's energy buzzed. "It's a small universe."

"Everything is ready." Freya motioned toward the tall white candles that circled the familiar rug. Her runes sparkled in the candlelight as she crossed the room. She picked up a bowl of stones and placed it at the center of the rug.

A sweet taste lingered in the air, and my head swam at the heavy magic that surrounded us.

"You okay?" Jasper whispered in my ear.

I nodded. "Just sensory overload." I slid my mental shield into place. Having the ability to siphon energy had its perks, but it also had its downsides.

Bright moonlight reflected through French doors in the front living room, facing the river. I wandered over to the glass and peered out onto a wraparound porch. A luminous glow glinted off the top of rippling black water that raced with the current. The moon was in the last phase of the gibbous and would be full by tomorrow.

"It's a Scorpio moon." Freya's voice floated near. "Many will give in to desires they've withheld. Do you feel its energy?"

"I do." My hand brushed the doorknob. "May I?"

"Of course," Freya answered.

I twisted the knob and pushed open the French doors. The river air whipped with ferocity. I gripped the porch railing to steady myself and lifted my face toward the night sky. The energy of the moon was high as it neared the completion of its cycle. After tomorrow, it would wane, and emotions would calm, like the flow of a river before the next tide change, but for now, it vibrated with the intensity of a hot beacon about to explode.

The creak of cables whined from the docks visible below the hilltop of Victorian homes. The wind and current sped up together. Whitecaps crested atop the choppy dark waters, causing the moored boats to rock in their slips. I pushed away from the railing and went back inside, where candlelight lit the warm space.

"You have a lovely home, Freya. Thank you for allowing us in once again."

She inclined her head and motioned her hands toward the rug. "You and Neil will sit here. Your Shield"—she motioned to Jasper—"will wait outside the circle with Anya." She eyed Jasper, making sure he understood.

Jasper glanced at me, and when I nodded, he stepped back with Anya, but I sensed his unease at being banished from my side.

I settled myself in a cross-legged position. A bowl of incense burned in the center of the rug, and my head wobbled heavily as I breathed the billowing smoke. Its woody scent grew stronger when I tried to shift out of the growing cloud of smoke. My limbs and even my lips tingled with numbness.

"What's in the smoke? Why do I feel numb all over?" My voice echoed in my ears, and I placed my hands flat against the floor on either side of me for balance.

Jasper darted toward us, but Freya halted him with a sharp "Tsk!" and a wave of the arm.

"Don't worry, Everly. It's only the effects of resin from the bark of an ever tree. They will subside soon. The resin will aid in expanding your senses, but you mustn't fight it." Freya's words floated like a breeze in a field.

My jaw clenched, but when I glanced over at Neil, he wore a goofy grin as his head wobbled. I drew in a breath, letting the tension release from my temples, and my muscles relaxed as I sank deeper into the round meditation cushion beneath me. When my vision slightly blurred, I closed my eyes to focus on the rhythmic thumping of my heart. I cracked one eye open and peeked over at Neil. He still wore an expression like he was enjoying the dizzying feeling. I definitely wasn't.

A warm finger ran down my forehead between my brows. I reached up and felt a sticky, thick salve smeared on my skin. The scent of fresh-cut wood grew strong.

"Don't resist. Allow your mind and body to merge with the spirit of the earth. Let the roots awaken in your sacral, and as you become grounded, clarity will be unveiled."

I stopped fighting the urge for control and imagined roots entwining beneath me. The dizziness subsided, and the numbness faded until only a light tingle remained, similar to the sensation when my arm wakes up from falling asleep, except the sensation wasn't limited to just my arm; it was my entire body, and my senses felt more attuned than before. The runes painted on Freya's skin were no longer gold and black; they shimmered as though surrounded by a halo. I glanced around. Every color danced with life. Each scent was so potent, the taste of it lingered on my tongue. I spun around. Voices echoed from a distance. They were coming from the docks. I turned back to Freya. "How?"

"There'll be time for explanations later. The effects will not last long."

Neil straightened at the urgency in Freya's words.

"It's time for your part, Neithropolis."

He clasped his hand over mine, and the familiar buzz of our magic syncing coursed through me. I knew what to do this time. I closed my eyes and directed my magic. When I opened them again, what I saw within my own sight vanished. My mind raced as I searched in a sea of darkness. I connected with Neil's ability to project thought, and I called out across space and time.

Darion. Can you hear me?

"I hear you, Ev." His voice was weak.

Why can't I see anything? It's just darkness. Do you know where you are?

"Ugh …" Darion moaned, and I heard something that sounded like metal rattle across a surface. "I don't know where they've brought me. The bastard has me blindfolded. I can't see a damn thing, and my hands are bound in spelled chains, so I can't use my magic either." Darion breathed hard. "Molly … is she … okay?"

Yes, she's perfectly fine. And you'll be proud to know she kicked a shifter's ass.

Darion sighed. "Thank the stars. I don't know what I'd do if anything happened to her. She took out a shifter? That's my girl."

Focus, Darion. We don't have a lot of time, and I promised Molly I'd bring you home. Do you know who took you?

"It's definitely Orien. I don't know how, but he's still alive. And, Ev …"

Yeah?

"You can't come for me."

What! What's wrong with you? No way I'm leaving you or Lucas. Is Lucas there with you?

Darion didn't respond.

What about Lucas? Do you know if he's there?

"When I get my hands on that shifter, I'm going to—"

Don't worry about him. He's taken care of, but I need to know if you've heard Lucas or felt his presence.

"Yes," Darion finally answered. "I think he's here, but …"

But what, Darion?

"His energy is weak. I'm sorry, Ev. I can't tell how long he has, but Orien has been …"

My stomach lurched with dread. *What's happened to him?*

"Orien's been drinking his blood … and mine. He's been using blood to replenish his magic and maintain his longevity. He wants all of mine and yours. Once he absorbs the magic of Ever twins, he'll restore himself and won't need to sustain his life on blood any longer. So please, Ev, don't try to find me. If you do, he'll kill us both."

Damn it, Darion. I'm not leaving you to be tortured, or Lucas either. If you can't see anything, then tell me what you hear and smell.

"No. Orien knows about the curse. He knows that if he kills me, you'll die before he can consume both of our powers, and he needs our magic. This time, don't play the hero."

You are such a pain in the ass sometimes, Darion.

A voice from somewhere else whispered in my ear. "Spread your roots and use all of your senses."

Then I remembered the smoke from Freya's and how much clearer everything had looked, sounded, and smelled once I'd stopped fighting the dizziness. I stopped trying to see, and instead, I breathed through Darion's nose. *Dirt. Moss. Water. Blood.* I listened through Darion's ears. In the distance, a train roared atop tracks; its horn blared somewhere nearby. A trickle of water dripped close to Darion, and the farther I reached out, the more I homed in on a louder rushing of water somewhere not far. I focused on what Darion felt. He was on the ground. Not concrete, but hard, damp dirt. Moist air clung to his skin, but heavy dust made it difficult to breathe.

Darion. I think you're in a cave or a tunnel somewhere. There's a train and water nearby. Please try to find where he's keeping Lucas. I'm coming for you both.

I broke the connection, and my eyes snapped open. "Darion's in a cave or a tunnel, and there's a waterfall or creek nearby. Freya, my brother and I are bound by a curse. Can you use my blood to track his location?"

"I can try." She knelt over the candles.

That's when I saw the blade near the stones on the rug. I

175

glanced back up at Freya and wondered more about her specific magic. She picked up the knife, and Neil left the circle to stand by Jasper and Anya.

The point of the blade hit my skin. My jaw clenched as a hot sting tore across my palm. All I could think about as I stared at the open gash was Orien drinking blood from Darion and Lucas. My stomach twisted. What kind of monster was he?

Freya directed my dripping hand over the stones. She chanted as my blood trickled down, coating the stones as they rose from the bowl and arranged themselves onto the rug.

"Whoa," Neil mused as we all watched the drops of blood pool together and slither across the stone formations until it stopped.

Freya's chanting ceased. "Your brother is somewhere here." She moved her hand over a cluster of stones and pointed.

I lifted a brow, and she explained. "The stones represent landmarks." She pointed. "East, west, north, south, and the river runs through the center. This line of stones here leads up to Vernonia, and nestled between the highway and Vernonia is …"

Jasper bent over the stone map. "Crown Zellerbach Trail. Ev, there are caves along the trail for miles. Darion might be in any of them."

I squeezed my cut hand into a fist, thinking about the curse that linked my life to Darion's.

Why has Orien kept Darion blindfolded?

Unless he suspected that Darion and I shared the same Sight as he and Oria had. He was taking precautions. And if Orien didn't want me to see where Darion was being held, then he wasn't ready to come face-to-face with me again. He was strong but not what he used to be, forced to survive on the blood of others.

But Orien couldn't know about Neil or that I'd be able to use Neil's ability to project thought to speak with Darion. He also didn't know about Freya and her ability to use the curse I shared with Darion to pinpoint his location. I had to act now before Orien found out that I was onto his location.

"Freya, will this spell continue to work away from your presence?"

Her charcoal eyes brightened. "Yes. I will gather some stones. And you must take this knife and use it to reopen your wound each time you wish to use your blood to trace your brother." She sheathed the blade and handed it to me. "The blade and stones are both bound with the magic for this spell," she said in answer to my unspoken question.

I nodded and tucked the blade away.

Neil followed Freya as she collected stones for me to bring.

Anya motioned for me to follow her through the living room and into the kitchen, which during the day would have a spectacular view of the river. She turned on the sink faucet and then glanced over her shoulder as she guided my hand under the running water. The scent of jasmine surrounded her as she leaned closer and whispered in my ear. "I sense a terrible loss for you. It'll happen soon."

A lump of dread hardened in my chest. "What do you mean?" My voice rose louder than I'd meant it to.

"Shh," she whispered.

I glanced back to make sure my blunder hadn't caught anyone's attention. "You have powers?" Since Anya was half-human, I hadn't been sure she had any magic until now.

She nodded. "Sometimes it comes as images, and other times it's just a feeling, like now." She looked down like she wanted to say more.

"There's something else," I prodded. "What is it?"

She sighed. "I don't enjoy knowing these things."

Footsteps were heading our way. "Just tell me, Anya, quick!"

Her glossy topaz-blue eyes penetrated mine, and her shoulders tightened with her regret-filled words. "I've seen images of your uncle. And you ..." She clicked her nails on the counter. "The only way for you to defeat your uncle is to embrace the part of yourself that's like him."

I gripped the counter with my free hand. "I don't understand." But deep down, I did. I knew the darkness she spoke of. I'd felt it creeping to the surface this past year.

"The part you've kept buried. It is not Siobhan's magic; it's yours. You must accept the darkest part of yourself if blood is to defeat blood."

Jasper rounded the corner into the kitchen.

"Remember," Anya said quickly. "Stop fighting your true nature. And don't tell my mother you know of my magic." She smiled at Jasper as she rubbed a healing salve on my hand and began wrapping it.

"Is this even necessary, since I'll be cutting it back open?"

"Of course," she said. "The salve will protect against infection." She handed me a small container of it. "Reapply it when you are able."

Freya brought me the pouch of stones. I tucked them away but slid another stone from my pocket. Freya tsked when she saw it. "How did you get that?" She took a step back.

"You know of this stone?" I asked her. "Can you tell me anything about it?"

Her gaze followed the bolts of electricity that rippled across the stone, and a shadow darkened her features. "It's called an ever stone, and it can only be found inside caves within the

Ever Forest. They carry dangerous magic. This one holds the essence of life within. Someone has used it with dark magic. That's all I can tell you." She pressed her lips tight and shook her head. "Handle it with care." She closed my hand over the stone and pushed it down. "Good luck on your journey."

I tucked the stone back inside my pocket and wondered at Freya's reaction as Neil and Jasper said their goodbyes. It had been more than simple unease. Something about the ever stone haunted her, but what?

~

"*H*ow well do you know Freya?" I asked Neil as we drove back to his club.

Neil shrugged. "Freya's father was a hunter. My mother traded fabrics for rare ingredients that only he could procure. I remember I would trail behind Freya while my mother bartered with her father. I'd ask her a million questions while she gathered stones from anywhere she could find them."

I wanted to ask Neil more about the stones Freya would collect, but we were pulling up to the club with Jasper right on my bumper. His motorcycle headlight flooded my rearview mirror.

"Someone's in full Shield mode tonight." Neil opened the passenger-side door, then leaned over and kissed my forehead. "I'm a call away if you need anything, darling."

"Thanks, Neil."

He closed the door and went inside the club.

I drove away, with Jasper following close behind and Anya's warning echoing in my mind. If there was even a chance she was right, I had to track Darion alone. The loss she sensed could be anything. But Orien had already attacked three people I cared about, and I couldn't risk anyone else getting hurt.

Jasper's motorcycle pulled up beside me in front of the main house.

I got out of my car and hoped my plan would work. "Will you go let my mom know what we found out? I'm running into my place to grab Oria's ring. Then I'll meet you inside."

Jasper latched his helmet behind his motorcycle seat and furrowed his brow. "Are you sure you should bring the ring?"

My arms shivered, and I folded them tight across my chest. "Yes. Oria and the ancestors may have the knowledge to help defeat Orien. It's worth the risk to bring it."

Jasper didn't budge as he studied me. He had the whole overprotective stance going on, and for a second, I didn't think he'd go inside. "Okay." He relaxed.

I blew out the breath I'd been holding and waited until he disappeared inside the front door before I ran to my apartment.

The shifter's body was nowhere in sight, and a thick sheet of plastic covered the broken window.

I hurried to my bedroom closet and pulled out the long rectangular box and slipped the lid off. The silver sword lay sheathed inside. This had been the queen's sword—Oria's sword. And now it belonged to me. Its weight felt just right as I secured the belt around my waist. At a height of five feet four inches, the sword was expertly forged to match a woman of my proportions. It hugged my hip perfectly. I gripped the hilt, and the weapon sang as I slipped the dangerously sharp blade from its sheath. My finger slid across the edge of the glittering silver as I traced the runes burned into the blade, leading up to the embedded gem at the top of the handle, which I now recognized as an ever stone.

A section of the hilt clicked loose when I passed my finger

over the stone. No one but Oria and her sword maker had known of the secret compartment before she'd shared the knowledge with me when I'd worn the ring. I'd put the ring inside for safekeeping after retrieving it from Felix's. The familiar auras hummed with life as I scooped the ring out of the compartment and slipped it inside my pants pocket. Prisms of light danced across the sword as I lifted it high and slammed it into its scabbard.

Creeping from my apartment back to my car, I stayed low to avoid the windows. My heart skipped a beat when a shadow crossed in front of a window facing the driveway and paused. I ducked and opened the driver's side door, reaching in and shifting the gear into neutral. When the shadow moved from the window, I turned the steering wheel and rolled my car backward so it faced the exit of the driveway. I'd parked close enough to the road that I could give it another good push and roll far enough away before starting the engine and speeding toward the highway.

Sorry, Mom. But I can't give Orien the chance to hurt anyone else I love. I have to do this alone.

Energy pulsed from Oria's ring, tucked inside my pants pocket. Jasper was right about it being too risky to bring it with me, but I couldn't leave it at my apartment—not after Orien had already sent one shifter to look for it there—and I didn't have time to drive back to Felix's.

I parked along the dark street in front of my yoga studio. The only visible movement was shadows of tree branches cast by the dim streetlamps, but I still kept my senses heightened as I crossed the sidewalk to the studio entrance and went inside.

Leaving the lights off so I could move without being seen from outside, I hurried to the locker room. The lingering incense from recent classes reminded me of the ever resin

Freya had burned tonight, and of all the secrets of Aenoas-Vita I had yet to learn.

Inside the locker room, I scooted one side of the lockers forward to reveal an area of the brick wall that needed repairs. I shimmied out a loose brick and set it aside, then pulled Oria's ring from my pocket. The auras swam wildly inside the tiny glass globe, and I wondered if the spirits of the ancestors inside sensed what was happening in the world of the living. I wrapped a cloth around the ring and tucked it inside the space in the wall. After carefully arranging the brick and lockers back in place, I left the studio.

~

*T*he drive to the entrance of Crown Zellerbach Trail took about twenty minutes. I pulled up next to the only other vehicle. The leather-clad figure waited atop the parked motorcycle. I should have known I hadn't fooled him. Jasper's amber eyes stalked me furiously as I got out of my car and walked forward.

"Really, Ev? What the hell were you thinking coming out here alone?"

I huffed out a breath of fog. "I was thinking I didn't want anyone else getting hurt. Orien wants me and Darion, and I want to keep you and everyone else I love safe."

Jasper lifted himself off his motorcycle. "And what do you think is going to happen if he gets what he wants? He didn't come out of hiding after hundreds of years just to vanish again."

"No, he didn't." I leaned against the hood of my car.

Jasper peaked a brow as he glanced at the sword dangling at my side.

"My premonitions have started." I kicked at nothing on the ground. "And the vision I saw was horrific. Orien doesn't just want my and Darion's magic; he wants to destroy Aenoas-Vita."

Jasper cast his gaze up at the sky, then back toward me. "Your mom sent a message to Felix, but she hasn't heard back. Shouldn't we wait for Arden?"

"There's no time for that. Orien is drinking their blood, Jasp. And he's done something to Lucas; the shifter told me himself that Orien used Lucas to test his spell with this"—I reached into my pocket and pulled out the ever stone— "Freya said someone used it with dark magic. Lucas may not have much time, and I don't know what's taking Arden and Rheya so long to return, but Orien has to be stopped before it's too late."

"Then let's go stop him." A puff of fog billowed away with his words. He scooted closer and nudged my shoulder. "Together."

I rested my head against his arm. "Do you know Anya has magic? She warned me I'm going to suffer a terrible loss. What if I can't save our planet and Orien destroys everything and everyone?"

Jasper turned me to face him and put his gloved hands over mine. "Anya told me of her magic. Premonitions are interpretations of possibilities. They are not facts. One event can influence a multitude of changes."

I shook my head. "Oria's premonitions have never been wrong. She saw me generations before I was born."

Jasper moved my chin and held it in place. "Anya is not Oria. She told me herself that the glimpses she gets can alter. Nothing is set in stone. The future can always change. It's what we do now that matters."

"What would I do without you, Jasp?"

He squeezed his long arms around me. "I ask myself that same question all the time." His body vibrated with laughter.

"Hey!" I pinched his side.

"Ouch! Okay, I'm sorry. But I'm not just your best friend, Ev." His laughter died, and his tone darkened. "I'm your Shield, and it's my sworn duty to stand at your side and to protect you, at any cost." His gloved finger tilted my chin until our eyes locked. Flecks of gold glinted in his amber eyes. "We walk into those woods together, or neither of us goes at all."

I nodded. "Together."

"That's my girl." He pulled me against his hard chest, and I breathed in the worn leather scent of his jacket and relaxed against him.

He wrapped the unzipped sides of his jacket over me, and my hands bumped up against cold metal.

"Great minds think alike," Jasper laughed as I slid my hands under the sword strapped to his back.

"I love you, Jasp."

He squeezed tighter. "I love you too, Ev."

"Okay." I exhaled and separated myself from Jasper's embrace. "Let's go find Darion and Lucas, and bring them home." I opened the passenger-side door of my car and grabbed the pouch of stones. I'd already strapped the knife Freya had spelled and given me to my belt.

The forest loomed ahead. A year ago, I never would have imagined the two of us heading into the woods in the middle of the night, armed with swords, and yet here we were, doing just that.

Jasper's shoulders shook, and his serious expression melted into an amused grin.

"What?" I asked as I scanned the area for any other energy signatures.

He shook his head. "I was just thinking about how different things are now. We used to be just a couple of teenagers, and now look at us: a queen and her Shield, preparing for battle."

"I'm no queen, Jasp. It's a role I've been forced to play, and I have absolutely no talent for it. I'm not even a true Vitarian. Earth is the only home I've known, and life was so much easier when I thought I was human. How can I rule a planet of people I don't completely understand when I've never even set foot on Aenoas-Vita's soil? Vitarians won't accept me as their queen."

Jasper snatched a leather glove off, and my fingers warmed as he entwined his with mine. "Oria and the ancestors wouldn't have chosen you if you weren't fit to rule. You just need to believe in yourself. And maybe it's time we visit our planet. You'll feel differently once you've seen it and *your* people." He squeezed my hand.

"Maybe." I untangled my fingers from Jasper's and walked to the trailhead. "But first, it's time to get Darion and Lucas back."

Three paths split in different directions. The stones tumbled out of the pouch as I turned it upside down over the ground. I arranged the labradorite crystals into three connecting lines, with each line facing a path. Then I peeled the bandage back from my hand and whipped out the knife. Fresh blood dripped down onto the stones, and a hot sting spread across my palm as I replaced the bandage over the oozing cut.

Crimson blood pooled together, as before, and rolled atop the stones to the farthest line of rocks. "We take that one." I pointed to the path on our right, then scooped up the stones and secured them in their pouch.

As we made our way deeper up the trail, our surroundings blackened without any city lights. Vitarians saw better in the dark than humans did, but it was still a challenge. I slipped a small flashlight out of my jacket pocket and clicked it on the lowest setting and kept the light pointed down at the ground, hoping it wouldn't attract attention if any unseen eyes monitored the woods.

We had walked for at least an hour when I heard what could have been water rushing somewhere in the distance.

"Do you hear that?" My blood pumped with renewed adrenaline. The wind soared, rustling leaves and branches in the tall ancient oak trees closing in around us.

Jasper closed his eyes and listened. "It sounds like the rush of a waterfall. Do you feel anything?"

"No," I shook my head. "I've been trying the entire time. I don't even sense the animals. Orien must have created a spell to hide the auras around this area."

"Test your other abilities."

I tilted my head up toward the top of the forest and connected my magic to nature's elements. The wind roared at my command and swarmed around us, picking up twigs and nettles and dried leaves. I released it, and the debris fell back to the ground.

"Lift your shield," I instructed Jasper.

I didn't feel the heavy, invisible energy that normally exploded from Jasper when he cocooned us in his impenetrable wall. Nor did I see the watery substance or feel the high vibrations that usually surrounded us. "Did it work?"

"Yes, it's up. Orien must have specifically done something to block your Empath abilities."

A twig snapped nearby, and we both turned, searching the woods.

I pointed the flashlight into the bushes where the noise had come from. Thanks to Orien, I couldn't sense if there was another aura nearby, but my skin crawled with warning. As soon as we turned to continue on the trail, a squeal erupted from behind us, and someone jumped from the bushes.

Bree slapped her head furiously and shook her entire body.

"What the hell are you doing here?" I hissed.

She stomped madly on the ground, crushing something under her foot. Then she looked up with accusing eyes. Her finger shot out, shaking in midair. "You … I saw what you did with the wind. And … and I heard you talking about a spell. What are you?" Bree asked, shaking like a frightened mouse.

I stood speechless and glanced at Jasper. He locked his attention on Bree, as if she were a snake ready to strike.

Fiery anger coursed through me. "You didn't see or hear anything. Why are you following us?" I propelled myself forward, ready to throttle her, but Jasper snatched my arm.

"She's not worth it." He narrowed his amber gaze at her, and she shriveled back a few inches.

"Answer me, damn it." My voice came out in a growl.

"Okay, okay. I saw you going into your studio and got curious, so I followed you when you left."

Heat boiled inside me. But this time, I wasn't angry at Bree. This type of behavior didn't surprise me coming from her. I was angry at myself for not paying better attention. If Orien hadn't spelled the woods so I couldn't sense aura energy, I would have felt her behind us. I depended too heavily on my magic these days.

"What are we going to do?" Jasper asked. "With her." His scowl deepened as he glanced back at Bree, whose ponytail was a mess. Leaves stuck to the side of her head, and she had dirt smudged all over her face.

I quirked a brow at her stretch pants and tennis shoes. She hadn't given the impression of a person who dressed for comfort. What was she doing prowling around this late at night?

As I smoothed my ponytail back, I squinted my eyes to

get a better look at the trail ahead. "I've come too far to turn back now. I have to find Darion and Lucas. You take her back."

Jasper scrunched up his face. "No way! I'm not leaving you. She found her way here. She can find her way back by herself."

I dug my fingernails into my palms and winced at the searing pain in my injured hand. We were wasting time. "These woods are dangerous," I whispered, so only Jasper could hear. "We can't let her go back alone."

Bree inched forward and rolled her shoulders back, seeming to have regained her courage. "Wait. Look, I'm sorry I followed you. I know you don't like me, and the feeling is mutual." Her tone took on the familiar air of superiority. "But let's just forget for now about what I saw and heard, which I expect you to explain later. I don't want to walk back alone. If you let me stay with you, I can help."

Jasper and I both barked out a laugh simultaneously, causing Bree to cross her arms over her chest and narrow her gaze at us. She tapped her foot, waiting for us to compose ourselves.

"Okay, seriously," I said, rubbing at the aching muscles in my abdomen. "How are you going to help us?"

One of Bree's hands flew to her side, and her elbow arched high. "I've been hiking these trails every morning since I moved here. I've gotten pretty familiar with the area."

When neither Jasper nor I responded, she continued. "I can prove it. Do you hear rushing water?"

We both nodded, cautiously.

"There's a waterfall just around this corner. It's the first of many along the trail."

My head tilted to the side as I considered. "You could have guessed that."

Bree huffed and rolled her eyes. "There's a fallen tree

across the trail about a quarter of a mile up. We'll have to climb over it." She marched forward, not waiting for us to agree to let her join our group.

Jasper's silhouette leaned closer to me. "Should we follow her?"

I shrugged. "I don't think we have any choice. She might know where some caves are. But if Orien or any of the Shimera find us, I want you to protect her."

Jasper stiffened. "Your safety is my priority, Ev."

Bree's voice floated back to us. "Are you two coming or what?"

I grabbed Jasper's shoulder and squeezed through his leather jacket. "You said the Vitarian people will accept me as their queen. Well, you are one of those people. I need you to do what I ask. Promise me."

I might not have been able to use my Empath ability while in these woods, but I knew Jasper well enough to know that the creases forming at the corners of his eyes meant he battled with his emotions. He bowed his head against mine. "All I can promise is that I'll do my best to keep her safe as long as it doesn't put you at risk."

"Thank you," I whispered.

We ran up the trail and caught up to Bree. It wasn't long before we found both the waterfall and the large fallen tree, just where she'd said they'd be.

"Bree," I called ahead, and she paused. "Do you know of any caves or underground tunnels along this trail?"

Her eyes lit up. "There's an old railroad that runs through here. I found a path that leads down to an underground tunnel the workers used to use. It looks like it's been abandoned for years."

My pulse quickened. "What direction is it?"

Bree pointed forward. "If we keep going a bit, there's a trail that breaks off the cliffside." Her arm moved sideways with her finger pointing down the side of the trail we were on. "If we follow it, it'll take us directly to the cave's entrance."

I extracted the pouch of stones from my pocket and arranged them on the ground in two long horizontal and vertical lines. I slipped the knife from its case on my belt.

"Don't freak out," I told Bree, who watched me wide-eyed as I lifted the bandage from my hand and cut through the open gash once more. Once enough blood had pooled, I tilted my hand over the stones.

Bree grimaced. "Yuck! What are you doing?" Her tone quivered with disgust. She backed up a few steps, gawking at my blood like it was a contagion. "Wha... what's happening?" Her finger shook at the drops of blood that gathered and slithered over the rocks.

"Would you settle down? It's just a little blood," I told her.

"Yeah, well, blood doesn't just coagulate and travel over rocks on its own."

Jasper coughed to hide his snicker.

I rolled my eyes at both of them. "It does when it's infused with magic."

A jolt shot through me when the blood stopped. "He's down there." I hurried past them.

"Who's down there?"

I ignored Bree's question and sped up the trail. My hamstrings were on fire by the time Bree called out, "This is it."

It was barely a path. The only signs of use looked to be recent. If Bree hadn't known it was here, I probably wouldn't have noticed it. "Are you sure?"

She nodded. "Yeah. I hiked up here with Ty a few days ago. He wanted to go check out the old tunnel, and I nearly broke my neck making my way down when my foot got stuck in a pile of vines and I tripped."

"You saw the tunnel? Did it look like anyone else had been in there?"

She shrugged. "All we saw was a bunch of old beer cans and candy wrappers, probably left behind by teens who come down here to party. Follow me." Bree took the lead.

"Stop!" Jasper said. He took off his jacket and unsheathed the sword on his back.

Jasper had been training with his father for most of his life, and he was an expert swordsman, as was every member of the royal guard, and he'd insisted on giving me regular lessons this past year.

Jasper moved past Bree, who sneaked in a brush of her hand across his back.

I swallowed hard, fighting back the urge to snatch a handful of her hair and yank. She was supposed to be dating Ty, yet she flirted with every good-looking guy she crossed paths with.

The gleam of my sword illuminated the night as I unsheathed it, relishing the way its hilt fit so perfectly in my grasp. Bree's startled expression brought a smile to my face. A little fear would do her good.

My attention was abruptly pulled back to the present by the sound of a swift blade slicing through the grass and bush. I nodded for Bree to proceed behind Jasper, who started down the trail, hacking away overgrown foliage that threatened to scratch out our eyes in protest at being moved aside.

The hill was steep and littered with fallen branches. Ferns brushed our legs, and our feet squished in the damp moss that had taken over where the path had become overgrown and barely visible. A screech echoed in front of me as Bree slipped and fell back. I dropped my sword and caught her from behind just before she hit the ground.

"Thanks," she mumbled, and accepted Jasper's hand. He

gave her a powerful pull, and she jumped back to her feet. "So, who are you two looking for in the middle of the night?"

"Huh." I sighed, and my breath dissipated in the misty air. "My brother and Lucas."

Before she could ask another question, I had one of my own. "Why were you following us?"

She didn't turn around when she said, "I don't sleep well, and I was checking on my new sign—I'm sure you've seen how awesome it is—and when I saw you creeping around your studio without the lights on, I got curious." She shrugged like curiosity gave someone the right to sneak around, spying on other people.

I fumed I couldn't use my Empath powers on her. "First, I wasn't creeping around. And second, your sign sucks!" I knew it was a cheap shot, but lashing out felt good.

Bree tossed her head back. "Not everyone has taste as sophisticated as mine."

"Sure, that's it," I mumbled under my breath, and rolled my eyes at her back.

We reached the bottom of the hill and came to a narrow creek. "It's just this way." Bree went left at the creek. The ground turned to mostly crushed rock, and our legs wobbled over the sharp edges. Bree jumped over the creek and pushed through a thick area of leafy bushes.

"She didn't strike me as the woodsy type," Jasper whispered as we neared the creek.

I eyed the rocks on the other side, determining which one would be easier to land on. "I've been thinking the same thing. She's hiding something. I'm not buying that she followed me out here and tracked us through the forest out of some morbid curiosity." I jumped and landed firmly on a flat rock.

Jasper sprang off the ground with no hesitation. "I agree. And she's not Ty's type at all. I mean, she's gorgeous in that

Barbie doll kind of way, but Ty's never been into girls like her before."

Bree's voice echoed through the woods. "Everything okay back there?"

"Yeah," I responded to Bree, then more quietly to Jasper, "I hear you. I can't figure her out. She's just a human, but I can't shake this feeling ... I don't know ... I can't explain it."

Jasper lifted the branches back for me. "I know what you mean. She makes the hairs on the back of my neck stand up, and not in a good way."

We huddled behind the bush a moment longer. "We'll let her show us the tunnel," I told him, "and when we get back, we'll do a memory spell, so she forgets all this, but we'll keep a close watch on her for a while."

Jasper puckered his lips to the side and nodded his agreement.

A scream came from the other side of the bushes, followed by a loud thump. We rushed through the thick branches, not caring about scrapes or pokes to the eyes, and found Bree kneeling over a body and holding a heavy rock above its head.

Jasper pried the rock from Bree's shaking hands, and she twisted her quivering body into his.

"Wha... what is that thing?" she stuttered. She curled herself around Jasper's torso, and I couldn't help but think she was taking advantage of the situation. But then I chided myself. She was just a human girl who'd knocked her first monster unconscious.

I bent down to examine the body and had to check the human way to see if he was still alive, since I couldn't feel his energy or see his aura. My fingers pressed against the wrinkled and deteriorated skin of the Shimera. The eyes, nose, and mouth weren't abnormal; they resembled human and Vitarian features, but every visible part of his skin appeared decayed. And the odor of rot permeated the air all around him.

A faint pulse beat against my fingertips—that was until Jasper came over and shoved the tip of his sword through the Shimera's throat. A gurgle bubbled from his mouth, and I glanced up at Jasper and lifted my brow in a question.

"He would have done the same to us, given the chance, and alerted any others inside the cave."

The cave. I stretched and stepped over the dead Shimera.

Just ahead of us, nestled within the moss-covered mountainside, was a large cave entrance.

"This has to be where they're keeping Darion and Lucas," I said to Jasper, who was already surveying the area for more Shimera.

"Um, are either of you going to tell me what that freaky zombie thing is?"

I flicked my gaze toward Bree. *What the hell. We're going to erase her memory, anyway.* "He's a creature from another planet who can take the form of anyone he wants to. That rotting, mutilated thing is his natural appearance."

Bree dragged her gaze from the Shimera's lifeless body. "And you two?"

I huffed. "We don't have time for this. We're both"—I pointed to Jasper and then myself—"from another planet and have magical powers. No more questions. You wait out here and hide in the bushes. Quietly," I added.

"Um, that's not happening." Bree stomped her foot. "No way I'm waiting out here alone to get attacked by another pus-filled monster. Besides, you wouldn't have found this cave if it wasn't for me." She placed her hand on her hip. "I've been inside and explored the different tunnels. I can help navigate."

My chest tightened. Of course, there would be multiple tunnels. I ground my teeth. "How many tunnels are there?"

"I don't know. I was too afraid to go very far, but they looked to go pretty deep under the mountain." Bree shoved her hands into the pockets of her tight-fitting sweater.

"Well, you'll be a brilliant navigator." Sarcasm oozed from my tone. I spun around and hacked at a bush. It was unnecessary but made me feel better. "Okay, you can come with us, but stay close and keep quiet."

Jasper sped in front of me. His gaze was sharp as he glanced inside the cave. He tightened his grip on his sword. "I'll go in first. Both of you stay behind me."

Bree leaned toward me, her breath hot on my ear. "He's so hot when he's all protective."

I resisted the urge to turn and elbow her in the jaw. Instead, I whispered back, "Just stay close and keep quiet."

A chilled, dusty air hit my skin inside the dark cave. Bree shivered behind me, her teeth jittering in my ear. My right hand rested on the hilt of my sword as I tried sparking light from my left fingertips as Calista had shown me. Only a weak glow sparked before dimming out, like every other time I'd tried. Jasper was no help in that department, either. Besides mastering his shield and combat training, he put little effort into learning other magic. I gave up and pulled out the flashlight and pointed the beam ahead.

We stood in a large, empty cavern, facing four separate tunnels.

"This is as far as I've gone," Bree admitted, her words echoing off the dirt walls.

My palm pulsed with pain as I renewed the gash once more. I winced at the pus pockets forming inside the cut. When the blood trickled over the line of stones, indicating the tunnel at our right, Jasper scoped it out. I couldn't sense his shield, but I knew it was there, and nudged Bree to follow behind him so his shield would safely encompass her.

We stepped into the tunnel, our feet crunching over a

mixture of dirt and crumbled stone. A damp mildew breeze hung in the air, and my skin prickled with the familiar buzz of the curse that Darion and I shared. "He's close," I whispered.

Jasper nodded and continued to lead the way.

The air grew colder as we moved deeper beneath the mountain.

Our steps slowed as the scent of rotten eggs wrapped around us. Bree coughed, and Jasper's sword flashed ahead. The Shimera hadn't expected the invisible shield nor Jasper's speed. His blade sang as it slashed through the Shimera's hand, then down across his body. The Shimera thumped to the ground.

"Where did he come from?" My heart raced as I spun, checking behind and over the walls on either side of us. "There could be more." I shook a clinging Bree off my back.

"Oh my God! We're going to die in here," she quivered.

"You're not going to die," I assured her, even though it was entirely possible that we would. "It's not too late for you to go back." My whispers echoed overhead.

Bree's head bumped against mine as she shook it from side to side. "Uh-uh … no way. I'm staying with you two."

We kept moving. The decaying odor grew stronger, burning my lungs with every breath. A shiver crawled down the back of my neck as something scraped nearby. I twisted side to side, bathing the walls in light. Bree spun, blinding me with her cell phone light, and my foot bent awkwardly as I tripped over a rock. Arms snaked out from the wall and slammed me into hard earth. Metal clanged as my sword hit the ground. I grasped toward my belt and yanked Freya's blade free, and in one swift movement, I whirled around and buried the knife into the side of the Shimera's throat.

"You okay?" Jasper scanned my body for injury.

I snatched my sword from the ground and kneaded my

throbbing temple. "Yeah. My head hit the wall, but I'm fine. Why couldn't we see them?"

"I don't know," he answered, monitoring the walls for further attack. "I don't really know much about the Shimera, but it appears they can blend in with their surroundings."

"Great!" Bree screeched, brushing dirt from her pants. "So now we have to worry about invisible monsters." She sidestepped the Shimera's blood pooling near her feet.

I blocked my eyes. "Bree, get that light out of my face."

She pointed the light toward the ground. "Look, I want to help find your brother and boyfriend, but maybe we should all go back, and you can come back with the police."

"That's not an option," I bit back, and ground my teeth. If I left now, Orien would move them. This could be my only chance to save them both.

The curse hummed stronger within me. "We have to keep going. Darion is near."

"Okay," Jasper agreed. "Let's keep close in the center of the tunnel and pay attention to any sound or movement."

We huddled together, watching the walls as we inched forward. If there were any more Shimera, they kept hidden and didn't attack.

Jasper paused.

"What is it?" I asked, not wanting to take my eyes off the tunnel behind us.

"A light ahead. Looks like another cavern."

I risked a glance over Jasper's shoulder. "Darion's in there; I can feel it. Let's keep moving."

Jasper hesitated. "It could be a trap."

"I know, but what choice do we have?"

Jasper continued forward, with Bree and me pressed to his back. He tapped my shoulder, signaling for us to creep to one side of the tunnel. He used the point of his sword to check the wall for unseen threats as we shuffled toward the light. When we reached the entrance to the cavern, two more tunnels broke off on either side.

Jasper held his finger to his lips and motioned for Bree and me to stay where we were. Knots twisted in my stomach as he peeked around the entrance, then slipped inside the cavern.

Bree fidgeted at my side. I nudged her away to get her hot breath off my ear. Seconds passed before Jasper popped his head out and whispered, "It's clear."

"Darion!" His body lay limp on the ground. Dread knifed at my insides when I saw Lucas wasn't in the cavern. We'd have to keep looking for him.

I pulled Darion's blindfold away. Dried mud smudged his face, and I carefully brushed the dirt pebbles from his eyes. His skin felt ice cold, but I knew he was alive—our curse still hummed inside me.

His eyelids flickered as he rolled to the side with a low moan.

"Ev? Is that you? Are you really here?" His voice cracked.

"Of course I am. Can you move?"

His head dangled as he groggily scooted into a sitting position, and I noticed the teeth marks and crusted blood on his neck. Rage boiled inside me.

He blinked, his eyes adjusting to the light of the torches staked in the ground, and settled a dark scowl on me. "I told you not to come." Then his face twisted into a grimace as he glanced behind me. "What's she doing here?"

I'd forgotten all about Bree. "I'll explain later," I told him without paying Bree any attention. "Let's get these bindings off."

Jasper bent down to help.

"I wouldn't do that if I were you." Bree's change in tone hit me like ice.

I gripped the hilt of my sword and turned to face her. "Why not?"

Her green eyes sparked with a devilish glint. And then a deeper voice sounded from the tunnel just outside the cavern.

"Because if you remove his bindings, I'll finish this one off." Orien stepped into the cavern, holding a limp Lucas in his arms.

Acid burned in my throat at the sight of Lucas. His head hung forward; he was barely conscious.

"Hey, baby," Bree cooed at Orien.

Baby? My jaw clenched. I hadn't trusted Bree, but this didn't add up.

Bree laughed hysterically as she slinked near Orien and ran a finger down the back of his neck, licking at his ear. "Oscar worthy, right?" She cackled some more.

"We could do without the PDA," Darion jeered, earning himself a hard stare from Orien.

"What?" Darion kept going. "It's like watching myself being fondled by a hyena."

"Shut your face, pretty boy, or I'll shut it for you," Bree threatened.

"Oh, you wish," Darion taunted her.

"Enough." Orien settled his cold sapphire glare on Bree. "Did you get it?" His words came out impatiently.

Bree shoved her hand into her pants pocket. "Of course I did. You were right. She's naïve and careless and not fit to rule our people."

"Our people?" The words left my lips as I studied Bree with fresh eyes. "You're Vitarian?"

It was Jasper who asked, "How did we not sense you?"

Bree shrugged. "It's my dominant gift. I can hide my essence and that of others. I've got a talent for persuasion, too." She winked, then ran a long red fingernail down Orien's arm. "Isn't that right, baby?"

That was why I hadn't been able to use my Empath abilities. She'd been blocking my magic the entire time. "You nasty little rat," I ground out. My hand ached to throttle her.

Bree's lips twisted into a satisfied smirk as she slipped something from her pocket.

No! How did she ...? What have I done?

A bitter taste filled my mouth as Orien greedily reached for Oria's ring and grasped it between his fingers. "Finally," he whispered.

My heart froze as images of my premonition filled my mind. I'd failed everyone. I lunged forward and caught Bree by surprise, wrapping my arm around her throat and pressing the edge of my sword into her flesh. "How did you get the ring?"

Jasper flew to my side with his sword arched to defend.

Bree's shoulders shook, but not in fear. She laughed even as my blade inched closer to her skin. "I've been watching you, you silly girl. What kind of queen can't sniff out her own kind? You were as easy to fool as Ty was to persuade." She attempted to twist out of my grasp, but I cut into her skin and kneed her in the side.

Her body stilled. "You bitch! You cut me! Orien! Do something!"

Orien didn't seem at all concerned with Bree's safety as he ogled the ring.

I pushed the knife deeper and felt Bree's wet blood drip over my fingers. "Let us go, or I'll kill her."

A heaviness settled in my stomach at the wicked smile that spread ear to ear across Orien's face. Even before he spoke, I knew Bree was useless leverage.

"Go ahead," he said. "It'll save me the trouble."

Bree thrashed. "You bastard! I did everything you asked. I'm going to rule at your side. You promised."

Orien barely took his eyes off the ring when he used Bree's own words against her. "And you were so easy to fool. When I finish with Aenoas-Vita, there'll be nothing left to rule." A chuckle vibrated from his chest, causing Lucas's head to bob around.

Whatever magic Bree used to block my ability stopped. I sensed the vibration of Jasper's energy shield and saw its watery substance encasing us. I focused on Lucas. He wasn't just weak. Something was off about his energy. His aura ...

My legs trembled. I held onto Bree tighter, using her body for support. "Lucas! Can you hear me?"

My heartbeat thrashed in my ears when no response came from Lucas. "What did you do to him?"

Orien didn't even look at Lucas as he spoke. He just held him like a dirty piece of laundry. "Your boyfriend here helped me accomplish my promise to the Shimera."

My thoughts raced with dizzying speed. "What are you talking about?"

Darion's chains rattled from behind as he struggled to free himself.

"He drained Lucas of his life force and put it inside the Shimera," Bree blurted.

Orien's nostrils flared, and when his eyes landed on Bree, her entire body shook in my arms.

Inside the Shimera. The stone! Now I understood why I sensed something familiar about the energy it held. It was Lucas's.

Just then, at least a dozen Shimera moved past Orien and filled the cavern, surrounding us.

"It's true," admitted Orien. "I've finally reverse engineered the spell the sorceress used to make this." He held up the ring. "And I've rewarded one of my Shimera with his"—he gave Lucas a shake—"life force. He can draw on it continuously to maintain his form, or could when he was still alive."

I pieced Orien's meaning together. He'd stolen Lucas's aura and transferred it into the ever stone, which he implanted into the Shimera.

"Why assassinate one of your own?"

Orien sneered. "He outlived his usefulness."

I released an arm from Bree and dug into my pants pocket. "Or you didn't want us to know about this." I held up the milky-white stone that flickered with tiny bolts of lightning. "Does this hold Lucas's aura?"

Orien stood unfazed by the appearance of the stone. "Clever girl. You are my blood, after all." I could have sworn his eyes flashed with a hint of pride, which made my skin crawl.

"Give Lucas back his life force," I demanded.

Orien clicked his tongue. "My dear niece, I'd love to help you, but you have something I want."

My head throbbed as I tried projecting energy into Lucas, as I had with Molly, but nothing happened.

"Your magic can't help him, niece. Without his vital essence, he's nothing but an empty shell."

An uncontrollable heat seared my insides. "You have the ring. You've won. Lucas has nothing to do with this. Restore his life and let him go. Please." For a moment, I thought I saw a flicker of emotion cross the hard surface of Orien's expression.

"Humph." Orien smoothed his fingers over the ball of the ring, watching the auras swim inside, and then whatever emotion had surfaced dissipated. "I need something else from you and your brother."

The Shimera tightened their circle, and Jasper tensed at my side, ready to strike. But as long as Orien had Lucas, he held all the cards.

"I'm tired of surviving on the scraps of life I must drain, and you two are going to restore me to what I once was. I need the magic inside both of you, the royal twin descendants of Oria, my dear beloved sister, who betrayed me and took everything from me." Orien's fist balled at his side. "But the curse that binds your life forces has made things complicated. If I kill one of you, the other dies before I can take their power. So you're going to simplify things for me."

A lump formed in the back of my throat. Orien knew about the loophole in the curse. If I siphoned the curse from Darion, I would absorb all of his magic, and only he would die.

Orien smirked. "I know Oria showed you the magic you needed to save your brother from his wicked stepmother, and I know you can siphon energy as she could. You will take the curse into yourself, and all of his magic with it. Then you will submit your life to me afterward."

Jasper dashed in front of me, flashing his sword. "You're not getting anywhere near her."

Spiders raced down my back as Orien laughed like Jasper had said something funny.

"I won't take my brother's life."

His laugh ceased as quickly as it had started. "Then you don't want to save this one after all."

Jasper flinched, and I heard a grunt. Then something thumped to the ground. I released Bree, who darted past Orien and down the tunnel.

My body smashed into Jasper's hard chest as he tried to block me from pushing around him. "Ev, no."

I shoved past Jasper, and my sword clanged to the ground as I dropped to Lucas's side. "Lucas!"

Blood oozed over my hands as I pressed them against where Lucas's liver had been located. His eyelids fluttered open, and a flash of recognition stared back at me as the last spark of life faded.

"No! Lucas!" I breathed into his mouth and pumped his chest. "Please come back." Tears flooded my eyes, blinding me, and my head crashed down on top of Lucas's chest. No heartbeat. He was gone, and he wasn't coming back.

The stone that held his life force lay dark at my side, no longer pulsing with energy. Fire burned inside every part of my body. My hand locked on the stone, and I roared as I snatched my fallen sword and charged.

My arm froze in midair when I saw that Orien now had Jasper clutched behind his blade.

Orien nodded to one of the Shimera, who broke the circle and made for my sword. I sent him flying backward with a blast of energy, then faced Orien, but my magic had no effect on him.

He barked out a laugh. "Oh, niece. I do regret having to end your life. I see a part of myself within you. But my life means more to me. Now, try that again, and you'll have another dead friend on your hands."

"We're nothing alike!" A Shimera stalked toward me and gripped my armed hand. I chewed my lip as I fought the urge to slice him down with the blade as he unhooked my fingers from the hilt, while another monster, younger and less rotted, grabbed my other arm and twisted it behind my back.

"I've waited too long to let anything stand in my way," Orien went on. "Oria wasn't the only one with tricks up her sleeve." He wiggled a finger encased in an onyx band, and next to it, the ring from the photo with my father.

"Your Shield has no power against me. Neither do you," he continued. "Now, I'm hoping this one means more to you than him." He flicked his dark gaze at Lucas with a careless glance. "I intend to get what I want, or he dies next."

Jasper's amber eyes bored into mine. "Don't do it, Ev. It's

my honor to die for you. We'll see each other in the afterlife." Jasper meant it. He was ready to die for me, but I couldn't let that happen.

"Did you kill our father?"

Darion's chains quieted as his struggles ceased, and we waited for Orien to answer my question.

Orien's lip curled. "You figured it out. What gave me away?"

"You bastard!" Darion jumped to his feet. "I'm going to kill you!" His chains stopped him in his tracks, and one of the Shimera lifted a sword and hit Darion behind the head with the hilt, causing Darion to stumble back onto his knees.

"Ahh ... What a family we could've been if I didn't need your magic." Orien sucked air between his teeth as actual regret shadowed his aura. "I could teach you both so much."

I balked at the idea. "You're demented. We'd never want to learn anything from you. Why did you kill our father?"

Orien shrugged. "An opportunity I couldn't pass up. Creagan was so desperate to save his son from the curse his wife had placed on him he let his guard down, and his power now flows through my veins. But it fades as we speak."

Darion pounded his fists on the ground. Orien had taken our father's life, but I knew Darion would blame himself.

The fire that I'd denied this past year sizzled at the surface of my skin. An unnatural wind stirred around us, and the surrounding torches flared.

The cavern rumbled with Orien's laughter. "Enough of that, niece. Do as I say, or best friend here loses a liver, like boyfriend over there."

Orien tightened his grasp on Jasper as he struggled to break free, but Jasper went rigid when Orien shoved the tip of his knife into his side.

My head throbbed like it was going to explode. I couldn't take my brother's life, but I couldn't sacrifice Jasper's either.

No matter what choice I made, someone else I loved would pay the price.

"It's okay, Ev," Darion said. "Save Jasper. He deserves to live more than I do."

I bit back a frustrated scream as Anya's words rang in my memory. And the resistance I'd clung to for so long melted away. Something inside me cracked, and the fire that festered beneath my abdomen churned to a boil.

Orien's sardonic laugh ricocheted against my ears. "So honorable. If only my sister had been as loyal, we could have ruled together and been unstoppable."

"Why are you doing this? Why can't you just be grateful to be alive?"

Orien seemed to consider my question before he answered. "Because I crave power, and I enjoy destruction, and why settle for a half-life when I can be whole again?"

"I'm ashamed to be related to you." I spat in his face, and the Shimera clutching my sword swiftly struck my mouth and cheek, leaving a fiery tingling sensation. The coppery taste of blood filled my mouth as I clenched my jaw, determined not to show any signs of weakness to the Shimera.

Orien studied my reaction as he wiped my spit from his chin. "You can rejoice in the fact that you won't be here much longer to endure my presence, niece."

"You disgust me!"

His icy sapphire eyes froze on me.

"My beloved sister once said those very words to me after I killed her husband." He stroked the globe atop Oria's ring, which he now wore. "What will it be? Best friend lives or everyone dies?"

My feet dragged beneath me as I approached Darion and dropped to my knees, and clasped my hands around his.

"Wise choice," one of the Shimera sneered.

I ignored them as I focused on what I needed to do.

"How do I know you won't kill Jasper after this is done?"

"You don't, but what choice do you have?"

I sucked in a deep breath before turning to look at my best friend. "Take care of my mom."

"No! Don't do it, Ev. He's lying. He'll kill me anyway." Jasper jerked against Orien.

Darion squeezed my hand and clutched the stone I'd tucked between our palms. "I trust you, Ev." He understood my unspoken plan and was permitting me to do what was necessary, even at the risk of failure.

"I love you, Darion." I hadn't said these words to Darion before, but somewhere along the line this past year, Darion had become a true brother to me.

He pulled me against his chest. "I love you, sister. Thank you for giving me back my life, and for giving me the chance to have a real family."

My entire body shook in his arms. "Mom will never recover."

"Shh." Darion cupped my tender cheek with his free hand. "You can do this."

"Enough!" Orien growled. "Your mother will live, and that's what matters. Once I've absorbed your magic, I won't need hers, but if you don't get on with it, I'll have her taken and brought here so you can both watch her suffer the same fate as your father."

My chest heaved as a roaring filled my ears, and every muscle in my body tensed. Orien would always crave more than just the magic that Darion and I possessed. He'd go after our mother next, just like he had our father and his own family.

The heat churning within me turned to a boil as the fire sparked to life, nearly ready to bend to my will; all I needed was the boost Darion's magic would give me.

Darion's silver eyes reflected the same hate I felt toward

Orien. "Kill him," he whispered through bared teeth, just loud enough for my ears.

We gripped the stone between our clasped fingers as I put my free hand over Darion's chest. Our two hearts beat as one as I latched onto Darion's life force and siphoned the curse.

Bolts of light shot through my arms as they vibrated with Darion's power. Memories of his past flooded my mind while tears streamed down my cheeks. His skin paled as his energy slipped away and his body slumped against me. I gently laid his head down on the ground as I bent over him. "Hang on, brother," I whispered in his ear as I tucked the vibrating ever stone into my pocket.

Hot power coursed through me as I turned to face Orien. The gloating expression fell from his face when he saw the fire flickering at my fingertips.

Without hesitating, I lit each Shimera up into a burning blaze, starting with the one that had hit Darion in the head. Their bodies twisted and thrashed as screams filled the cavern.

The fire responded to my command and clung to the Shimera without spreading. A snarl peeled back my lips as I turned toward Orien. "Looks like having tricks up our sleeves runs in the family. Your ring might protect you from magic, but let's see how well you fare against fire."

A stream of blue and white flames swirled from my fingertips, stretching toward Orien. Sweat trickled down his forehead as he yanked Jasper backward into the tunnel while keeping the sharp edge of his blade pressed into Jasper's throat.

I focused my energy on Orien's dagger until it burned a deep orange. Orien's hand shook as he tried to hold on to his last piece of leverage. When his hand sizzled, he hissed and flung the blade to the ground. He thrust Jasper toward me and turned down the dark tunnel. I picked up Oria's fallen sword, which lay near the Shimera ashes, and chased after Orien.

Orien chanted as he ran ahead of me, and the wind he conjured pressed me backward. A familiar watery substance took form ahead of him.

"No!" Fire tore loose with my scream and carried my sword as I threw it. The flame rippled through the tunnel, singeing Orien's back while the blade sliced across his arm just before he vanished through the portal, taking Oria's ring with him.

The wail that escaped me shook the mountain above us, and rocks crumbled from the tunnel walls.

"Ev!" Jasper hesitated as he approached me and shuffled back a step when I turned. "Sorry." He held up a hand and squinted into the dark. "It's just your eyes ... How?"

I blinked, trying to shake off the red haze that clouded my vision.

"I don't know, but we have to save Darion."

"He's still alive?" Jasper chased after me.

"Just barely."

We ran back to the cavern, and I slid to the ground beside Darion while tearing the stone from my pocket.

"Most of his life force is in here."

Jasper's eyes widened as he watched the tiny bolts of lightning flash across the ever stone.

"I just hope I can put it back in time."

Darion lay motionless as I settled the ever stone on his heart and closed my hands over it.

Spirits of my ancestors, please give me the strength to save my brother.

Jasper's large hands clamped down atop mine. "Let me help. Siphon as much as you need."

"Thank you, Jasp." I hadn't thought it was possible to love

Jasper more than I already did. Warm, salty tears ran past my lips, and words became stuck in my throat.

"I know," Jasper whispered as I latched onto the source of energy that fueled his being.

Flecks of gold ignited in his amber eyes, and a glow of light exploded around us. Bolts of sizzling electricity traveled up my hands and arms, zapping me as I siphoned Darion's life force from the stone. My entire body vibrated with both Jasper's and Darion's magic combined.

My heart raced as I commanded Darion's energy to move through me. When the familiar feeling of the curse buzzed between us, I knew it was working. I continued until Darion gasped for air and his eyes flew open.

Jasper caught me as I slumped sideways.

"It worked, Ev. You brought him back." He cradled my head as I sobbed against his chest.

Darion's chains rattled as he came to his hands and knees. "What happened?" he croaked.

I drew myself out of Jasper's embrace and flung my arms around Darion's neck. "You're okay!"

"It worked, then? I knew you could do it." Darion glanced around as Jasper and I undid his chains.

Jasper dug out a bottle of water from his backpack and handed it to Darion, who gulped it down in one long drink.

"How long was I gone for?" He examined the piles of ashes. "Where's Orien? Is he one of these roasting blobs?" He rubbed his freed wrists and ankles, then slowly stood while testing his leg strength.

I cast my eyes down. "Orien got away with Oria's ring. It's not over. He'll come back for us." With a burst of frustration, I pounded my fist on the ground, the thud echoing in the air. "I failed! I let him get away, and I couldn't save Lucas."

Darion bent down and wrapped his arms around me. "No! You saved me for the second time." He kissed my forehead. "I'm so sorry about Lucas." He held me tighter. "We'll get the ring back from Orien and avenge our father and Lucas."

I didn't have the energy to tell him about the premonition I'd had, and what would happen if Orien succeeded in his plan. I could only hope that since Orien had failed to steal our magic, it wasn't too late to stop him from destroying Aenoas-Vita and all its people.

I pushed Darion away and crawled over to Lucas. "He'd still be alive if it wasn't for me. I never should have let him into my life." I buried my face in Lucas's chest and choked on the tears that flooded down my cheeks. My fingernails dug into the dirt and pressed hard until it felt like my nails would rip backward. Unintended flames sparked from my finger-tips and rippled across the ground.

Darion and Jasper stomped across the dirt, putting out the stray bursts of fire. They worked together to lift me gently off Lucas, but I clutched onto him with all my strength. "We can't leave him here." My voice was hoarse and thick, and mucus completely plugged my nose.

"We won't leave him," Jasper promised. "I'll carry him back."

Darion shook his head. "That's too dangerous—someone could see us. We need to get this mess cleaned up, and we need a portal. Did you bring a phone?"

While Jasper rummaged through his pack for his phone, and he and Darion talked of cleanup, I sat on the ground and pulled Lucas's head onto my lap. His face was gaunt, and his skin a sickly gray. I took off my jacket and covered his bloodied stab wound.

Only yesterday Lucas had been full of life and love, and now he was this: an empty shell. He'd died incomplete, with a vital part of his being missing. I smoothed his hair back, remembering all the times I'd run my fingers through it, hearing his laugh echo in my memory. My fingers traced his closed eyelids. I would forever remember the pain in Lucas' eyes the last time he had truly looked at me. I'd caused that pain, not Orien. Lucas had loved me with every part of himself, and I'd betrayed that love and gotten him killed.

"If I hadn't been so selfish, you wouldn't be lying here lifeless. This is my fault," I whispered. "I promise I will never feel the happiness of being loved by someone again, just like you won't."

Fire might burn inside me, but icy darkness encased my soul. My hands slipped from Lucas's body to lie flat on the hard ground.

I'm just as destructive as Orien.

His words came back to me: "You are my blood, after all." And the truth of those words clung to me, rancid with shame.

I was vaguely aware of the heavy energy that appeared as the portal took form in the cavern. Voices and bodies moved about the space as Darion and Jasper explained what'd happened. Gentle fingers caressed my face.

"Honey." My mom cupped my cheeks and searched my numb expression. Worry etched deep around her sapphire eyes. The once tranquil color now served as a reminder of our shared resemblance to Orien.

My eyelids squeezed shut as I tried to block out the world around me.

"We need to take Lucas now. Jasper's going to lift him from you, okay?" My mom smoothed the hair at my temples as my head tilted forward.

When they took Lucas away from me, a cold tingle shot through my legs. I forced my eyes open and followed Jasper's movements as he carried Lucas through the portal.

This can't be real. My fingers clawed at my legs. *It has to be a dream.* My nails raked across the skin on my arms. When blood prickled to the surface, my chest heaved forward with a guttural cry.

"Oh, sweetie." My mom tried to hold me. "It's time to go now, baby girl."

My torso twisted as I shook her away. I had no desire to move. The hollow ache in my chest expanded as I curled into a ball and lay shivering against the cold earth.

"She's in shock." I heard Calista comforting my mom. "She just needs time to heal."

Strong arms slid beneath me and lifted my body from the ground. Arden's energy wrapped around me like a blanket as he tucked my head under his chin. "I've got you." His breath warmed my ear as I breathed in his familiar scent and felt ... nothing. I shut everything off inside me except the burning hatred I felt toward Orien.

"Where were you?" Hot anger laced my words.

As the portal whisked us away, Arden's gentle whisper of "I'm sorry" lingered in my ears.

CHAPTER 6

*B*urnt copper stained my mouth and stiff bones ached as I tried to orient myself. My hand flew to my calf, massaging the cramp that lasted for several minutes. Light filtered through the blinds, reflecting off the familiar gray walls. November Rain was the name of the color. Lucas had helped me paint this room. We'd laughed about how fitting the color choice was. I squeezed my eyes shut as memories of the day came rushing back. Rain had poured that entire day, and a stormy breeze had flowed through the open window while we painted. The night had been perfect for a scary movie, so we'd made popcorn after we finished painting, and snuggled on the sofa. We fell asleep in the living room and woke up entangled in each other's limbs with popcorn spilled between us. Lucas plucked a piece from my hair and popped it in his mouth and joked that it tasted like my homemade lavender-and-honey shampoo.

I slammed a door on the memory and yanked the blanket tight over my head, wishing for utter darkness. My stomach roared with a traitorous growl. The thought of eating made me feel sick, and I tried to ignore the aching hunger as images of Lucas lying gaunt and lifeless filled every sector of my brain. I tore back the blanket and leaned over the bed, gagging on my breath. Hot acid burned up my esophagus, and I waited with my head hanging for the tears to come, but my eyes were as dry as my mouth. I had nothing left. Every cell in my body felt dry, like a desolate desert. I tried to swallow, but the sides of my throat burned and felt as rough as sandpaper.

How long have I been asleep?

The angry growls continued painfully, and I finally gave in and shifted my legs over the side of the bed. My head spun with the movement, and I gripped the sides of the mattress to steady myself. I didn't remember changing into the pajamas I wore, or going to bed, for that matter. All I remember is Arden carrying me through the portal, then I blacked out.

A full glass of water sat on the bedside table. I picked it up and swirled the clouded liquid. It was cold. Someone must have brought it in recently. I tentatively wet my cracked lips. The water had a powdery texture, with a hint of citrus flavor. I drank slowly at first, until I could swallow without the pain, then drained the glass. The water calmed the acid bubbling in my belly, but my hunger only intensified, and I knew I had no choice but to eat.

When I dragged myself out of my room, it didn't surprise me to see my mom in the kitchen, making scrambled eggs—I had sensed her energy as soon as I woke up.

She dropped the spatula when she saw me and rushed to my side. "Oh, honey, I'm so glad you're up."

I put my arms out to stop her before she drew me into a hug. I didn't want comfort. The rejection shone in her eyes, but she respected my boundaries and kept her distance.

"How long have I been asleep?" I knew by the way I felt it had to have been longer than a day.

My mom filled another glass with water and tossed in a scoop of powder. She swirled the powder around until it dissolved, then handed the glass to me. Her skin smelled of fresh lavender, a scent that used to lift me up, but not anymore.

"You've been out for three days." Her brows wrinkled together as she scanned every inch of me.

I coughed when the water went down the wrong pipe. "Three days!"

"I tried getting you to eat, but all I could manage was giving you a small amount of water each day, mixed with electrolytes, protein powder, and a secret ingredient of my own. Everyone has been so worried about you. Only magical restraints have kept Darion, Jasper, and Arden from breaking in and forcing you up, but I knew you'd come out when you were ready, and I've been here each day, watching over you."

I turned from her watery gaze and pulled myself up onto the barstool at the kitchen island. The task was harder than it should have been, but my throbbing limbs ached with a heavy weight. A shiver tightened my shoulders, and I hunched over the warm coffee my mom handed me. My stomach twisted into knots when she slid the plate of scrambled eggs in front of me, and I snatched up the fork and stabbed into a chunk of fluffy yellow egg.

The creases in my mom's face relaxed as I ate, and she filled herself a plate and took a seat next to me.

I took a few bites, then quickly devoured the plate and went to get more eggs. We ate quietly and sipped hot coffee. When my mom finished eating, she cleaned up while I sat numbly watching her move around my kitchen, rinsing dishes and putting things away. She didn't speak of Lucas. She knew I would ask when I was ready.

His name stuck in my throat. "Luc... Lucas?"

She stopped wiping the counter and set the cloth aside,

pushing her hair behind her ears. She came around and took my hand. I didn't pull away this time. "Let's go sit."

I followed her to the sofa. My feet lifted with the weight of lead, and I wrapped my arms around my chest as I lowered myself down.

My mom unfolded a couch blanket and tucked it over my shoulders, then smoothed my matted hair.

I sat frozen, staring down at my legs. A high-pitched whine rang deep in my ears as she explained that they'd had to make it look like an accident, that Lucas had crashed his car when he'd tried swerving to miss a deer. His car had caught fire, and by the time the responders had arrived …

Her words trailed off, and I glanced up to catch her swiping away a tear. I waited without speaking for her to finish telling me what had happened.

She gave my hand a squeeze. "At the request of his family, they cremated his body and sent his ashes back to them in Australia."

She stood, walked to the bookshelf, and picked up a new wooden box. It rested next to a photo of Lucas and me. She carried the box over and sat back down, gripping the box in her lap. "Sam helped me secure this for you. If it's too much right now, I'll take it away, but I thought you might like to say goodbye." Tears slid from her eyes and dripped onto the box.

My jaw clenched, and the room spun. I reached out for the armrest next to me and dug my nails into the sofa's smooth fabric. "Are those his …?" It was impossible to say the words.

"Some of his ashes," she whispered, and offered me the box.

My fingers trembled as they smoothed the surface of the four-by-four-inch wooden cube that held the last piece of Lucas I would ever be near.

"His family must be devastated," I said, wiping my nose on the corner of the blanket. "We talked about taking a trip so I could meet his parents." The memory was so recent, but now it felt like a distant dream. "Before I broke his heart," I added in barely a whisper.

My mom cast her eyes down. "Losing a child is the worst kind of pain. My heart goes out to them."

I knew my mom was remembering the loss of her own child, when Siobhan had stolen Darion from her for the first nineteen years of his life. She'd nearly lost him forever until I'd saved his life.

When the box drifted back to my mom's lap, I reached toward it and clasped my fingers around its edges. A pain like a knife ripped down my chest. *How can this be happening?*

With the box in my grasp, I ran my free hand over the sofa cushion, as if trying to capture the essence of Lucas's presence that still lingered from where he'd sat just days ago.

Inhaling sharply, I hastily wiped my eyes and pulled the blanket snugly around me. Clutching Lucas's remains, I walked out to the porch and dragged a chair away from the patio bistro table.

My gaze drifted past the field of wildflowers to the forest that rustled in the wind.

"You deserved better than this, Lucas." I cradled the box close to my heart. "I'm so sorry I let this happen. If I could trade places with you, I would. You should be here, smiling and laughing and playing your music." Tears streamed down my face; the tepid liquid dripped between my fingers and pooled on the wood. "You meant so much to me. I'm sorry I couldn't love you the way you deserved. I wish ..." Hoarse sobs wracked my body as words caught in my throat. With my knees tucked under my chin, I leaned forward and rested my forehead gently on Lucas's box.

I didn't know how long I'd sat arched in the chair, but my

body ached and a migraine pulsed at my temples from the kink in my neck. Footsteps crunched over gravel, followed by the creak of worn wood as someone walked up the steps to my deck. There was no need to glance up. I sensed Darion's energy as he set a vacant chair down next to me.

"I'm sorry, Ev." Darion smoothed his hand over my back. "I had a lot of respect for Lucas. What happened to him was a tragedy, but I know he wouldn't want you to let his death break you."

My head snapped up. Darion's silver eyes locked with mine, and I saw the understanding in them and *felt* his concern, neither of which I wanted, but he pushed on. "I know better than anyone what shutting off your emotions can do to you. Lucas would want you to lean on the people who love you, grieve, and find healing. He wouldn't want you to shrivel into a hollow shell."

A shell, like Lucas was when he died.

My legs fell to the deck floor. "I don't need a lecture on how to mourn, Darion. And unfortunately for Lucas, he's now dust in a box and won't ever get to express his feelings again." I slammed a fist down hard on the table next to me, causing the glass centerpiece to rattle.

Darion didn't flinch. "You need something to focus on. Mom told me of your premonition. Only you, me, and Jasper are aware of Orien possessing the ring. Let's devise a plan to get it back."

Heat flushed within me. "That damn ring is the reason Lucas is in here. I hope I never see it again." I jumped up and went to the railing. The clear blue sky stood in stark contrast to the somber atmosphere. I cringed under the sun's bright rays and longed for the shelter of dark, stormy clouds.

Darion stood and grabbed my arm. "I know you, sister. Even in your darkest state, you would never leave innocent people to that fate."

My skin burned hot, and Darion jerked his singed fingers from my arm. His brows furrowed in a silent expression of frustration before he reluctantly stepped aside.

I moved towards the door and stopped. Without turning, I told him, "Send word to Arden and Felix that I need to speak with them in person. Tell them to meet us at the cabin tonight. And tell Arden that Rheya should attend. I'll take care of the rest."

I felt Darion's eyes on my back as I walked through the door, leaving it open, and carried Lucas's remains back to my room.

~

The drive to the cabin was quiet. Darion took the corners with careful precision as I stared blankly into the shadows of the forest. A pair of glowing eyes flashed as they watched us approach. Pointed furry ears turned in our direction before the four-legged creature slunk away and vanished. A part of me longed to have that freedom, but as much as I yearned to slink away, it wasn't an option—I had a snake to catch.

"Are you sure you're ready for this, honey?" asked my mom from the front seat.

I shifted my attention from the trees. "I won't let Orien get away with what he's done, and I won't hide from my duty. Orien has the ring because of me, and the others should be prepared for what could happen if we don't get it back." The fire magic remained a constant heat under my skin, fueled by my pain and anger. My blood warmed as I imagined burning Orien to cinders.

When we neared the cabin, I spotted Jasper's motorcycle parked next to his parents' car. Darion pulled up next to Calista's red Mustang. She'd picked up Selkie on her way. I sensed the vibrations of all those we expected for tonight's meeting, waiting inside the cabin. A lump stuck in my throat as I got out of the back seat of my mom's 4Runner. Explaining that Orien had taken the royal Ever ring was only part of tonight's plan. The other part would take far more courage.

The cabin vibrated with powerful energy. My hand lingered at the knob before turning it and pushing the door open. All eyes turned toward the three of us as we walked into the cabin's quaint living room. I avoided making eye contact with the blue-green eyes that seared my soul and went to stand in front of the blazing fire. I wasn't cold. In fact, I'd been on the warmer side since I'd accessed my new ability, but the flickering flames gave me something to focus on while I calmed my nerves.

"Everly, my dear." Felix stood. I hadn't seen him since he'd returned to Aenoas-Vita at my request. Being back on his home planet and away from the aging toxins of Earth had been good for him. His champagne hair flowed down his back with a glowing sheen that appeared fuller and more radiant. His skin was smoother, and a renewed vitality emanated within his aura. I threw up a hot wall to block the healing light that Felix expanded as he neared me. His features tightened, and he paused when he sensed my reaction, but then continued forward as if nothing had happened.

"You are a sight for these old eyes." He opened his arms, and I reciprocated his hug out of obligation but restrained from allowing myself to feel comfort in his embrace. "Stay strong, my dear," he whispered in my ear, then looked me over. The wealth of knowledge hidden in the stormy sea of his eyes had dizzied me when we'd first met, but as I grew familiar with Felix, the deep sense of his knowledge had turned to a feeling of calm. But now I darted my eyes away, not wanting to see what he knew: that I had failed our entire planet. He squeezed my shoulder reassuringly before moving to my mother.

Rheya's familiar laugh drew my attention to where she bantered with Arden. I'd been envious of their closeness when we'd first met, but now I was glad for it—Arden would need her.

When Rheya noticed my appraisal of her, she bolted up, returning the gesture as her green cat eyes scanned my appearance. I'd chosen my outfit meticulously for tonight: tight black cargo pants, black combat boots, and a short-sleeved black cotton T-shirt. I'd kept the knife Freya had given me strapped to my belt, along with Oria's sword, which I had slung across my back. Both had always been within reach since I'd awoken after Lucas's death.

"Nice outfit," Rheya approved, slinging her twisted, long red braid over her shoulder. Rheya wore the same battle gear she had the first time I'd seen her in the woods when I'd been training with Arden. She hadn't changed a bit, which was exactly what I had been hoping for. "My *queen*," she said with a hint of mockery, though I knew she spoke in jest and not disrespect. She dipped her head and touched her fist to her heart.

My thoughts raced as I rehearsed my interior monologue and fought the desire to be back in my room, curled in a ball. The jovial banter quieted, and Jasper and Darion closed ranks at my sides. I drew on their steady energy and inhaled a deep breath.

"Thank you all for coming at such short notice." I cut straight to the point. "Aenoas-Vita is in danger. My ancestor Orien lives, and he has taken Oria's ring. And that's not all." I told them of my premonition of what would happen if Orien succeeded in his plan, and how he was working with the Shimera. "But I don't believe he has the power he needs to move forward without my and Darion's magic."

"I agree," Darion added. "While Orien held me captive, he required several doses of blood to maintain his strength. Without our magic, he won't be able to access the ancestral link to the ring."

"He can't access the power he needs elsewhere?" Jasper's father's baritone voice boomed from his seat next to his wife.

"No," Darion answered. "He needs the magic that bonds Ever twins."

I nodded when eyes looked to me for confirmation of Darion's words.

Rheya paced the room. She wasn't good at managing her emotions. "How could you let this happen?" Her aura burned hot and then chilled to freezing, which I knew was an effect linked to her unique gifts.

"Don't forget you address your queen." Darion's stony stare met Rheya's prowling glare.

I touched Darion's shoulder. "Rheya's right to be angry. I've failed you all, but I won't let Orien get away with this."

"You already have," Rheya accused.

I was glad she didn't hide her anger toward me. I deserved every bit.

"I will do whatever is necessary to get the ring back and destroy Orien."

"Does *the queen* have a plan?" This time Rheya meant her mockery.

Darion tensed, and I shook my head at him. He fought back the urge to respond to Rheya with a nasty retort, which wasn't an easy feat for him, but I appreciated he kept quiet, though there was no way Rheya missed the fury building in his posture.

"How can we help?" Jasper's mother asked. Jocelyn was soft-spoken and shared the same amber eye color, dark hair, and golden skin as her son. Her husband, Ryker, Jasper's father, sat with a protective hand on his wife's knee. As a former member of the royal guard and my father's trusted Shield, he brought his family to Earth to assist my father in a different capacity when Jasper was a child. They waited patiently for my answer.

"Orien can create portals at will. It was how he escaped with the ring."

Ryker shook his head. "Orien is an Ever, and weakened or not, he will still be formidable and capable of more than the average Vitarian."

"Indeed," said Felix. "He's not to be underestimated. He's survived centuries under the radar to accomplish his tyranny."

Arden followed my movements but observed quietly as everyone spoke their minds.

"Jocelyn." Jasper's mother met my eyes. "You're a Portal Tracker. I need you to watch for any signs of portal travel on Earth and report them to me."

She nodded her agreement. "I'll start right away."

"Felix," I said. "Is there another Portal Tracker that you trust on Aenoas-Vita?"

He nodded.

"Good. We don't want to create any unnecessary fear or panic. Please handle the details with care and only tell who you must."

"Of course, my dear."

"Neil had business that took him out-of-town tonight, but he will monitor his clubs for any sign or knowledge of Orien's whereabouts. Calista, Selkie, and my mother will work on creating a spell to trap Orien in his portal once he's located. I have contact with a local Vitarian who will help me work on a tracking spell using my blood."

Felix's eyes shot toward me, but he said nothing, though his thoughtful expression hinted that he guessed I spoke of

Freya Moon, who had declined to be present at tonight's meeting.

The fire crackled, and a wave of heat blew through the room.

"Arden." His name rolled off my tongue with mounting tension.

When his watchful stare met mine, the hairs stood up on my arms as a shiver raced across my skin. I hardened myself against the power he had over me and forced my body to ignore its traitorous response as I focused on my words. "I trust whatever decisions you make to protect Aenoas-Vita. When you speak to the council, you speak for the queen."

He nodded, and I turned away from the lingering question in his eyes.

"Felix, you are head of the council and rule as my proxy. Please make sure the rest of the council members understand Arden's place as commander. His decisions are not to be questioned unless a direct order comes from me."

"You have my word."

I nodded. "Rheya, may I speak with you?" I motioned for her to follow me.

Rheya gritted her teeth, her defiance heating her aura. But she stood from her place next to Arden and followed me outside and down the porch steps.

"You've changed," she mused. "You're no longer the uncertain girl finding her way, but it's more than that."

Flecks of yellow glowed in her emerald eyes as she stalked toward me. Her hand shot out and touched my skin. "You have fire magic." She snatched her hand away. "It burns hot inside of you, just barely controlled," she accused.

I matched her challenging stance. "That's not what I asked you out here to talk about."

She quirked a pointed auburn brow. "No, I thought not. Is the reason tall, buff, and handsome, and currently brooding from rejection?" Her taunting grin fell when my expression remained hard.

"It's time for Arden to move on and find someone else. We can't be together, and I want him to be happy."

Rheya glared at me, her nostrils flaring. "Is this because you think Arden failed you? He was furious he couldn't return to Earth in time. Someone tampered with our portal. Didn't Arden explain?"

"Of course he did. I'm not doing this because I think Arden failed me. It's because of my own failure, and it's what I have to do, no matter how much it hurts."

Rheya shrugged her muscular shoulders. "What do you want me to do? The man loves you, though you cause him nothing but grief. You don't think I've tried to convince him to find someone on our own planet to take his mind off of you? He won't listen to me if you're asking me to talk to him." She folded her arms across her chest.

I exhaled a frustrated sigh. "I need you to guide him in another direction. There must be someone he's cared for or can care for."

She stared at me hard for a long moment, and then her eyes softened as they lit up, and she glanced up into the dark, star-filled sky. "I have someone in mind who may be interested in the challenge."

A heaviness settled on my chest as my inner voice screamed at me not to let Arden go. But I silenced the part of me that loved Arden too much to lose him. I made a vow to Lucas in the cave the night he'd died. My actions caused his death, and now it is my duty to repay him with my sacrifice. "I need one more favor."

"What am I? Your personal genie?" Rheya placed a hand on her hip. "Okay. What is it?"

I stepped up to stand face-to-face with her. "Promise me you'll protect Arden with your life."

Rheya narrowed her gaze. "That's not a promise you need ask of me. I would give my life for the commander a million times over."

I nodded. Her answer didn't come as a surprise to me; she meant every word. I'd once been jealous of Arden's feelings toward Rheya. But she was his best friend and second-in-command. They loved each other deeply, but there nothing romantic about their love.

"Arden will not give up on you. He spent the past year brooding and rejecting the attention of every woman that even looked his way, all while you were dating your human. How do you expect this to work?"

"I plan to break his heart." The words hung bitter on my tongue, and for a second, I thought Rheya might reach for her sword and cut me down. But after we stood frozen, eyeing each other, she finally nodded.

"It's the only way." The same regret that coursed through my veins laced her voice. She hated everything about my plan. "This is a mistake," she said bluntly. "I know you do this to punish yourself and you think this is for the best for Arden, but you'll only cause more pain to yourself and to him. Believe me, I know." She closed her eyes as if shutting out a threatening memory. When she opened them again, she was about to say more, but the front door cracked open and Arden walked out. "Anyway," Rheya said. "You have my two cents." She quickly brushed past me.

"Walk with me?" Arden asked. A vulnerability shone in his uncertainty of my answer.

As much as what I was going to do would hurt, it had to be done, and this was my opportunity. I nodded toward the woods.

Arden came down the porch steps, his muscles tight, his gaze fixed on me as if he could sense my intentions. I swallowed hard, making myself forget what it felt like to feel those powerful arms holding me tight. I sensed his restraint as he stepped to my side, then moved past me, and I followed him through the line of trees where we had once had our first kiss. My skin flushed as the memory raced through my mind, and the emotion passed as I turned everything off, like flipping light switches, until all I felt was void and ... *numb*.

Arden stopped. "I can't tell you how sorry I am about Lucas."

I spun away. "I don't want to talk about it. We can't change what happened." I bent and picked up a pile of dried leaves, crushing them in my palm, and watched as their broken pieces blew away with the wind, just like Lucas's ashes would.

Arden's feet crunched over fallen leaves as he strode back to face me. "I should have been there with you. Why didn't you wait? You could have been killed."

A defensive buzz rushed through me and aided in hardening my resolve. "I did what I had to do. You have no right to question my choices." My words came out with harsh authority.

Arden's brow creased. "That's not ..." He placed his hands on my shoulders. "Everly, if anything happened to you, I ..." His fingers trailed down the bare skin of my arms until they interlaced with my own. His warm breath brushed my lips as he spoke. "Don't you know how much you mean to me?"

He pressed our bodies together, and I could feel his heart race against his chest. "Let me be here for you, my love."

I sucked in a breath. My resolve nearly melted in the security of his embrace. His aura wrapped around me, and my arms ached to lace around his neck and tell him how much I needed him.

"Everly, I—"

I froze. *No, no, no. I made a vow. I owe Lucas this sacrifice.*

My mind filled with the image of Lucas and the pain I'd

caused him before my deranged uncle took his life. I yanked my hands free from Arden's and inhaled a sharp breath. "Stop. Don't say it." I looked into the blue-green sea of his eyes. "We can never be together, Arden. I am your queen and nothing more."

He flinched. Waves of confusion washed away the blue, and only a deep green stared back at me. "You don't mean that." And for the first time since we'd met, Arden's words held uncertainty.

He drew me back into his arms. "This isn't you talking. You've just lost someone you cared for. You're angry and hurting. Don't push me away, Everly. Let me in."

Flames consumed my heart as the lie passed my lips. "I don't love you. Losing Lucas made me realize that. You are the commander of Aenoas-Vita's guard, and I'm its queen. That's all there is or ever will be between us."

Heat licked beneath the surface of my skin, and Arden released me. His brow furrowed, and when his eyes met mine, I knew I'd succeeded. He backed away from me, drawing in his emotions and locking me out.

"Are you doing this because I failed you? You're punishing me for not being there to save Lucas."

"No," I answered. "What happened to Lucas was my fault."

"Then you're doing it to punish yourself. I love you, Everly, and you love me." He grabbed my arm, waiting for me to tell him he was right.

I channeled every ounce of pain I felt, allowing it to flow through my words and imbue them with a raw, undeniable truth that I hoped would convince Arden. "I don't love you," I told him with a coldness that felt wrong and yanked my arm from his grasp.

A brisk wind stirred, and the weight of my lie formed a glacier between us. I turned and ran without a glance back.

When I reached the cabin, Rheya paced out front. "He

needs you" was all I told her, and she bolted past me in the direction I'd come from.

I slumped onto the stairs, fighting back the emotions that banged and slammed behind their wall to be free. I choked on dry tears as I bent forward and grabbed the porch railing.

A blast of warm air came from behind, and footsteps creaked toward me.

Darion stepped down the stairs and reached out his hand. "Let's go, sister."

I slipped my hand into his, letting him lift me to my feet. "What about Mom?" I asked when I realized she wasn't with us.

"She's riding home with Cal and Selk. When I felt you shut off your emotions, I told her you need a night out with your big brother." Darion maneuvered the 4Runner out of its parking spot and got us turned around.

"Big brother, huh? And here I thought we were twins."

Darion shifted gears as he rounded a corner. "I'm pretty sure I was born first. Besides, I was stolen from the womb, so I'd say that gives me dibs on firstborn rights."

"Okay, you have a point, big brother." I went along with his theory and gripped the grab handle as we jostled over potholes hidden by the night.

"Thank you, Darion. This curse we're stuck with sucks, but I suppose it has some perks after all."

Darion's cheek lifted as he grinned.

～

The bass coming from Neil's club was a welcome distraction.

I recognized the host who greeted us. She sat in Neil's usual place, pumping her blue Converse shoes to the beats. Streaks of a brighter pastel blue decorated her hair. I felt a pang of guilt at being relieved that Neil wasn't in the club tonight. He'd left me a message earlier that he'd be out of town for a few days, sorting out some things. He hadn't said what those things were, but I guessed they had to do with the management of his Eugene bar now that Lucas was … gone.

"You two have fun." The host blew a large, stretchy bubble from her mouth, then sucked it back in with a series of pops.

I didn't miss the way her eyes lingered on Darion before we mumbled a thanks and passed through the red velvet curtains.

Neil changed the lighting theme frequently, and tonight it was all neon, glow-in-the-dark colors. He even added special black lights to the glass fish tank that made up the entire length of the bar. The fish swam back and forth, creating a mirage of twirling colors.

"Hey, D," the bartender greeted Darion.

I looked at Darion and mouthed, "D?"

He shrugged, then talked to the bartender in Vitarian, who then uncorked a fresh bottle of the evernescence.

Neil considered his new name for the drink to be a clever play on words as it was created from the extract of the ever flower on Aenoas-Vita and produced fleeting sensations of euphoria. The lavender liquid glowed under the dark light as the bartender filled two martini glasses, and the familiar vapor floated atop the liquid.

"To letting go," I said, and touched my glass to Darion's.

"To getting revenge," he smiled, and a glint of the old Darion shined in his eyes.

We drained our glasses in seconds. The extract's potent effects overwhelmed me, making my head swim. The lights stretched across my vision, and I had the sensation that I was floating as I left Darion sitting at the bar and moved out onto the dance floor, drifting into the crowd of gyrating dancers.

The bass filtered through my chest as warm bodies closed

in. My skin tingled when arms brushed my skin, and I didn't resist when soft hands lifted my hair and equally soft lips touched the back of my neck. Long fingernails trailed down my back and slipped around my waist. When I entwined my own atop them, I realized the stranger's hands were slender and feminine. I twirled and locked eyes with the woman holding me tightly.

Makeup glittered over her dark caramel skin, and long curls cascaded past her shoulders. When she moved, I moved with her. Sparkling powder coated my fingertips as they trailed up her gold-dusted arms. When my hands combed through her thick waves, her head bent toward mine, and my lips crushed hers. The kiss was filled with a raw and insatiable desire fueled by magic, and I couldn't help but succumb to its power.

Drinks and dancing continued throughout the night. I didn't remember leaving, but at some point, Darion was carrying me out of the car and into my apartment. He made me drink something tangy with herbs and said I'd thank him in the morning. The last thing I remembered was crashing face-first onto my bed and falling into a spinning, dark sleep.

~

I circled the room, drawing the dark clouds of energy toward me. They no longer resisted, eager to enter a willing host. I held my arms open wide, feeling the sweat drip down my body as each tangled wisp of darkness came to me, filled with the negative charge I needed. When the weeping echoed throughout the room, I ended class.

Ever since word had gotten out about Lucas dying in a car crash, students filtered out of each class without their usual rush of questions, and today was no different. The room quietly cleared, giving me the time to do what I'd been itching to do all day, and what I'd stored up an excess of negative energy for.

I grabbed a piece of chalk and bent to the floor. My hand scribbled furiously until the large white eye encased in a circle looked up at me with its tormenting gaze. I sat in the center of the eye and picked up Freya's blade, cleansed and respelled for a new purpose.

After my meeting with everyone at the cabin, Felix had sent me a warning to be careful of how much help I accepted from Freya Moon. His message didn't elaborate beyond warning me not to fall into her debt, but I needed Freya's spells, so once again I shut off all thoughts about the dangers of working too closely with her as I stabbed the blade into each of my palms and cut a long slice down their centers. I'd done this so many times over the last few weeks that I didn't even notice the pain any longer as I held my palms open and watched the blood pool, then quickly flipped them over and placed my bleeding hands flat on top of the white chalk on either side of me.

The room spun as a dark tunnel swallowed me. Energy sizzled and zapped in the air. Wind ripped past, threatening to send me to oblivion as I searched for any sign of light, and then I saw it: a crack. It was more like a hairline fracture, but it got bigger each time I discovered it. I ran and ran toward it, but as usual, it drifted farther away as I advanced. His laugh filled the void, taunting me, as it did every time. Flames blazed from my hands, but I knew it was no use. The fire hadn't made a difference before. I screamed into the nothingness and filled the empty portal with searing fire.

"I'm going to find you, Orien."

"Everly!"

My eyes snapped open. Darion and Molly glowered over me. Darion crouched down and snatched my hands off the floor and hauled me to my feet.

S. L. WATSON

"What are you thinking? You didn't even lock the door. What if one of your students had forgotten something and come back?" He flung my hands away, shaking his head.

I ignored his berating and picked up a towel to dab the sweat trickling down my brow.

"Stop this, Ev. You're taking in too much dark energy. You're not sleeping or eating the way you should. Look at yourself." He tugged my arm and forced me to face the mirrored wall.

I stared numbly at the sunken sapphire eyes that reflected back at me. The circles underneath had turned to a dark purple, and my once radiant hair hung limp and dull, with greasy strands falling loose from my bun. I didn't want to think of how skinny and frail my arms and legs had gotten, but Darion wouldn't relent. He scowled at my reflection.

"You're skin and bone, Ev. You need rest and food." His eyes softened into a plea. "Even if you find Orien, you're in no condition to fight him. Please—"

I yanked my arm away and spun from the mirror. "I'm getting closer. There's a crack. If I can just break through, I'll see what he sees, and then we can find him and get Oria's ring back and avenge our father and Lucas." I glanced side-ways to see Molly wiping up the chalk on the floor.

"I want those things too, Ev. But you've been at this for weeks. Please, just take a break. Your students are noticing the change in you. They've approached Molly with their concerns."

My attention flew to Molly, and she acknowledged the truth of what Darion said with a nod.

My head drooped, and I stared at my bleeding hands.

Molly rushed to me and cupped her hands over mine. "Darion's right, Ev. You can't beat Orien like this, and please remember that if you put your life in danger, you put Darion in danger, and I need both of you in my life." Molly's voice cracked and tugged at something buried deep inside me, but I stifled the emotion before it surfaced.

When I lifted my head to look at Molly, something unexpected caught my eye through the window from across the street. My heart thumped, and I barely listened to Molly's words.

"Come on." Molly urged me forward. "Let's get these cleaned up, and then you're coming to dinner with us, and that's an order." She dumped antiseptic over my hands.

"I think I'll just take a quick shower here in the locker room." I withdrew my hands from Molly's, but offered the best smile I could muster. "Why don't you two go on ahead, and I'll meet you at the café?"

Darion narrowed his eyes. "We can wait."

I gave Molly a pleading look, and she patted my shoulder before going over to Darion and taking his hand. "Babe." She turned on her "you can't refuse me" voice. "Let's give Ev her space. She'll meet us there, won't you?" She flashed me a stern appraisal.

"I promise." I tried for another smile, but it came out as more of a twitch. But thankfully, Darion caved and followed Molly to the door. He stopped just before he was through and held the door propped open with his elbow as he turned back. "If you're not there in thirty, I'm coming back."

I sighed and shooed him with a wave. "I'll be there. Now get out of here so I can get ready."

I waited a minute until I felt Darion's energy turn the corner, and then I walked outside. The energy I sensed from across the street reappeared, and so did the person it belonged to. Bree stood in the open doorway of her studio, which had remained abandoned until this moment, and faced my seething glare. My chest tightened as the desire to rip her to shreds tore through me. She was the reason Orien had Oria's ring. If she hadn't stolen it from me, Orien wouldn't have killed Lucas. He would still have needed him to barter with me. She was just as guilty as Orien.

My skin burned. Bree jumped back when she heard the explosion above her head, and then her sign caught fire and crashed to the ground.

This time when I smiled, my lips peeled back from my teeth, and my cheeks lifted painfully high. When Bree's eyes met mine once more, she cringed and doubled over, grabbing both sides of her head. Energy poured from me as I crossed the street. Even if Bree had tried to use her power to block my Empath abilities, it wouldn't work. I twisted the onyx ring on my finger, which I'd had Freya make me, and stepped over the fallen sign.

A sardonic laugh escaped my lips as I glared into Bree's pleading eyes.

"Make it stop!" she begged.

My nails dug into my palms as I circled her bent form. "I told you that sign sucks."

"Please," she moaned. "I can help you find Orien."

Black tendrils burst from my palms and consumed her. I kicked the door closed behind me, barricading in her screams, and dragged her to a back room.

Folding chairs sat propped against a wall, and I slid one over and snatched Bree by the hair, forcing her onto the chair.

I didn't know what game Bree was playing coming back here, but I intended to find out.

Bree's phone buzzed in the purse, still slung over her shoulder. I took her bag and dug the phone out. A text from Ty lit up the screen, and I ground my teeth.

"You won't be getting anywhere near Ty," I growled as my fist tightened and shot out, thumping its target. Bree's head slumped as she fell unconscious. I scanned the room for something to secure her to the chair with.

Blue flames hissed through the air as they poured from my fingertips and imprisoned Bree. Even if she got the towels I'd bound her with loosened, she wouldn't be going anywhere.

My stomach roared, and I checked the time on Bree's phone. Darion would come to find me if I didn't hustle to the café.

"Sweet dreams," I chuckled, tucking Bree's purse under my arm as I ran back to my studio and stuffed her purse and phone inside a locker.

After changing into clean clothes, I gave my hair a quick ruffle before twisting it back up in a fresh, messy bun, then hurried to lock up the studio. With a satisfied glance across the street, I ran down the block and around the corner.

Just as I swung the door open to the café, I collided with Darion, slamming into his hard chest. His hands flew out, grasping around my shoulders and balancing our wobbling bodies. "I was just coming to find you." A frown shadowed his silver eyes.

"Well, I'm here." I shimmied past him to the table where Molly sat, eyeing her menu. "Let's eat. I'm ravenous." I smiled inwardly as I thought of returning to Bree.

THANK YOU

Thank you for reading Last Descendants. I hope you enjoyed it.

Help other people find this book by visiting S.L.'s website and writing a review at S.L. Watson author.com.

While you're there, check out some of S.L.'s hand crafted book-inspired goodies like fabric book covers, book marks and bundle deals available for purchase and sign up for her newsletter to receive great discounts and special offers. Have a wonderful day!

Everly's journey continues in Stone of Fire (Vitarian Chronicles Volume 3)

Stone of Fire: Vitarian Chronicles Volume 3

Visit my website for exclusive updates and newsletter goodies: www.slwatsonauthor.com

Come hang out with me on:

Facebook: https://www.facebook.com/slwatsonauthor
Instagram: https://www.instagram.com/slwatsonauthor/

www.ingramcontent.com/pod-product-compliance
Lightning Source LLC
Chambersburg PA
CBHW030110260626
47156CB00008B/2597